JUST BEFORE NIGHT
A ZOMBIE ANTHOLOGY

JOE TONZELLI
&
ANTHONY GIANGREGORIO

OTHER LIVING DEAD PRESS BOOKS

BLOOD RAGE & DEAD RAGE (BOOK 1 & 2 OF THE RAGE VIRUS SERIES)
DEAD MOURNING: A ZOMBIE HORROR STORY
BOOK OF THE DEAD: A ZOMBIE ANTHOLOGY
LOVE IS DEAD: A ZOMBIE ANTHOLOGY
BOOK OF THE DEAD 2: NOT DEAD YET
BOOK OF THE DEAD 3: DEAD AND ROTTING
END OF DAYS: AN APOCALYPTIC ANTHOLOGY VOLUME 1 & 2
DEAD HOUSE: A ZOMBIE GHOST STORY
THE ZOMBIE IN THE BASEMENT (FOR ALL AGES)
THE LAZARUS CULTURE: A ZOMBIE NOVEL
DEAD WORLDS: UNDEAD STORIES VOLUMES 1, 2, 3 & 4
FAMILY OF THE DEAD, REVOLUTION OF THE DEAD
RANDY AND WALTER: PORTRAIT OF TWO KILLERS
KINGDOM OF THE DEAD
THE MONSTER UNDER THE BED
DEAD TALES: SHORT STORIES TO DIE FOR
ROAD KILL: A ZOMBIE TALE
DEADFREEZE, DEADFALL, DARK PLACES
SOUL EATER, THE DARK, RISE OF THE DEAD
DEAD END: A ZOMBIE NOVEL, VISIONS OF THE DEAD

THE DEADWATER SERIES

DEADWATER
DEADWATER: Expanded Edition
DEADRAIN, DEADCITY, DEADWAVE, DEAD HARVEST
DEAD UNION, DEAD VALLEY
DEAD TOWN, DEAD SALVATION
DEAD ARMY (coming soon)

COMING SOON

DEAD HISTORY: A ZOMBIE ANTHOLOGY
THE WAR AGAINST THEM: A ZOMBIE NOVEL by Jose Vazquez
DEAD WORLDS: UNDEAD STORIES VOLUME 5
THE CHRONICLES OF JACK PRIMUS by Michael D. Griffiths

JUST BEFORE NIGHT: A ZOMBIE ANTHOLOGY

Copyright © 2010 by Anthony Giangregorio & Joe Tonzelli
All stories contained in this book have been published with permission from the authors.
ISBN   Softcover ISBN 13: 978-1-935458-42-5   ISBN 10: 1-935458-42-6

www.livingdeadpress.com

Table of Contents

BILL

JOE TONZELLI & ANTHONY GIANGREGORIO

"Bill, breakfast is ready," his wife called from the kitchen. He could hear her setting the table as he sat in their cramped living room, his eyes glued to the TV. A news reporter was reciting the latest event in a recent rash of unmotivated attacks perpetuated by random people.

"Mary, have you heard about this one?" Bill called, crouched over in front of the TV, his face two feet from the news broadcast. "It's another one of those weird murders! They don't have a lot of details; something about a bus driver being bitten at a bus stop!"

"Oh, Bill, I've had enough of that macabre stuff. And so have you. Turn that thing off and let's eat breakfast like normal people."

Bill checked his watch and saw that it was 8:30 a.m.

"Why did you make it so late?" he asked, his eyes darting back to the TV. "We'll never make it in time for church."

"Bill, I make breakfast the same time every Sunday morning, and every Sunday morning we sit down and eat, and we *always* make it to church on time. Now, get in here before I feed all the bacon to Willy."

Bill smirked as he looked into the kitchen to see their dog cock his head at the sound of his name being spoken. His tongue fell sloppily out of his mouth, spotting the wet strips of bacon Mary was laying on her plate next to her eggs and fried potatoes. "Paws off, Willy," Bill said, straightening up. He reached to turn off the TV, hovering over the knob for a moment, but instead turned up the volume. He then walked over to the kitchen, pulled his chair back, and slowly lowered himself down, glad to be off his feet.

"You take it easy on the bacon, Bill, I mean it."

He waved her off, grunting in response.

"I just saw Dr. Burke, and he said I'm fine."

"*Except* for your heart. He said you're a good candidate for heart disease. It's probably all the fatty foods you eat. I just read up on a study in Japan about it," she said, pouring two glasses of apple cider. "If he could see you now, he'd never let me hear the end of it."

"I'm a grown man, and if I want bacon for breakfast, I'm going to have it," Bill muttered, popping a piece in his mouth to punctuate his defiance of the good doctor's orders.

"You just take it easy, mister. You're only getting the one strip, so you make it last."

Mary sat down in her chair and patted Willy's head which he always stuck in the crook of her arm to patiently wait for an offering from her plate. She cut a small sliver of egg white, laid it over a piece of buttered toast, and took a bite.

"*Similar reports of such strange occurrences have been steadily coming in since the first attack was reported yesterday evening...*" the newscaster said from the other room.

"Really, Bill, can't we just eat in peace? If I hear one more report about some crazy biting another person, I think I'll go crazy."

"It's important, Mary. It's getting worse, and they still don't know what it is yet. Now me, I'd like to be up to date on it," Bill said, reaching for the butter that Mary automatically moved further from his reach.

"All those hippie kids with their pot smoke, I bet. They probably got bored giving poor President Johnson grief about the war," Mary complained, taking a sip of her cider.

"And they're right to. That war is a travesty."

Mary didn't respond to this, and she snipped off another piece of egg. Bill looked at his wife, smiled at her as his hand crept to her plate towards the bacon. She spied this and slapped his hand away.

"Uh-uh-uh," she scolded, and smiled. "I'll call Dr. Burke and rat you out."

"Lousy piss-ant," he muttered. "My heart is fine. He just wants me to run out and buy whatever prescriptions he writes in his little notepad. It probably puts more money in his pocket, too. He was telling me they're coming out with some new medicines that people can take that will actually lower my chance of a heart attack." He waved his hand in a dismissive gesture. "I bet it's all a scam, too."

"You're too cynical for your own good. He's just trying to help you."

Bill made a disgusted noise as he concentrated on his food.

They ate in silence then, and as Bill spooned bits of fried potato lathered in ketchup into his mouth, his heart suddenly skipped a beat.

"*...strange men and women have been seen in packs, wandering around populated areas and attacking others around them for no apparent reason. The first report came in yesterday evening when an elderly man opening his newsstand for the morning rush was allegedly attacked and bitten by an unknown assailant...*"

Mary rolled her eyes at these words and snapped off a piece of bacon and fed it to Willy, who gratefully slapped his wet mouth around it.

"Aw, c'mon, honey, are you really gonna do that in front of me?" Bill groaned like a child. She giggled in response.

"The way Willy chases those rabbits around the backyard, I'm sure his heart can handle it. Maybe if you chased some rabbits, you could have some more bacon, too." She fed Willy another piece, which he chewed, his small, wet eyes on Bill's almost tauntingly. "They say exercise is good for you."

"I go into Charlie's General Store twice a week just to keep food in this house, and kibble for Willy is always on my list. I don't pay top dollar for that bacon just so I can watch you feed it to him!"

Bill's heart skipped another beat, and he sat back against his chair, his breathing becoming ragged, the piece of toast in his mouth refusing to be swallowed. He rubbed his chest as he made a face.

"Damn heart burn," he muttered.

"Again? See now? Look at you. You're complaining about wanting more bacon when you can barely handle what I made you. You and that heart burn. Being married to you is like having a child!" she responded, annoyed, sipping from her cider again.

Bill's heart began pumping rapidly, and sweat formed across his suddenly-pale forehead as he gripped his right arm. He gritted his teeth against the pain, let go of his arm and gripped the sides of the table. His eyes lolled around in his head, almost as if he was in a daze.

"Can't...oh, Mary...it hurts..." he managed, his head clouding over. "This... isn't...heartburn."

"Bill, oh my God, are you all right?" Mary asked, getting up from her chair.

Sharp pain rocketed across Bill's chest and his eyes bulged out after each jolt of pain. He tried to get up, knocking his plate and silverware to the floor with a loud clatter, a hunk of egg still stuck to the fork for which Willy greedily lunged.

"Bill, wait, sit down!" Mary pleaded, running to his side, forcing him to sit. "Sit! I'll call Dr. Burke!"

She pushed him into a sitting position and rushed into the living room where Bill could hear her pick up the phone. Sweat dripped down his face onto his best suit, the dark brown one Mary had gotten him for his birthday, the one he always wore to the first Sunday mass of each month when he volunteered to do the reading.

"Dr. Burke! Please, I need help! It's Bill! I think he's having a heart attack!"

Bill lost all control of his body, his head suddenly feeling like it weighed a ton. He pitched forward, slamming his head on the table, flipping Mary's remaining plate of breakfast up in the air. Mary's voice began to gradually drift away, akin to when she would try to wake him from a deep sleep and her voice would carry over into his dreams.

Eventually, Bill saw nothing through his open, glazed eyes, so he didn't hear Mary's panicked cries for help on the phone, nor the news broadcast on the TV about rumors of people recently deceased inexplicably rising from the dead...

BILL

*   *   *

Bill opened his eyes as he felt something nudging him from the side. He slowly raised his head, turned to look at whatever it was that was pushing against him, and saw that it was Willy, staring at him curiously and whining. Bill cocked his head in confusion, but then dropped his mouth open, spilling drool and unchewed bits of dry toast onto the table. He moaned and reached towards Willy, who cried and skittered backwards across the floor. The animal fled from the room, and Bill lunged for him, falling facedown on the floor. Mary looked up from her spot from a chair in the living room, the phone falling from numb fingers, her face streaming with tears. She looked at him and gasped in relief, getting up and rushing over to him.

"Bill! Oh, thank God! You weren't breathing for a minute, and I thought…" Mary trailed off, likely grateful not to have to say those words out loud. Bill, however, didn't understand what she was saying. He turned to look at her from her place on the floor, rubbing his forehead across the dirty tiles. She continued to speak to him, and though he couldn't understand what she was saying, he was attracted to the sound of her cries, anyway. Mary knelt down, grabbed his arm, and pulled him to his feet.

"Let's get you back in the chair," she said breathlessly, her head down while trying to support his weight. He groaned again and reached for her, grabbing her hair and pulling her head back sharply. She let out a scream, shrill and piercing. She clamored at his face, pushing him back, and Bill momentarily lost his balance, rocking backwards against the table and letting her go.

She backed up away from him, her hands in front of her.

"Bill, what's the matter with you?" she called to him, her voice still quivery from her mournful sobs, but still he didn't understand what she was saying. He approached her again, reaching out his arms, his mouth opening slowly.

There came a knocking on the front door and the bell began chiming.

"Mary? Mary, are you in there?" called a voice from the other room, following the slamming of the front door. Bill, his arms still raised, turned his whole body around to see Dr. Burke clutching his small, leather bag and rushing towards them. The man stopped when he saw Bill's condition, fear washing over his face as he slowly realized what was happening.

"Christ! Mary, get away from him!"

"Oh, God, what is this? What's going on?" she whined, still shrinking back into the corner of the kitchen.

"Mary, that's not Bill anymore! He's one of them! Get away from him, get out of there!"

He stepped into the kitchen and soon found himself the focus of Bill's attention.

Bill crept slowly after Dr. Burke, who stood very still, keeping his eyes on this once-normal man that had morphed into a monster. He lowered his bag to the kitchen tile which was covered with Mary's apple cider after spilling from the table, his other hand raised to show he wasn't a threat.

He straightened up and gently waved Bill towards him.

"C'mon, Bill, that's right. Come this way. That's it. I won't hurt you."

Bill obliged, walking towards him, moaning. When he was close enough, Dr. Burke shouted, "Run, Mary! Get behind me!"

Dr. Burke pushed Bill back over the kitchen table hard enough that he flipped back over the top and landed on the floor behind it.

Mary's feet slapped against the floor as she ran across the kitchen, panic in her eyes, still not understanding why her husband suddenly wanted to hurt her. Dr. Burke grabbed Mary by the arm, picked up his leather bag, and they ran through the living room to the front door. He whipped it open and pushed her outside as she called out to her husband one last time. Bill's eyes met Mary's for a brief second before she disappeared from his view; Mary saw her husband, but Bill only saw warm flesh.

He shambled through the living room, bumping clumsily into a small table that held several framed photos of Bill and his wife, knocking them onto the hardwood floor. Cracks ricocheted across the plated glass, and those that survived the fall didn't survive Bill's heavy footsteps that crushed them as he walked towards the front door in pursuit of his prey. The sound of the clattering frames sent Willy sprinting from his hiding place behind Bill's heavy recliner and he tore out the front door, yelping in fear.

As Bill made it to the door, he could see Dr. Burke shoving Mary, still in hysterics, into his brown, Ford Falcon station wagon. Willy tore off in the opposite direction, dashing across the road and narrowly avoiding getting hit by a passing milk truck. Bill stepped out of his peach-colored rancher and looked around him, trying to spot an easy meal. Their road was unpaved, and the small houses that lined the street were identical in construction and design. Nothing about them immediately interested him, so he turned his attention back to Dr. Burke's station wagon.

Mary clawed at the front passenger window at Bill, silently sobbing his name as Dr. Burke frantically drove off. Bill stepped onto his lawn and began following the car, intent on feeding on its occupants to quell the hollowness building inside him. The vehicle eventually vanished from sight, but Bill kept following, unaware of the likelihood he wouldn't be able to catch up.

An oncoming car honked at Bill, who didn't move, and the driver swerved out of the way to avoid hitting him.

"Goddamn fool!" the driver shouted, spinning tires and shooting dirt onto Bill's clean church suit. Bill spun, looked at the car as it sped away and then began following the receding vehicle, spotting new potential. His feet clomped awkwardly on the dirt road as he pursued the speeding car.

Bill continued to walk, though the car was long out of sight, and now there was nothing around that appealed to his desire to quench the hunger overpowering him. He eventually walked for so long that the houses on either side of him disappeared and were soon replaced by tall maple trees.

Bill walked across a field and saw the wrought-iron gated entrance to Evanstown Cemetery. On the gate were a few crows and as the birds flapped their wings and cawed at one another, Bill headed for them, attracted to the noise and motion. As he swatted at them dumbly from the ground, the birds cawed a final time and took off into the air.

He watched them go and then slogged through the open gate, finding himself among tombstones that jutted unevenly out of the ground like broken teeth, and despite not seeing anything living, he continued to walk, directionless.

He stumbled around the cemetery for more than an hour, chasing after small rodents or birds when they appeared. A few times he found worms or beetles, but they never filled the hole inside him, never seemed to quench that something in his gut that needed to be filled.

Then, off in the distance, Bill suddenly spotted two figures moving about in front of one of the tombstones. It was a man with glasses and a woman, the latter holding flowers.

Bill grunted, wiped the back of his hand across his sloppy, drooling mouth, and pursued them, his suit now filthy from the times he'd tripped and spoiled it in the wet grass from the afternoon rain shower. As he moved closer to the couple, he could hear them arguing, the man saying something to the woman that seemed to scare her. Then he pretended to be pulled behind a tombstone as the woman looked on, not the least bit amused.

The man then pointed right at Bill and he could see the man looking at him. The man whispered something to the woman and ran off behind a tree as the woman turned and shouted at him, her face filled with anger...and something else, too. Fear, perhaps.

With his hands in his pockets, the man now casually began walking back to his car.

Though Bill's stomach was useless and could no longer growl, his hunger intensified as he watched the woman shifting about impatiently on the green lawn.

She began walking away back to her car, following the man that was already heading that way. She tried not to make eye contact, looking at her shoes with her hands in the pockets of her coat to ward of the chill off the coming night.

Bill approached the woman, and when he was no more than three feet away, she glanced up at him, a slight hint of a smile coming to her lips. She was assuming Bill was going to say hello to her and she was ready with the required greeting herself, so her face changed to one of shock when Bill lunged for her, grabbing her shoulders, his mouth widening to take a selfish helping of her.

The hunger was unbearable now, and soon he would consume her. Soon this growing pain inside him would cease. She raised her hands on instinct and cried out, Bill dwarfing her by almost a foot.

They struggled for a few seconds as she fought off this madman who was attacking her for no reason. But just before he could sink his teeth into her, he was suddenly tackled from behind and was forced to let go of the woman as he was thrown sideways, the man with the glasses now holding onto him.

"Russell, help me. Help me!" the woman cried out in fear as she ran to a tombstone and wrapped her hands around it for support.

Not caring who he had in his grasp, Bill attacked the man now, encircling his arms around him as they struggled. Bill's right hand went to the man's face and he raked the eyeglasses off him as the two struggled like dancers battling for the lead in the school play.

The man's attempts to free himself caused the two of them to pitch forward, the man's head smashing against the corner of a low tombstone. A large gash on his forehead immediately began flowing blood, and just as Bill was about to take a bite, the woman began screaming. Bill looked up at her sharply, attracted to her terrified screams, and was no longer interested in the man. He advanced on her again.

The woman ran off, dodging in and out of tombstones as Bill followed close behind. His slow footsteps were a disadvantage for him, but he would not give up. Not this time.

As she ran, she fell forward, sliding in the wet grass, but she pulled herself to her feet, glancing over her shoulder to see Bill advancing on her. With a frightened scream, she ran on, reaching her car and climbing inside. She slammed the door locks home, but for some reason she didn't drive away.

That was fine with Bill, and though he was losing his reasoning powers, he still had enough memory left to pick up a brick, knowing this would break the glass of the car.

He began banging on the glass, his face distorted in an expression of anger and death as he pummeled the driver's side window, shattering it and dropping the brick.

Reaching inside, he pawed at the woman, but she continued to dodge him. She reached under the dash and released the emergency break, the car beginning to roll down the steep embankment.

Frustrated she was escaping him, he began to chase after the car as it outdistanced him in seconds.

The tire tracks now pressed into the lawn were an easy trail to follow, and he stumbled forwards, the brick he'd used now forgotten behind him.

He would track her for as long as it took. He needed to satisfy the hunger inside him, and he would pursue her until he was finally wrapping his hands around her throat, until he was grabbing warm, steaming handfuls of her entrails between his dead fingers to then shove into his vapid mouth.

Mary had escaped him, and so had the doctor.

This one wouldn't.

This one was *his*.

THE DINER

JOE TONZELLI

The man tightened his grip around the steering wheel of his idling car as he stared at the onslaught of attackers coming towards him from every angle. They looked like regular people—hell, they *were* regular people—but at the same time, they weren't. They were people taken over by something, and what that something was, he didn't know. The normal people he had encountered on the road had a bevy of theories, and the radio claimed to know as well, but the *why* or *how* wasn't so important when you were surrounded by an army of them. They wore shirts and ties and their best Sunday dresses, but that didn't mean they were human. *Couldn't* mean they were human. Because above their Windsor knots, their Sheffield blue shirts, and their frilly, floral sundresses, their mouths were agape with a film of drool cascading slowly down their bloody chins; their skin was pale white.

Their eyes were wide, as if in a permanent state of surprise, but at the same time were so very blank. To look into the eyes of one of these *things*, you would think they had never witnessed the birth of a child, never laughed so hard they had to lean on their own knees for support, doubling over from whatever stupid joke had set them off in the first place, or never held another human being in love and intimacy.

They were mindless.

They were monstrous.

But they were *us*.

The man turned quickly when he heard soft flesh slapping against the backside of his sky-blue '57 Ford Fairlane. He let his right hand drop from the steering wheel to grasp the tire iron sitting beside him on the passenger seat as he stared down the thing that was behind his car. Slowly and methodically, he grabbed the tire iron, cast a look into each mirror to gauge how many of them there were, inhaled a single deep breath, and lunged from his car.

They were upon him almost at once, and he swung the tire iron into their faces, one after the other. Some were instantly killed, some merely stunned, while some barely reacted at all. The sound of metal against skin and bone was nauseating, and in a less surreal situation, it would have turned his stomach, caused him to dry heave the morning's ham and eggs. There weren't many of them, at least not on this side of the road, and he was able to kill most of those that were an immediate threat. He broke through several attackers that were still advancing and jumped through the hole he created in the middle of them, running towards the squad car that had skidded off the road to avoid hitting what the police officer inside must have thought were people in need.

The man with the tire iron skidded to a stop at the car, which had smashed into a tree at intense speed, mangling the driver's side door and shattering its window. The man steadied himself from his sprint by leaning on the hood, and as he beat against the window on the passenger side, he could see inside the car that the police officer was motionless. Blood was dripping from a horizontal wound on his forehead, drop by drop, onto his navy blue slacks, and it formed a large black stain on his left thigh.

The man furiously pounded on the passenger window, trying to wake the police officer from his stupor, trying to determine if he was still alive. There was no sign of life coming from him, and the man was about to give up when he saw the police officer stir. Despite all the moaning coming from those slowly advancing things, he heard a groan of pain emanating from inside the car. The man peered through the window and was able to just make out the name on the officer's badge.

"Hey... Hey, Riley! Riley, can you hear me?" the man shouted at him.

The police officer, maybe twenty-five years old, maybe younger, held his head wearily up, his hands blotting the cut on his head. The man continued to tap on the window, trying to alert him to the danger growing as the small crowd surrounded them. Riley looked over at him, smiled a half-smile, and said, "I'm all right, partner. Just skidded off the road over there. Let me call this in."

"Get out of the car!" screamed the man, pounding again. "They're coming!"

Riley, still woozy from the crash, finally looked around and spotted the pack of drooling things stumbling towards them with their blood-drenched shirts and outstretched arms.

"Oh, shit! Holy, holy shit!" was his response.

As the man turned behind him to see how close they had gotten, Riley quickly picked up his car radio and began screaming into it. "Dispatch! Dispatch: this is car sixty-eight! We have us a riot situation! Repeat! We have us a riot situation! Request immediate assistance! Over!"

"Get out of the car, man! They won't get here in time!" the man pleaded.

"*This is dispatch. Request for assistance denied. No officers available. I repeat, no officers available. All are responding to emergency calls,*" someone on the radio responded, though there was sympathy present in the otherwise firm female's voice.

"Dispatch, request immediate assistance! This *is* an emergency! Over!" he repeated desperately, and then, "Damn it, Shirley, I need backup!"

"Listen, Riley, you need to get out of that car and help me! I can't fight them all myself! There's too many of them!" the man pleaded.

Riley threw the radio down in anger and took another quick look around at the approaching crowd. He beat against the driver's side door with his shoulder, but the mangled frame had locked the door permanently in place. He crawled over to the passenger seat and pushed the door open. He got out, yanked his gun from his holster—a .38 Special—and took aim at the approaching people.

"Halt! I said halt!"

The approaching people did not halt.

"They're not going to halt, Riley! Shoot! You have to shoot them!" The man swung the tire iron into an approaching attacker's face, knocking the nose clean off and sending it through the air like a golfer would a ball. Riley shouted in surprise and turned his gun on the man instead of the oncoming horde.

"Freeze, sir! Do not engage! I am the only one authorized to use deadly force!"

"You better wake up," said the man, readying his tire iron for another swing, his eyes on the adversaries. "Or you're not going to make it out of this alive."

Another attacker, this one a baseball player adorned in a red and white striped uniform, reached his hands out to Riley, his mouth wide open, ready to bite. Riley pushed him back and stuck the gun in his face.

"I will shoot, sir! Don't do this!" Riley shouted in warning. The baseball player made no sign of stopping or understanding and advanced again.

"Shoot him, goddamn it!" the man shouted, furious and frustrated.

Riley obliged, shooting the baseball player in the arm. He stumbled momentarily, but began advancing again. He didn't grab his arm in pain, nor did blood pour from the wound. It was as if the shot had no effect at all.

"What the hell?"

"The head! Shoot him in the head!" the man yelled.

"But I just shot..."

"Now!"

Riley aimed the gun at the baseball player's face, grimaced, and pulled the trigger. The baseball player went down immediately, the escaping bullet tearing a hole through the back of the hat and knocking it off.

"Now keep doing that!" the man shouted.

Riley took aim at the closest attackers and fired. An elderly man in a brand new suit, a nun with a chunk of flesh torn out of the right side of her face, a young girl in a flowing poodle skirt with a notepad stuck in the front pocket of her black-and-white checkered shirt, whose body stumbled around on a broken foot; they all went down one by one. Meanwhile, the man with the tire iron fended off attacks of his own, bashing the people in the temple—their weakest spot—or plunging his weapon directly through their eyes.

"What is this, mister? You seem to know an awful lot," Riley said, taking aim at the next thing that was once human, waiting for him to get closer before firing.

"There's no time for that, Riley. You just keep firing that gun, and you best reload. You fired five shots already, which means you only have one left."

The police officer grabbed immediately at his belt, felt around for his extra bullets, found them, and shot his last round before refilling the chamber. He gave the man a quick, bemused look.

"Who are you anyway, mister?"

"I'm Duane," the man answered, striking the head of an attacker so hard on his soggy head that his left eye flew through the air like a ping pong ball.

"How do you know what's going on? You sure act like you do," he said.

"I don't, really. Not much, anyway. No one seems to know what's happening. Normal people just started going crazy, attacking and biting folks. I think some of them…" he trailed off, not knowing how to finish his sentence. Despite the madness in front of them, despite the fact that he knew it in his heart it was true.

"Some of them what?" Riley demanded.

"I think some of them…came back from the dead. They were dead, and they just…came back."

"That's crazy!" Riley said, but he paused for a moment as he considered the enemy around him. "That can't happen!"

"I think the whole world is going to redefine the word *can't* after today."

Duane swung his tire iron in the face of a doctor dressed in a large white lab coat with a stethoscope wrapped around his neck, a mouth-shaped chunk of flesh missing from his neck. Riley fired a round into the head of a nurse with a bloody mouth, shattering an almost-perfectly round hole through her teeth.

"I'm getting on that radio and we're going to call in the Calvary! Forget this!"

"You heard them, there's no one to send! Don't fall back! We're doing all right! We might make it out of this alive!" Duane pleaded.

"The day I take orders from one of you people is the day I'll put a dress on and sing at Easter Mass."

Duane shook his head, then sliced off an attacker's ear with an unfocused swing.

"Nice, man, that's real good," he said bitterly.

Riley jumped into the passenger seat of his squad car and grabbed the radio from the floor.

"I don't know what I need to say to make you realize there is no help coming!" Duane yelled, shaking his head in frustration.

"And I'm gonna listen to the guy who's telling me that we're fighting ghouls from the grave?" Riley retorted.

"I don't want to believe it, either, but after what I've seen...yeah, man. I believe it. Now get your ass out of that car or neither of us is gonna make it out of this thing alive!"

Two attackers rushed at Duane from both sides, knocking the tire iron out of his hands and him onto his back. They fell on him, snapping their teeth above his face. He held both their heads away, grabbing one by the chin and the other by the neck.

"Hey, man, help me!" Duane cried, trying to dodge the falling globs of disgusting spit coming from their wretched mouths.

"This is Officer Riley for God's sake, and I'm on Route 10 out past the reservoir. If I don't hear verification that additional officers have been dispatched, I'm going to come down there and rip your head off, Shirley!" Riley spat desperately into the radio.

Duane grappled with his two foes, furious at Riley's inaction, and smashed their heads together with such force that when they fell away, their heads were flattened where they had connected. He jumped to his feet, grabbed the tire iron, and turned to Riley still sitting in the passenger's seat. He still had the radio to his lips and was about to speak again.

"You stupid..." Duane started, stepping forward, when another attacker suddenly sprang up on the other side of the squad car and grabbed Riley through the shattered driver's side window.

"Watch out!" Duane cried, far too late. The thing that was once a middle-aged man yanked Riley close to the driver's side window and bit down on his throat—hard. Riley exhaled an awful scream, high-pitched and gurgling wet.

"Help, Duane! Help!" he managed, blood spraying from his mouth in misty, wet clouds. It was too late for him, and Duane knew it, but he grabbed at Riley's flailing hand through the open passenger side door, anyway.

"Hold on, man!"

As Riley fought the dead man off with one hand, trying desperately to push him away by the forehead, his other hand fumbled into his holster and withdrew his gun. He shot blindly around the roof of the car in a stupor of half-dead shock, trying to shoot the thing in the head, but by then Riley was useless to defend himself. One shot after the other went off directionless, tearing through the car's roof or into the tree in which the car had smashed. Finally, Riley fired one last shot, which blew a hole through his hand that was holding the dead man at bay, as well as the dead man's head. The attacker had bitten far enough into Riley's throat that he had been chewing on the base of Riley's tongue, and when he flipped over backwards, his jaws that were still clamped down on Riley's tongue yanked it through the jagged hole in the officer's throat. Riley's tongue now rested on top of his destroyed neck like a tie, blood spurting from the wound underneath. He spoke soundlessly to Duane, reaching his arm out for help, grasping his blood-covered gun. The tongue convulsed like a flapping fish out of water overtop his bloody throat, responding to the muscles Riley was desperately using just enough to say two garbled words. "*Kill me.*"

A torrent of blood fired out of Riley's throat and splattered against the windshield, projected outward from his further attempt to speak. It rained down in small crimson rivers as Duane stared at the misplaced tongue in shock and morbid fascination. The way it moved reminded him of that schlocky movie he had seen years ago at the drive-in with that guy from *The Great Escape*.

Duane took the gun, slick with Riley's blood, his eyes still on the mangled tongue. Riley thrashed in pain, breaking Duane out of his trance. He raised the gun, said, "Sorry, man," and shot Riley through the left eye. Duane stared at him for a moment, feeling guilt and regret surge through his heart before realizing there was more than just his morality at stake right then. He turned to see a middle-aged woman with hair done-up like a schoolmarm reaching for him, a clean bite mark missing from her left ear. He easily pushed her aside and ran, ducking past another that snarled in his face. He shot one attacker in the chin that was lunging at him, and as he turned to finish the man off, the gun clicked at him. He yelled in anger, tossed it aside, and ran back to his car, which thankfully was clear of the dead. He sat down in the seat, shifted the car into drive, and stepped on the gas.

While he drove, he raised his hand up to his face and stared at Riley's blood. He grabbed some newspapers from the floor of the passenger side and wiped it off as best he could.

The car sped forward; passing a road sign that had been battered and beaten by years of abusive weather.

EVANSTOWN: 3 MILES.

Duane checked his gas gauge and saw he had half a tank; more than enough to reach civilization, to find people, to get help.

He flipped on the radio, turned the dial until he found a clear station, and waited for the emergency interruption that was going to occur at any moment, if it hadn't already.

* * *

Duane roared past a wide graveyard on his right during his journey to Evanstown. He craned his neck to see inside, though he wasn't sure why. Was he looking to see hands reaching through their grave blankets, or the shuffling dead wandering between tombstones? He wasn't sure. Except for a lone white car traveling slowly through the graveyard's inner roads, the place looked quiet. He thought a moment about finding a way into the graveyard, of warning whoever it was that slowly circled within, but he opted to keep driving, to find help. If the people in the cemetery were in a car, they could at least make a quick escape if they had to. This was what he reasoned, anyway.

Several news networks on the radio had interrupted normal broadcasts to alert people about rioting taking place along the East Coast. Very little was known about the rioters, but they had promised to keep listeners informed when newer information was available.

"Rioters. Right. And I'm Curly Howard," Duane said to himself, shaking his head.

He saw a sign approaching in the distance, and he leaned forward; he read that it was a sign welcoming him to Evanstown. And just beyond that on his left was a small roadside restaurant and gas station. A large sign lettered with small yellow bulbs, barely visible on this overcast, thundering day, spelled out *Beekman's Diner,* with a newer looking sign below it which read "**Gas!**"

"Thank God," he whispered, screeching off the road and into the sandy parking lot of the quaint diner. He parked crookedly in a spot between a blue Oldsmobile and a big rig truck. Turning off his engine, he jumped out, still gripping the tire iron. He ran past the handful of cars parked in front of the diner and tore through the front entrance.

"Hello? Where is a ph…I need a phone!" he stammered, the occupants of the diner barely giving him the time of day. Most turned to acknowledge his presence, but none seemed to be in a hurry to direct him to a phone, even though he was very clearly rattled.

An elderly woman, a waitress, came over, notepad in hand and a pencil behind her ear.

"Help you?" she asked, eyeing him suspiciously. Duane realized he was still holding the tire iron in faintly bloody hands and he looked down at it, confused as to why it was there.

"I, uh…I need a phone. Do you have a phone?"

The waitress continued to eye him warily, but she pointed to the back of the diner, her thumb crooked over her shoulder.

Duane went to the phone, grabbing it off the handle and dialed the number for emergency services. He leaned his head against the cool phone stand, waiting for the operator to pick up. As it rang, he looked down at his hands, seeing the remnants of Riley's blood. He held the phone against his shoulder and rubbed his hands together, trying to rub away the blood. As he did so, he looked around the diner again. Sitting at the front counter, a mother stared at him over her steaming cup of coffee as her young son ate his scrambled eggs. A burly man in a brown beard and dressed in a flannel shirt, overalls and a wicker fedora, stared at him the hardest from one of the booths. A cigarette rested between the lone man's fingers, and had been ignored for so long that a half-inch of unbroken ash jutted from the smoldering filter. Duane met the man's gaze for a moment, but then turned back to the phone, realizing that no one had yet answered. He pressed the receiver down until he heard a dial tone, then he dialed again. He hung up after four rings and turned with hands on his hips, head down. He walked quickly over to the counter where the elderly waitress was counting out change for a customer.

"I need to talk to you, miss. It's important."

"Hang on just a sec', honey," she said, not trying to sound friendly. "Let me just take care of this gentleman."

"But you don't understand, there are…"

The waitress made it a point to cut him off by counting the change louder, and then slid it across the counter to the customer, who picked up most of it and slid fifty cents back to her.

"For you, Francine."

"Aw, thanks, Donny. I'll see you soon. Say hi to the kids for me."

"You bet," said the man, shoving the rest of his change in his pocket and leaving, the bell on the door twinkling merrily on his way out.

"Okay, sir, what can I do for you? Were you able to make your phone call?" she asked, talking to him as if he were a child, a slight frown on her face.

"Listen, I don't know how I should go about this. I really need to get in touch with the police, but the operators aren't answering. I…something's wrong out there. Haven't you been listening to the radio today? Watched any TV?"

"Honey, this is a diner. People come in here and they wanna eat, so you know what we do? We cook for 'em. We don't have time to be sittin' around and listenin' to no banter on the radio."

Duane sighed and rubbed the top of his nose, impatient and beginning to grow angry.

"There are…things out there that used to be people. I don't know what they are, but… these people are going crazy, I think. The radio's calling them rioters, but they're not. They're…" he trailed off again. He hated having to say it. He'd said it a few times already, baffled at his awful luck that he continued to run into people who had no idea that something so completely unbelievable was happening.

The young boy sitting next to his mother at the counter looked at Duane, waiting to hear what he would say. Duane looked at the boy for a moment, and then back at Francine. He leaned in close.

"There are people coming back from the dead," he said, and though it was barely a whisper, the boy audibly gasped and clung to his mother's arm. Francine looked quickly at the little boy before snapping her head back to look at Duane coldly.

"Mister, I don't know what you're on, but I think you should leave our diner before I call the police."

"Francine, I would love for you to call the police. In fact, I'm *begging* you to call the police."

Francine stared at Duane for a moment, unaware of what he could possibly want from her, but the look on her face said it all. She thought he was crazy. This normal looking dark man, reasonably dressed in brown slacks, a blue and white striped button-up shirt underneath a cream colored cardigan sweater, and who was gripping a tire iron. This man who rushes into her diner with this cockamamie story about people *coming back from the dead*.

"Hey, Earl? Ya wanna come on over here?" Francine called behind her, not taking her eyes off Duane.

"What is it, Francine? I'm busy," called an unseen voice from the back.

"Someone out here wants to talk to you. He's got something *real* important to tell you." Her sarcastic emphasis of the word 'real' did nothing to allay Duane's fears that these people, no matter how dramatic a story he told them, weren't going to take him seriously.

"Hold your horses, girl, I'll be right there."

"He'll be just a minute," she said, continuing to give him that cold, distant look.

"Goddamn it, we don't have time for this!" Duane yelled, pounding his fist on the counter, causing everyone within earshot to stare at him with even deeper curiosity.

"And what exactly is it that we don't have time for? Your little fairy tales about the dead walkin' around?"

"If you would just put on the radio, or a TV, you could *hear* them talking about it!"

Francine made no attempts to entertain Duane's obsession further. He turned wildly, at the end of his rope, and looked out among the rest of the diner patrons who were all watching him intently.

"All you people need to listen up!" The remaining customers in the diner, the young mother and her son, an elderly couple, and two young men, including the one who had eyed Duane while he was on the phone, all sat quietly, their attention on him. "I don't even know how to put this, so I'm not gonna pussyfoot around. I'm just going to come out and say it." He still had their attention, so he sighed once and said: "The dead are...coming back to life." He shut his eyes, flinching at how bad and ridiculous it sounded when he said the words. He was greeted with the reaction he had pretty much expected; the two lone truck drivers laughed and turned back to their meals, the elderly couple simply turned without any perceivable reaction at all, and the mother continued to look at him, maybe to see how long his charade would continue, how ludicrous it would get.

"Just now I was driving down Route 10, and I was attacked by a bunch of these *things*," Duane said. "I was in the city earlier today, and I saw people...going crazy. They were chasing other folks and biting them. Ripping...parts of them off and eating them."

The mother of the young boy stood up just then. "That's just about enough out of you, mister. I don't know what your intention is here today, but you're scaring my little boy!"

Duane looked at the boy again, noticed for the first time that he was dressed as a cowboy, complete with a gun holster clipped to the waistband of his denim jeans and a plastic, golden badge pinned to his plaid shirt. The boy sniffled, his tears obvious. He ran the sleeve of his shirt against his face, trying to wipe away the proof of his fear.

"Ma'am, I assure you, I am just trying to help! If someone—*anyone*—would just put on a radio, you could all hear it for yourselves! Please!"

Earl finally came out from behind the counter, an older gentleman around the age of sixty. Dressed in a stained white shirt, he wiped his hands on the dirty apron hanging from his waist.

"Okay, mister. You just calm down. We'll figure this out. We don't want no trouble here."

"Figure this out? Listen to me, I'm not crazy! Someone, please, go get a goddamned radio so you can finally hear for yourself!"

"Now you wait just a minute, mister. You can't come in here and..." was all Earl could manage before Duane charged at him, grabbed him by his dirty shirt, and forced him into the back of the kitchen area.

"Earl!" shouted Francine. "Earl, I'm calling the police right now!" As Francine picked up the phone, tapping the receiver and waiting to hear a dial tone, Duane continued to push Earl deeper into the kitchen until they stumbled upon a small, cluttered office.

Earl's office.

Duane pushed Earl down hard into a chair and began tearing through the office, opening up a series of metal cabinets. Loose papers and pens, packages of napkins, extra menus; they all rained down onto the faded tiles. He ripped open door after door of each cabinet and threw everything onto the floor until he finally found what he was looking for. He grabbed the large, brown Zenith radio and awkwardly tucked it under one arm, and with his other, again grabbed Earl by his shirt and forced him to the front of the diner. Getting to the counter, he pushed Earl away, slammed the radio on the counter, plugged it in, and switched it on. He fumbled with the dial as the diner patrons got up from their seats to inch either closer to the exit or to the radio, curious to see if there was truth in Duane's claims. He finally found a clear station which was broadcasting an interview between two men. Knowing this was what he was hoping for, he raised the volume for all to hear.

"*...so if any of your listeners are in those areas, we recommend that everyone safeguard their houses as soon as possible. Find old wood if you can, board up windows and doors, turn off any outside lights when it gets dark. Stay still and keep quiet. Noise attracts them. We are doing our best to feed citizens information as it comes, but the National Civil Defense Headquarters is releasing very little information every few hours.*"

"*Dr. Grimes, what can a person do if they find themselves being accosted by one of these people?*"

"The best defense is a gunshot to the head. If you don't have a gun, grab a club, a heavy tool of some kind, and try to destroy the brain. We want your listeners to remember that these people are a threat to you and your loved ones. There have been no instances of these people acting passively. All have attacked when the opportunity was presented for them to do so. We ask that you please remember this in the event you come across someone you know. We know it will be hard to face such a situation, but remember, they are a threat. They will hurt you and kill you if they have the chance. We don't intend to sound so callous about it all, but knowing this beforehand could very well save your life."

"Thank you, Doctor, for your help. Uh, if you are just tuning in, we're sitting now with Dr. Grimes from the National Aeronautics and Space Administration. He's going to remain in the studio with us, and we'll be releasing information as soon as it becomes available."

Duane lowered the volume and looked at everyone. No one spoke. Everyone traded glances back and forth.

"Oh my God," Francine said, sitting down behind the counter.

"Now wait just a minute here," said one of the truck drivers. "You can't tell me you actually believe all this crap, do you?"

"You heard the radio, Ray," Earl said.

"Of course I heard it! I should ask you the same thing! Weren't *you* listening? And not once did I hear the word *dead* either. This is just a hoax! Some kind of joke!"

"It's no joke. I've seen these things," Duane said, looking to the trucker with pleading eyes.

"Sure, you did. What did they look like? Big, tall, and green, with square heads and bolts in their necks? Or did they have bandages wrapped around them? I know, maybe they wore long, flowing capes and tried to drink your blood," Ray laughed, using a terrible Bela Lugosi accent on his last three words.

"About ten miles back," Duane said, ignoring Ray's wisecracks, "I pulled off the road to help a police officer in trouble. He'd skidded off the road trying to avoid hitting a bunch of those things. Slammed into a tree. I went to help him, and we fought them off for a little bit. Got them in the head, like they said on the radio, and it was working. They got him, though—the officer. They bit his neck. Wide open."

No one spoke for a moment.

"What was his name?" asked the elderly woman, dressed like she had just come from church.

"His name was Riley. Did anyone here know him?"

"You say... Riley?" she asked, fear making her voice crack slightly.

"Yes, ma'am," Duane said. "Looked young, too."

"Oh my God. Billy Riley...?" she said, her hands creeping up to her face.

"Come on, Beverly. You can't honestly believe all this!" Ray said, turning to her. "Don't you remember that thing years ago? That thing on the radio? Hell, I'm sure you do. You were probably around when they invented the radio, for Christ's sake!"

"Ray Willis, you watch yourself," Earl said.

"You know what I'm talking about, Earl. That thing they did...What was it, thirty years ago, I bet? Aliens coming down? Taking over the world? And everyone believed it! There was panic in the streets! And then they all came out and apologized. They said it was just a radio show, said they didn't mean for folks to get all riled up, hurt themselves, thinking it was real! They play it every Halloween, now! This is the same kind of thing! And Halloween is just a few weeks away!" He turned now, pointed to Duane. "And this guy...I don't know if he's in on it, or if he just has an overactive imagination."

Duane could feel his anger rising again. "Why don't you let them make up their own minds, Ray?" Duane snarled through gritted teeth.

"You don't call me Ray, mister. You don't know me, and you never will. I don't know you..."

"I'm Duane."

"...and I sure don't want to know you or your kind of people. Now, you're scaring the hell out of my friends. And I won't stand for it."

"You want me to leave, Ray? That it?" Duane challenged.

"You bet your ass I do."

"Fine. Call the police. Have them come get me. I'll sit right down here at this counter, and I won't fight or struggle and I won't say another word until they get here." Duane sat down, slid his tire iron halfway across the counter for effect, and folded his hands.

"Suits me, mister," Ray said and turned to Francine. "Frannie, call Sheriff Kosana. Tell him we got us a...loon up here at your fine diner."

"Phone's out, Ray. I tried calling earlier, when..." Francine began, glanced at Duane, and then dropped her eyes.

Duane looked at Ray, who glared back.

"And I know you saw me try to use the pay phone earlier, Ray. I could feel your eyes burning a hole right in my back. I didn't get through then, either, did I?"

Ray looked at Francine again, then strode over to the counter and grabbed the phone off the cradle. He listened, dialed numbers, tapped the receiver. He dropped the phone into the cradle and held his head in his hands for a moment. Then he got up, pulled a few bills from his pocket, handed them to Francine, and began walking to the door.

"Tell you what, Frannie. I gotta pass the station on my way home, anyway. I'll stop in there myself and tell the sheriff about the situation with your new friend here. Oh, and I gave you a little extra. I'm gonna grab some gas on my way out. My pickup's damn near empty."

"Ray, listen, you don't know what's going on out there," Duane tried to reason. "Those things I left behind me on Route 10, they could be here soon. And that's not even considering what you might have going on in this town." Duane saw that Ray was still heading to the door. The man made no sign of stopping, nor was he listening. "Damn it, Ray! Please!"

Ray pushed the door open—the little silver bell on the door handle jingling merrily again—and let it slam behind him.

Duane looked at the diner full of people who were also staring at him. He opened his mouth to speak when a scream suddenly rang out. It was from the mother of the little cowboy, who was backing up slowly from the far window, her child in her arms. She squeezed her eyes shut, her face buried into her little boy's neck.

"What is it, dear?" asked Earl. "What did ya see?"

"I...I don't know. I don't want to look, someone please come look for me!" the young mother said. She turned away, squeezing her eyes shut and holding her son to her.

Duane and Earl ran over to the large window and looked out. Just at the edge of the parking lot, they saw a small crowd of disheveled, bloody people, maybe twenty or so, slowly approaching the diner.

"Oh my God!" Earl exclaimed, "Look at them all!"

"Earl, what is it?" Francine asked from behind the counter, craning her neck to see out the window.

Duane ran over to the diner's entrance and opened it, sticking his head out. He called over to Ray, who was sitting in his pickup truck, slowly backing out, completely unaware of the shambling threat on the other side of the diner. He pulled a U-turn and parked aside one of the few gasoline tanks next to the diner. He jumped out, leaving his door hanging wide open, and grabbed a pump from the tank.

"Ray, goddamn it! They're coming!" Duane yelled.

Ray, head down, sticking the pump into his gas tank, waved Duane away with his free hand.

"Ray! Just look behind you, for Christ's sake!"

Ray looked up at Duane, the annoyance on his face more than obvious. He turned to the lever to release the gas flow into his white Ford pickup truck when Duane called out to him one last time, seeing that the people had rounded the corner and were heading straight for him.

"You moron, Ray! They're right behind you!"

"You know something, Duane, I'm gonna come over there and stick my foot right up your..."

A wave of attackers was on Ray then, pawing at him, grabbing at him. Ray stared at them, a look on his face depicting a mixture of fear, defeat, and even slight bemusement. It was a look showing that, of all the scenarios possible in which to find himself proven wrong, he never thought in a million years that he would be so adamantly wrong about this one thing.

Duane stepped out of the diner when one attacker grabbed Ray's head and pulled him towards its gnashing teeth. Ray's wicker hat was batted off his head and stamped on by the ensuing crowd.

Duane sat a moment, trying to decide if his intervention would even make a difference. Ray had been brought down to the ground by then, the pickup thankfully obscuring what animalistic things the crowd was doing to him. Ray yelled out, the sound akin to that of a schoolyard girl, and Duane took another few steps forward in trepidation, knowing in his heart there was nothing he could do. He slammed his fist on the metal railing and ran back inside, shutting the door quickly and locking all three locks.

"They got him, the dumb bastard," Duane said. "They got him." Gasps rang out in response, while some steadied themselves on the counter. Duane hung his head a moment, but then compulsively swiped a nearby candy dish of after-dinner mints across the restaurant. He turned to the remaining diner customers and hated the look they were giving him. It wasn't a look he'd seen before, but he knew it plain as day just the same. They were looking to him for help. They were looking to him to protect them. Like it or not, Duane had been chosen as their hero.

"Is Ray...?" Francine started, her hand creeping up to her mouth.

"Earl, how many staff you got in this diner besides you and Francine?" Duane asked, ignoring the question in which the answer was painfully obvious.

"I got two cooks in the back. And Dora, my sister-in-law—she's our other waitress."

"Dora's not here today, Earl," Francine said, looking fearful.

"What? Jesus, is she at the house?"

"I don't know, she just didn't show, didn't call! I figured you knew!"

Everyone in the diner came to the same conclusion right about the same time, but no one dared speak it aloud.

"I'm sure she's fine. You know Dora, she probably just..." Francine began.

"All right, Earl, go get the cooks, bring them up here," Duane said, cutting her off before she had the chance to let her mind run wild with paranoid thoughts.

"We're here, mister," a voice called out. Duane turned, looked over to the counter, and saw two men staring at him from the back wall, confused looks on their faces, cigarettes hanging out of their mouths.

"Earl...what's going on?" one of them asked, the cigarette bouncing around between his lips.

"Listen, you guys, we got us a real situation here," Earl said. "Shut them ovens off and get over here." The cooks scattered, no questions asked, following their boss's orders.

"All right, listen, there's not too many of them out there," Duane said, wiping away the cold sweat forming on his forehead. "The only option I see is to get out of here, somehow, and into our cars. Start some kind of convoy into town."

Duane looked outside again, ignored the sight of even more approaching attackers, and tried to take a mental inventory of the cars. He counted them all, and including the big rig truck as well as his own car, there were five vehicles in the lot. Duane looked around the diner and took a quick headcount. Ten people.

"Who's got a car out there in the lot?" Duane asked.

Francine raised her hand.

"Earl and I drive in together every morning. It's that silver Pontiac out there."

The remaining truck driver, a portly man in a striped shirt and jeans, also raised his hand, before resting the palm on his head.

"The big rig out there is mine. I could fit two people in the cab with me, no problem."

The mother with the young cowboy stepped forward.

"The Oldsmobile...the blue car with the dented fender. That's me."

"And we got the red pickup out there."

Duane turned to see the elderly man, a cane in his hand and his nervous wife at his side.

"That's everybody, then? What about your two cooks?" Duane asked.

"They hoof it every morning. They live in Evanstown, so it ain't that far for them," Earl answered.

The sound of palms on glass startled everyone. They turned to see that the crowd had finished with Ray and had now reached the front entrance. Everyone watched as they slapped dumbly against the thick diner window glass. The door rattled, its locks safely in place, as they tried to fight their way inside the diner.

"How strong is that glass?" Duane asked, stepping slowly back from the windows.

"Strong enough. Won't shatter, that's for sure. After that freak hailstorm we had back in '65, I ordered the best they had."

With each hand striking against the glass, the little cowboy hugged tighter to his equally frightened mother, and the squeals he let out unnerved Duane each time. He turned to the little boy, wrapped in his mother's arms, and placed a calm hand on the boy's head.

"What's your name, kiddo?"

"Georgie."

"Listen up, Georgie the Cowboy. I need you to do something. Can you do something for me?"

The little boy nodded, tears spilling from under his black cowboy hat.

"Your mom is scared, little man. And so am I. Now, we need you to be brave, okay? For both of us. The braver you are, the braver we can be, too. Got it?"

The little boy nodded again, wiping away his tears with a red bandana he had bunched in his hand. Another bang from the window sent a shockwave of fear through everyone except Duane and Georgie as they looked at each other.

"Good man. Now repeat after me, I'm not afraid."

"I..." Georgie started.

"Go on," Duane said. "Say it with me. I'm not afraid."

"I'm...not afraid."

"Good, say it again."

"I'm not afraid."

"Good, now tell your mom what you just told me."

Georgie turned to his mother and told her the same thing. And then he added, "Don't be afraid either, Mommy." She hugged her son in response.

"I'm not afraid either, Georgie," his mother lied. "I'm not afraid. You're so brave. If only your daddy could see how brave you are." Though she tried her best to sound positive, Duane could see she was forlorn and scattered, and he was worried about her being able to hold it together.

"What's your name, Mom?" Duane asked her.

"I'm Marla."

"Marla, you've got an incredibly brave little boy there."

"Yeah, I sure do." Marla hugged Georgie to her, pushed his cowboy hat off his head and let it hang behind his neck while she kissed his forehead.

"Hey, mister, I hate to break up this wonderful moment, but what the Christ are we gonna do?"

Duane looked up sharply at one of the cooks leaning over the counter, the cigarette still bouncing from his lips.

"What's *your* name, boy?"

"Percy."

"Well, Percy, why not take your other cook buddy…"

"Name's Mac," his cook buddy responded, arms folded.

"*Mac*, into the kitchen and start rooting through whatever closets you got back there. Find some clubs, knives, oil or gas if you've got it; anything that we can use as a weapon. And you bring what you find up here and put everything here on the counter. You got that?"

"Sure thing, boss," Percy said, exhaling smoke through his nostrils. He turned and swatted the much taller Mac a couple times on the chest with the back of his hand, and they walked into the kitchen.

"Uh, Beverly, was it?" Duane asked the elderly woman in the church dress.

"Beverly," she said, nodding.

"Beverly, I want you to stay right here by this phone behind the counter. Keep testing it, keep trying to dial out. See if you can get someone on the line."

"Mind if I sit with her?" her husband asked. "I wouldn't be much good to anyone anyway." He tapped his cane against his bum leg to show Duane why.

"Sure, mister, that's fine. Tell you what, you put the volume up on this radio and keep listening. See if they release any new information on this whole mess."

"Will do. I'm Harold, by the way," he said, smiling meekly.

"Harold," Duane nodded and then looked at the truck driver, who stuck his hand out.

"Charlie. What d'ya got for me, friend?"

"Charlie, I haven't the slightest," Duane said, shaking his hand and looking to the wall behind him, spotting a red-handled fire axe in a glass case tucked in the corner. "Guess I couldn't convince you to take a walk outside and kill off some of the growing opposition, could I?"

"Not a snowball's chance in Hell."

"About what I thought. Grab that axe from that cabinet and just keep watch. Check out the windows where they populate and look for weak spots."

Charlie went to do just that as Duane turned to Earl and Francine, unbuttoning his sweater and tossing it on the counter.

"Okay you two, rack your brains and tell me what's around here. Police station, hospital, schools; hell, even a hardware store. Anything at all."

"Well, the sheriff's station's about, what, say ten miles or so down the road?" Earl asked, nervously rubbing the rough skin covering his elbows with either hand.

"About, give or take," Francine continued. "No schools, no hospitals. None close, anyway. We're about the only civilization from here to the sheriff's station. Just a smattering of random houses here and there," Francine finished.

"Damn it. We need people. We need a place that's more secure," Duane said, his brain working overtime.

"Well, I don't know about more people, but we got us a place down the road—me, Frannie and her sister, Dora—about two miles. A big farmhouse tucked away from the road some. No neighbors. It's got a bunch of windows, but nothing we couldn't cover. We even got us a gas pump, too. I had one put in when we had these pumps here put in a few years back."

"How far off from the road is it?" Duane asked.

"Enough where I think we would be safer than here, unless these things followed us, that is. Two right turns off of Route 10. The only turn you'll see for miles. Nice and quiet. Easy as pie."

"It might not be a bad idea," Duane said. "Once we can group together and find some weapons, maybe we should try making a run for the cars and…"

A shrill shriek from the back of the kitchen stopped Duane in mid-sentence. He jumped over the counter without hesitating and ran to the back. He rounded a corner around some metallic-colored machinery and quickly stopped.

Mac, motionless, was down on the ground, a man straddling the cook as he ripped strips of flesh from Mac's chest and chewed them sloppily. Blood whipped from the ragged flesh onto the floor and the massive refrigerator doors a foot away. Just behind this gory display sat Percy, mesmerized by what was transpiring. He held a large meat clever so tight in his shaking hand that his knuckles were the color of his bleached apron. And just behind Percy was an old screen door, slapping loudly in the wind against the wide-open door frame.

"Percy!" Duane screamed, trying to break him out of his trance. "Percy, goddamn it! Kill that thing!"

Percy only continued to stare, and as he did, there was movement just behind him in the doorway. Another figure stumbled in—a teenage boy—with yet another attacker close behind him. It was the boy's identical twin brother, right down to the same pair of tan khakis and blue ties. Seeing that the man on the ground was distracted with his meal, Duane ran quickly around the prone bodies and snatched the cleaver from Percy's hand. Duane spun quickly, slashed at the twin faces, back and forth, one after the other. The boys shot their hands up to their faces, blood pouring from their fresh wounds. And all the while, Percy still sat, mumbling, his hand curled as if he was still holding the cleaver.

"I need some goddamned help back here!" Duane shouted.

Earl came running up, saw the blood-covered man on top of Mac, then saw Percy useless and catatonic. Earl rushed at the two boys Duane was fighting. He pushed one of them hard enough out the door that it tripped over its own feet and landed on its back, cracking its skull on the hard sandy lot. Duane pushed the other twin outside as well, which tripped over its now-dead brother and landed on top of it, moaning in confusion.

Duane turned, saw the man still ripping strips of flesh from Mac's chest, and carefully approached him. He took a quick look behind him, saw a few approaching attackers outside that were still several feet away, and sunk the cleaver into the man's head. The body fell off Mac, immediately dead, thick blood spilling from the wound. Duane got up quickly, his shirt now peppered with crimson spots, and grabbed the dead legs of the corpse. Earl instinctually grabbed the arms and the two of them swung the body outside into the back lot, knocking the flimsy screen door off its hinges. Just before Earl slammed the inner metal door, Duane spotted an old, beat-up pickup truck parked crookedly against the back of the diner. Slamming the door, Earl slid the massive deadbolt home, just as more ghouls were reaching their dead hands out towards them.

"Whose truck is that out back?" Duane said, breathing heavily, leaning against the wall.

"Dunno, abandoned with the keys still in it. Sat around for a couple days until I called the sheriff. He told me to park it out back till he could get a tow-truck in. Why?"

"That might be the best way for us to get out of here. Most of those things are up at the front because they can see us. Back here, it's less crowded."

"Only one problem, tank's on empty. Probably kids boosted it and left it behind. A lot of folks leave their keys in the visor or the ignition. Not a lot of cars stolen in these parts."

Earl pushed off the door, started nervously rubbing his elbows again. "If we can maybe get to one of the gas pumps with it..." he started, but then stopped, finally seeing the aftermath of Mac's attack for the first time. "Oh, Jesus...Mac..." Earl said, grimacing. He didn't say anything for a moment, trying to get a hold of himself. "What should we do with him?"

"I don't know. Both doors are surrounded now. Is there a place we can lock him up?"

"What for?" Francine asked, suddenly making her presence known at the entrance to the kitchen. Her hand shot to her mouth in shock at the sight of Mac's body for the first time. The others stood behind her, trying to see what was going on.

"They get back up, Francine. This is just part one. Part two is even worse. Now, is there a place we can lock him up?"

"Well, there's the customer bathroom. Or we have a walk-in freezer," Earl said, looking to Duane.

"The bathroom we'll need. Let's get him to the freezer."

Duane, grabbing Mac's arms, and Earl, his legs, picked up the decimated line cook and carried him into the back corner of the kitchen. Earl dropped one leg to open the freezer door when Mac's body suddenly twitched. Earl screamed in response, letting the freezer door slam shut.

"Francine! Honey, come open this door! He's gonna wake up any second!"

She didn't move from her place at the wall, frozen in fear.

"Oh, Earl, don't make me, I can't come over there!" she cried, terrified.

"Someone open the goddamn door!" Earl yelled at them all. "I can't hold it open and throw him in at the same time!" Duane could see in their eyes that no one would step forward, each of them hoping and assuming that someone else braver than themselves would intervene.

Mac twitched again, and a barely audible moan escaped his lips.

"Christ Almighty!" Earl yelled in miserable anger. He dropped Mac, opened the freezer, and backed into the swinging door to keep it open with his body. He grabbed Mac's legs again, struggling to get a good grip on his bloody pant legs.

"Throw him in!" Duane ordered, and they swung Mac's resurrecting body onto the slick freezer floor. His body slid several feet, and as Earl was slamming the door, Duane saw Mac's head slowly turn and look directly at him. Earl slid a bolt through the latch and locked it, then leaned against the door as Duane rested his hands on his knees.

"This will hold him, right?" Duane asked through short gasps of breath.

"Hold him? It's gonna turn him into the Abominable Snowman."

"Any other doors in this place?" Duane asked.

"No more doors," Earl replied.

"Thank God for small favors."

It was then they noticed that Percy still stood in the same place in a vegetative, unresponsive state.

"Percy? Come on, Percy, snap out of it, man," Earl struggled to say through his short breaths.

Duane walked over, looked into Percy's eyes, and then gave him two sharp slaps in the face. Percy looked up into Duane's eyes then, wide and wet, but not much flickering behind them.

"It might be shock. Grab some water for him," Duane said, holding Percy by his shoulders and trying to lightly shake him to consciousness.

"Sure thing," Earl said, doing just that.

"And some hard stuff. I know a man like you has to have a bottle of something tucked away somewhere."

"Under normal circumstances, I would take offense to that. I've got some Jack in the office, bottom drawer."

"Good man. And grab some ammonia, too."

Duane led Percy to a chair near the front of the diner and lightly pushed him into a sitting position. He stepped into Earl's office, now a mess after ransacking to look for the radio, and grabbed the bottle of Jack out of the bottom drawer. He walked back to the counter, uncapped the bottle, and grabbed some cups from underneath.

"Any luck with that phone, Beverly?"

"Nothing yet, Duane. Just a weird tone."

"Well, keep at it. We might catch a break." Duane saw Harold eyeing the booze in his hand. "I won't make you ask for it, Harold. This one's on me." Duane poured a double shot into the small glass and fired it down the counter.

"You're good at that. Done that before?" Harold asked.

"I know my way around a bar." Duane poured himself a double and toasted Harold from afar. "To better times, huh?"

The two shot back their drinks as Earl came up with a pitcher of ice water and a jug of ammonia.

Duane uncapped the ammonia and splashed some onto a napkin. He slid the napkin back and forth under Percy's nose several times. The man's eyes watered from the fumes of the stuff, but he didn't otherwise react. Duane dabbed a bit more on the napkin and wafted it under Percy's nose again. He then dipped his fingers in the ice water and flicked some in the man's face. Finally, Percy shook his head and made a loud snorting sound, like someone who had dozed off watching TV and quickly woke up. He tried to stand immediately, almost knocking Duane backwards.

"Whoa, calm down, Percy. Just relax and sit."

"Give him some of the whiskey," Earl said, grabbing a glass from under the counter. Duane poured some into the glass and gave it to Percy, who drank it immediately. He gasped for breath once it went down, struggling to regain his poise. The soft pounding on the diner windows made him slowly recall their situation. The number of ghouls outside had grown since they last looked, and their circumstances were looking even more dire. They all slapped their hands against the glass, their blank eyes gazing into the diner, seeing their prey just a few feet away.

Percy looked around at the people in the diner, noticing someone was missing.

"Mac! Where's Mac?" Percy cried, looking from face to face, trying to find the answer to his question. When no one answered, when everyone chose to look at their feet rather than tell him, it was enough to realize the truth.

"We're sorry, Percy," Earl said, squeezing his shoulder. "We know you guys were buds."

"What... what happened?"

Earl continued to squeeze Percy's shoulder, but he looked down at the floor, words escaping him. Duane could see that no one else was going to tell him, so he sighed heavily and looked at Percy. "He didn't make it. He's gone."

And as if on cue, Mac beat against the inside of the freezer door, moaning loudly.

"What...what was that?" Percy asked, his eyes on Duane's, widening as he slowly realized what it was.

Again, no one spoke for a moment.

"It's Mac," Duane said finally.

"What the hell, Duane?" Percy said as he tried to get to his feet. Duane gently pushed him back down.

"Listen, Percy. That's Mac...but Mac's dead. You understand? That's not your buddy in there anymore. That's just a pile of meat. And that's all. Just understand that, okay?"

"He's right, Percy. It ain't Mac," Earl solemnly agreed.

Percy stared straight ahead, quiet, not sure what to think. He poured himself another shot and threw it back. "Just let me sit for a moment, okay?" he asked, staring down at the countertop.

"Sure thing," Duane said. He knelt behind the counter and grabbed some towels to clean up the mess left by Mac's exit. He pushed himself off the counter to head to the back when he saw Harold trying to get his attention, so he walked over to him. Harold had retaken his place by his wife, the radio pulled close to him.

"Anything on the radio, Harold?"

"Nothing yet. They just keep saying the same stuff over and over."

"Then what's up?"

Harold leaned in close to him. "I'm worried about Marla, the kid's mom." Duane looked at Harold a moment, then nonchalantly turned to look at her. She was sitting at a booth, rocking back and forth, her head in her hands. Georgie sat by her side, pulling on her arm.

"How long has she been like this?"

"Since all that ruckus in the back; you guys and those things. I think she's losing it."

Duane sighed heavily.

"This is the last thing we need." He clapped Harold on the back. "Thanks, Harold." The man nodded, pushing his glasses up over his forehead to rub his weary eyes.

Duane walked over to Marla and her son and knelt down beside them. He shook her gently, but received no response. He could hear her whispering, so he leaned in closer to listen. It was the Lord's Prayer, which she seemed to be reciting over and over.

"Hey, Marla," Duane said softly and shook her a bit more. No response. He shook her again, harder this time. "Marla!"

She looked up at him then, her eyes red from crying, her face soaked with tears.

"Everything's going to be okay, Marla. I promise you. You have to be brave. Georgie was brave for you, remember?"

"Yeah, remember, Mom?" Georgie asked, poking her arm.

"You have to be brave for *him* now," Duane reasoned.

"But he's so scared. He's terrified," she cried, seemingly talking more about herself rather than her son.

"I'm okay, Mommy. I was scared earlier, but I'm not scared now."

"He needs his father, Duane. He needs to get out of here," she said.

"Soon, Marla. We're making those plans right now. We just have to find some weapons, regroup, and come up with a plan. Okay?"

"Okay."

Duane stood up then, ruffled Georgie's hair, and walked back to the counter, giving Harold a shrug. "Keep an eye on her?" he whispered.

Harold nodded.

Mac thudded against the freezer door again, the loudest one yet, and everyone turned.

"I don't know if I can listen to that!" Percy screamed, clamping his hands over his ears.

"We're sorry, Percy, we just didn't have any other option," Earl said. He then looked to Duane. "Maybe we should..." he trailed off, hoping Duane would understand what he inferred without having to say it aloud.

"We can't, it would be too risky. What if he got by one of us, attacked one of us? I know it's hard to stomach, but leaving him in there is the safest option for now."

Duane rubbed his head, exhausted, frustrated, and especially hungry.

"Francine, do you think you could turn the ovens back on? Make something for us to eat?"

"Sure, Duane." Francine walked around the corner and tied an apron around her waist. "How about some steak and eggs?"

"That'd be just fine."

* * *

Everyone ate together at the counter, trying to ignore the rapping of fists on glass surrounding them, as well as the thudding and moaning coming from the freezer, coming from Mac. Beverly physically jumped with each bang against the sturdy metal door, her fork clattering against her plate of picked-at food. The radio continued to reiterate the same information and advised listeners to "stay tuned for further details."

"Stay tuned, my foot. This place is gonna be our grave in the next few hours," Harold muttered.

"Shush, Harold," his wife chided.

"He's right, though," Duane said. "We can't hang around here much longer, despite how strong that glass may be. It's only a matter of time. Maybe we should try for the sheriff's station. How we're going to do that, though..."

They all turned at once and looked at the sea of ghouls, separated from them only by a half-inch thick piece of reinforced glass.

"Yeah, right, mister," Charlie said. "Give us a wave when you get out there in one piece." A few people chuckled, in spite of their situation.

"What about that old truck out back, Earl? The one that was left here?" Francine asked, collecting the empty dishes. "You said there weren't so many of them back there."

"We talked about that already. That truck's on E, Frannie. It could get us to the station, sure, but it could also stall out by the time we reached the edge of the parking lot. It's too much of a risk. Our best bet..." Earl started, but then pointed out into the parking lot to their cars. He let that finish his thought.

"I guess I'd be wasting my breath if I asked if you had a canister of gasoline tucked away in the back for a generator or something," Duane said. "There are too many of those things standing near the pumps."

"I doubt it. We don't have no gas, right, Percy..." Earl started, turned, saw he was talking to no one. "Percy? Where'd you go?"

Everyone looked around from their seats, but Percy wasn't in sight. No one had even noticed him slip away from them.

"Where the hell did he go?" Charlie asked.

"He was hitting that bottle pretty hard. Maybe he's in the pisser," Earl reasoned. He was about to call out again when he heard the sound of the walk-in freezer door being opened.

"Percy, no!" Earl screamed, already running to the back. Duane ran behind him and rounded the counter just in time to see Mac, his frozen face and arms a light blue, lumber out of the freezer towards Percy, who stood in front of him holding a meat tenderizer.

"It ain't right, Earl! We gotta put him down! It's Mac, you know? It's Mac!" Percy bellowed.

The hulking ghoul that was formerly Mac lunged at Percy, his widening jaw dropping ice chips onto the ground as he advanced, his arms up, permanently frozen in a raised position. After just a couple hours in the freezer, his body had become almost—if not entirely—frozen. Steam lifted from his body as if wafting over a cup of hot coffee, and it poured off of Mac as he lumbered towards Percy. Mini blood icicles that hung from the deep wounds in his chest now fell in chunks and shattered on the floor, crunching under Mac's approaching, shuffling feet.

"You're dead, Mac!" Percy shouted, raising the tenderizer. "I'm sorry, but you're dead, damn it!" Percy brought it down over the head of the tall Mac, which made a dull *thunk*—like hitting a nail— and bounced off his undamaged, thoroughly frozen skull. Mac continued to come towards him, and Percy swung the tenderizer at the top of his head again, but he could see it was going to do no good. It bounced uselessly off his head like a doctor's rubber reflex hammer off a patient's knee.

Mac bit down hard on Percy's neck just under his cheek, ravaging his head like a wild dog, tearing away most of his face like it were a cheap, rubber mask. Earl ran to Percy's aid, pushing the ghoul back with his hands, and as Mac was pushed back, Earl found that he went right with him—his hands stuck fast to Mac's icy chest. "You've gotta be kidding!" he shouted in surprise.

"Charlie, bring that axe up here, now!" Duane yelled, not daring to take his eyes off Mac. Charlie, who had been standing behind Duane and had no choice but to watch the ensuing battle take place lest he get in their way, tossed the axe to Duane.

Percy ran screaming from the kitchen and into the diner, pawing at his faceless skull. The others shouted in surprise as he ran around them, bleeding, screaming...dying. Charlie chased after him, yelling to him to calm down so he could help him, though what he could actually do remained to be seen.

And meanwhile, Earl continued to attempt to free himself from the frozen man.

"Earl, get away from him!" Duane shouted, trying to ready the axe for the kill.

"I'm stuck to him! My hands are stuck right to him!" Earl yelled.

"What?" he yelled.

"Help me!"

The two men and the dead, frozen Mac took part in a dance of the most absurd; Earl and Mac spinning to the right as Duane sidled to the left, trying to aim the axe so as not to injure Earl. Mac gnashed his frozen teeth at Earl, all the while Percy screamed like a madman from the front of the diner.

"I can't get in a good shot!" Duane yelled.

"Just do it, already!" Earl replied in anger.

"I can't, man, I might hit you!"

"*Just do it!*"

"Goddamn it!" Duane shouted, bringing the axe down over Mac, the sharp edge entering his frozen head. The vibration that traveled up the handle was so intense, Duane had to let go, shockwaves of pain shooting through his hands. The axe wobbled loosely in Mac's head until it finally fell out, clattering to the floor.

"Hit him again!" Earl shouted, keeping his head ducked low, facing the ground.

Mac swung his frozen arms around in response to the hit, trying to get to Duane, and Earl had no choice but to swing with him in the same direction. With Earl now forced to block Duane's way, he stamped his foot down over the axe on the floor and kicked it between his legs to Duane, who stood behind him. Earl then stuck his feet behind Mac and pushed him hard, tripping him over backwards. Mac hurtled to the ground, sounding like a massive stone statue toppling in the heavy winds of a storm, bringing Earl with him. He held Mac down, though his frozen body wouldn't have let him sit up, and Duane picked up the axe. He aimed carefully as Earl moved as far out of the way as he could, and he brought the axe whistling down into Mac's mouth, separating the rows of upper and lower teeth—and the rest of the head with it. Duane scraped the top of the head away with the axe, and it bounced loudly off a metal oven. He breathed heavily, leaning on the bottom of the axe handle, the blade of which was resting on Mac's chest.

Percy stopped screaming suddenly and the front of the diner was now quiet, except for one last noise; Percy hitting the surface of a corner booth and toppling onto the hard floor. Passed out or dead, Duane had no idea, but the sudden quiet after the insane battle seemed foreign and unsettling.

Duane dropped the axe, fell to his knees, unsure as to whether he was going to laugh or cry. Looking at Earl, who struggled to turn from his affixed position to look at Duane, he did a mixture of both. It took him a few moments to shake it off, and when he did, Earl was looking at him with an expression of quintessential impatience.

"You got a minute or what?" Earl growled, wanting desperately to get his hands free of the frozen corpse.

Duane chuckled and climbed to his feet, grateful to have a break from all the madness, if even for a short while. Sure, Percy was probably dead, but Duane needed a release, needed to know there was such a thing still left in the world as laughter. To anyone else it would have seemed crazy for Duane to be carrying on in such a manner, but with everyone in the midst of the craziness themselves, it didn't seem to matter.

Etiquette had gone out the window of Beekman's Diner.

"Sure thing, Earl. Let me get some hot water," Duane said. He walked over to the sink, turned it on, and wagged his fingers in the stream, waiting for it to heat up. He grabbed a nearby pitcher and filled it up. It was when he shut the water off that he heard Percy moaning from the front of the diner, followed by the frightened cries of the others. He straightened up immediately, his reflexes kicking into gear.

This was followed by a sharp metallic crack and then another thud. Percy wasn't moaning any more.

"I got it!" Charlie called out from the front, signifying the temporary problem had been resolved.

Duane smiled and tried his best to control it, not wanting to appear cruel and callous to the others. But at the moment, Duane wasn't concerned about formalities. As he was walking over to Earl with the pitcher of hot water, his lighter mood was cut short when Marla let out an agonizing scream. It was the most terrifying scream Duane had ever heard. It was the scream of someone at the end of their rope, of someone whose sanity was slowly melting away like Mac's frozen body. The sound of it was infinitely more terrifying than even the sight of Percy running faceless through the diner, screaming and splashing blood across the floor.

"Francine!" Duane bellowed, rushing to the front of the diner. She came bounding around the corner, and he handed off the pitcher to her. "See to your husband!" he shouted, and she grabbed it from him with no questions, grateful to be away from the hellacious shrieking of the madwoman.

Duane came around and saw Marla standing in the middle of the diner, her hands plastered over her ears, her head down, screaming that intense, terrifying shriek. Georgie stood in front of the counter, Harold stooping to hold the boy's shoulders from behind. Georgie was crying and also clamping his hands over his ears, wanting to block out his mother's unholy screaming.

"Marla, you need to calm down!" Duane yelled, running to her and grabbing her shoulders. Marla continued her shrill scream, which agitated the ghouls outside. They pounded more furiously on the windows in response. "Marla, you're going to drive them crazy! You have to stop this!" Her screaming continued, and over her shoulder he could see them pounding harder and harder against the quivering windows. With no other option, he slapped Marla across the face.

Hard.

The screaming stopped.

"Mommy!" Georgie cried, shaking loose from Harold's bony grasp and running up to his mother and hugging her leg. Marla collapsed, falling hard to a sitting position on the floor, which knocked Georgie back as well. He started crying again and Marla looked at him, dazed, as if she didn't recognize this tiny human being crying for her. He crawled into her lap and forced her limp hands to hold him. Duane didn't know what to do, so he watched Georgie struggle in her arms before he walked away.

"Beverly, grab the kid. I need a break from all this," Duane said and lifted a cigarette from the soft pack in his pocket before walking to the back of the kitchen. "Charlie, put Mac back in the freezer. Percy, too."

Duane walked by Earl and Francine who were still in the midst of their detachment procedure. He heard the splash of water, a groan of pain from Earl, and Francine's shushing of him.

Duane lit his cigarette, jumped up on an old washer in the back, and shut his eyes. He focused only on his cigarette, on the bitter scent and smoke wafting around his face. He tried to picture that he was at a park, or on a beach, or anywhere else except atop a dingy washer surrounded by death.

But he couldn't.

Not for long.

Because his thoughts drifted back to Georgie, crawling into his comatose mother's arms, crying for her attention, for her love. Marla was never going to be the same after today. If she survived, that is.

None of them were.

*   *   *

Duane leaned his tired head on his hands on the counter, kicking idly at the wall below as he swung his foot off the stool. He stared outside at the darkening sky. It had been hours since the world had flipped out and spat demons into his otherwise peaceful existence. And in that time, people had died.

Officer Riley. Ray Willis. Mac. Percy.

Four human beings that Duane had tried to save, only to fail one after the other. Duane cast his eyes to the blood on the floor left by Percy's frenzied outburst. He shut his eyes, but tears brimmed anyway. Francine came over, reading his mind.

"Don't you blame yourself, Duane. Don't you dare."

He ignored her. He didn't know what to say in response, so he chose nothing.

"Listen, I'm scared, too," she said. "We're all scared. This situation is no one's fault. It's just happening, and we've got to deal with it. I can't control that. And neither can you." She cupped one of Duane's limp hands with her own. "God doesn't prepare us for something like this."

"Who?" Duane asked, not opening his eyes.

Francine caressed Duane's hand a moment longer before getting up and walking away.

* * *

Duane sat at a booth, a cup of coffee on the table in front of him, a smoldering cigarette in his hand. Smoke danced in front of his face as he stared through it at the still-growing crowd of ghouls outside. They were surrounded on nearly all sides now. He took a sip of the coffee, set the mug down, and continued to stare. Marla sat at the next booth over, her head still in her hands, continuing to repeat the Lord's Prayer.

Duane looked down at the piece of jewelry on his right hand ring finger. It was his college class ring that he had bought for himself upon graduation from the University of Pittsburgh. He turned the ring slowly on his finger with his other thumb. The University of Pittsburgh...roughly ten miles from where he was born.

Duane hadn't wanted to go away for school, though there were far better schools in the country better suited to his studies. Leaving home scared him, and though most of his high school chums had gone off to other schools, Duane opted to stay behind. And ever since graduation, Duane had worked a string of meaningless jobs that veered further and further off the path of what he had studied at the University. He had worked as a forklift operator in a warehouse, an editor's assistant at a local newspaper, and even tended bar in a restaurant in Philadelphia. A waste of an education he had determined.

Not that it mattered.

Not now, anyway.

Earl walked over and sat down, blocking his view of the ghouls, and of Marla.

"I've been thinking," Earl said. "Maybe sitting here in plain view isn't such a hot idea. Maybe if we go sit in the back, where they can't see us, they'll get bored and leave."

Duane chuckled, not because he found what Earl had said particularly funny, but because he felt asinine for being able to understand these dead things at all.

"Earl...these things...they've got nothing but time. We could go sit in the back kitchen, sure, but they're gonna stand right where they are now. They're dumb as dirt, but they know we're in here. And they're not gonna stop; not unless someone outside walks by them and waves."

Earl nodded solemnly for a moment, but then gave him a crooked smile. "I think I got something that'll cheer you up some."

He set a silver, brand new, Colt Six-Shooter on the table in between them, and tapped the gun with the same hand now wrapped in ace bandages. He had lost patches of skin during its removal from Mac's frozen torso.

Duane looked at the gun for a moment, then returned a crooked smile.

"Thought so," Earl said.

"When were you going to tell me?" Duane asked, the smile crumbling from his exhausted face.

"Easy, now, Duane. I only just remembered. We were robbed, maybe six months ago. I bought it the day after, and it's been tucked underneath the counter since then. Twenty-five years we've had this diner, and up until two months ago, I ain't never needed no gun. I ain't needed it before, and I ain't needed it since. But now...?"

Duane picked up the gun and opened the full chamber, the six loaded rounds glinting under the diner's fluorescent lighting.

"You got any more bullets than what's already in there?"

Earl looked down at the table top, ashamed. "No. I, uh...I bought just as many as I needed to fill it. I figured...if I needed more than that when the shit hit the fan, I'd be dead, anyway." He looked back up at Duane. "If only, huh?"

Duane smiled, spun the wheel, and snapped it close. He handed the gun back to Earl, handle first.

"Thanks, Earl. Hold on to that. I'm a terrible shot."

Earl took the gun, nodded to Duane, and got up out of the booth, tucking it into the back of his pants. He stopped on his way over to lightly cup the back of Marla's head. She continued to rock back and forth, not acknowledging him. Her behavior had so spooked everyone that Beverly sat Georgie with her at the counter as he enjoyed a cup of ice cream. Francine had begged Earl to retrieve the ice cream from the walk-in freezer where Mac and Percy were stored.

"Hey, little man," Earl said, walking over to Georgie. "Mmm, that looks good. Can I have some?"

"No!" Georgie yelled playfully, hugging the cup to him.

Earl laughed in response. "Okay, okay. It's all yours."

Earl looked up at the ghouls outside, pounding away at his windows. "God bless that Timmy Walen. I'm gonna have to call him when this is all over and tell him about how well these windows held up."

No one had any kind of response to this, so Earl shook his head, took his gun out of his pants and handed it to Charlie. "Hang on to this for a few minutes, would ya? I got some business to tend to." He walked to the bathroom, slowly, having to pass close by a section of the front windows. He kept his head down and walked stiffly, trying not to agitate the ghouls on the other side. He opened the door, gave them another quick nervous look, and ducked inside the bathroom. The door next to the phone Duane had fruitlessly used to call for help a hundred years ago.

Charlie held the gun up, popped the wheel out and then back in. He set it on the counter next to him and looked at Georgie, who sat two seats over from him. Charlie then got up, grabbed the gun, and walked to the last stool at the counter, far from where Georgie sat. He looked down the counter at Beverly and smiled.

"Can't be too careful with kids runnin' around." He set the gun down again on his left side and went back to tracing his fingers along the tile cracks in the counter top.

Francine, growing restless, had grabbed a mop and bucket from the back and did her best to clean up the blood splattered on the floor of the diner—Percy's blood. With each squeeze of the mop into the bucket, the red-tinted water grew darker until it looked as if her entire bucket was filled with only blood. Deciding she had done as good a job as she was going to, she pushed the mop and bucket into a corner.

Duane continued to stare out at the ghouls, and when he saw a familiar face, he got up suddenly and walked slowly to one of the windows. The action attracted everyone's attention in the diner.

"What? What is it?" Harold asked, spinning in his stool.

Duane walked right up to the glass and stopped just a foot away.

"I'm sorry, man," Duane said. He took a puff on his cigarette and stared at Officer Riley, whose wet, bloody, decimated tongue slapped against the window as he pounded against it. The hole in his throat was now wide open and fringed with blackened, rotting skin, having cured under the hot sun over the past few hours.

"Who is that?" Harold called out.

"That's Martha's boy, Harold! It's Billy Riley! Oh, that poor woman. I wonder if she knows..." Beverly said, trailing off.

Charlie turned around from his stool. He got up and walked over to Beverly. "Who was he?" he asked her.

"The son of a friend. So young, too. He was engaged to Molly Forrest, that pretty little thing who works at Christine's Crafts."

Duane held up his hand, made a fist, and pressed the front of it against the window. He made the slightest smile, but his eyes told a different story. All the regret in his life was present within *them*, and not just the regret from the day's events. Duane considered his own thirty-two-year-old life as he stood there, staring into the dead eyes of Officer Riley. He wondered if he had made any particular choice in life that had led him here to this moment. He looked around the room, saw Francine, the wife of Earl; Beverly and Harold, the old and happy couple; even Marla, though she was slowly losing her mind, still had her little boy and a husband, somewhere. Charlie hadn't said much during their time trapped together, but he strode about the place like a man with confidence and pride; a man who didn't seem to regret his choices in life, nor had any personal demons to deal with.

Duane wondered about his own family, long out of contact with him. He wondered about his brother David, who had a wife and three kids and lived in upstate New York. He wondered about his father, a drunk who had decided years ago to try and kill himself slowly with drink. And lastly, he wondered about his mother, who had died this past winter. Was she now awakened deep below the ground and scratching at the lid of her coffin, moaning that undead moan? The thought was too much to bear.

As Duane looked around the room, and as Riley bit stupidly at his fist still pressed against the glass, and as he saw everyone at the counter staring at him with sympathetic eyes, Duane suddenly realized that Beverly was no longer watching Georgie, and that Charlie had left the gun on the counter when he had turned his attention to the window. A quick look at the counter confirmed that the gun was missing.

And so was Georgie.

And so was his mother.

"*Marla!*" Duane screamed suddenly, running from the window towards the flash of a black cowboy hat he saw disappearing just on the other side of the last booth's wall. It was a mad rush to make it to the opposite corner of the diner as everyone came to the same horrifying conclusion at the same time.

A gunshot rang out, startling the silence, echoing in the small diner. Everyone reacted the same, their bodies flinching, looking in the opposite direction, their arms straight out at their sides as if they might have to hit the deck. Duane, however, never hesitated, and he made it to the wall with Charlie hot on his heels. He grabbed the corner of the wall to control his sprinting turn and stopped dead in his tracks.

"Mother of Christ..." Charlie muttered from behind him, grabbing Duane's arm in shock.

The bullet had likely struck Georgie in the chest, close to the heart, but with his cowboy hat now covering his chest as he lay motionless on the floor, and with so much blood on him and the ceramic tiles around him, it was hard to tell where it was coming from.

"Marla, what on earth did you do?" Francine asked, barely a whisper, trying to squeeze around Duane and Charlie to rush to the boy. Beverly held her fast by the shoulder, her eyes on Earl's gun still clenched in Marla's hand. Harold never made a sound, but the wetness from his eyes which sprung almost immediately was enough.

"He couldn't stand it anymore, Francine," Marla said, calmly, the calmest she had sounded since the nightmare had begun.

She had also very clearly lost her mind.

"He was just so scared. He hated being so scared, hated feeling like he was useless. It's better for him this way, I think. And for me, too." She whipped the gun up to her own face, holding it at an awkward angle, pointing it down into her mouth.

"Marla, wait! Don't you..."

There was a loud report and the bullet exited the back of Marla's lower neck, shattering the top of her vertebrae and spraying bits of meat and blood through the air like a sonic boom caused by an atomic explosion. The bullet whipped through one of the large windows behind her and left a spider web crack before Marla was even dead. Her body fell back on one of the many tables, her head making a sick smack on the hard surface.

"Oh, my Jesus, no!" Francine cried, collapsing into Beverley's arms behind her as Harold cradled them both.

Earl came barreling around the corner, buckling his pants.

"What the hell was that? Duane?" He stopped when he saw Georgie's body, and then Marla's. "Oh, Jesus."

Duane's mind shut down entirely then, like a struggling car engine that finally relented and sputtered to a dead quiet. What had just transpired was too much to process in his already fragile state. Duane stopped thinking, feeling, and reacting. He just stopped *being*. He'd had enough of this diner and the hungry dead pounding on the window glass just two feet in front of him. He'd had enough of letting down people that were depending on him, of seeing one life after another extinguished. It was so clear to him now, watching Marla's blood drip off the booth and plop onto the floor under her. He needed to survive this ordeal, and he needed everyone there with him to survive as well, because if they didn't—if they all fell victim to the walking dead just beyond the windows—then this horrid nightmare would have been for nothing.

Marla and Georgie.

Their deaths would have been for nothing.

Duane stepped forward, doing his best to avoid looking at the remains of Georgie the Brave, Georgie the Cowboy. All the while, the ghouls outside, agitated by the gunshot, began pounding at the now-weakened window. The hammering of their hands on the glass now emitted a terrifying cracking sound—each blow making the window weaker and weaker. Instead of the dull thump they had been hearing for the last couple hours—the sound of them coming nowhere closer to touching the patrons of the diner with their cold, clammy hands, of ripping them apart piece by piece— the slight crackling sound sent shivers down Duane's spine and bolts of fear directly through his heart.

Duane's mind, now rebooted, worked overtime. The cracks spread in every direction with each blow, and Duane knew it was just a matter of time before the entire window came crashing down out of the frame, allowing their most horrid waking nightmares to come waltzing in, to destroy them, and to make them reborn into something that nature had never intended.

Duane wiggled the gun out of Marla's dead hand, stuck it in his pants pocket, and stared at the cracked window.

"We need to find something to cover this window, and now. We have minutes before those things are in here." Duane turned to Earl. "Do you have anything? Wood paneling, old doors, anything at all?"

"Jesus...Georgie..." he muttered, unaware of Duane's presence.

"Earl...I need you to focus. Do you have anything?"

"Wood...won't do any good," Earl said, forcing his mind to work. "Those frames are metal. We'd be better off pushing something against the window, like one of those metal cabinets or..." Earl's eyes lit up. "Duane, help me! Charlie, you too! Come on!" Earl ran into the back with Duane and Charlie. He rapped his hands on the stainless steel refrigerator door. "We can push this bastard right up against the window! They'd never be able to move this thing, not in a million years!"

Duane's shoulders fell.

"It's no good, Earl. If we can move it, so can they."

"No, look!" Earl defended, kicking down a lever overtop one of the wheels. "Each wheel comes with a brake! Set all four of these suckers and this thing ain't rolling anywhere!"

Duane nodded his head. "It's all we've got right now, so let's hope so. Okay, let's get this thing moving!" They each grabbed a side and pushed or pulled with all of their might, moving it just a few inches. The contents inside rolled around, the sound of glass jars clinking against glass jars barely audible.

Duane stopped pushing, straightened up and looked over at the body of Marla. And then at Georgie. And then at Harold.

"Harold...there's no easy way to say this, so I'll just say it. Marla and Georgie are going to be getting up soon. Just know that. Watch over them, okay? I'd do it myself but we have to roll this thing. Can you handle that?"

"I'll have to, Duane. Don't worry."

Duane grabbed the gun from his pants pocket that he had wriggled from Marla's dead hand and slid it down the counter, nodding at Harold. Beverly looked worriedly to her husband and started to speak, but he held up his hand, shushing her, going for the gun.

Duane set himself against the fridge and began pushing with them again.

"Damn, this thing is heavy!" Charlie said, kicking against the wall, trying to push the fridge forward.

"Once we get it moving, it'll roll, no sweat! C'mon, put your backs into it!" Earl said, straining to get it rolling as the veins in his forehead popped out. The men rocked the fridge together and were finally able to get it moving steadily.

The ghouls continued to beat their fists against the glass, now whitened with cracks, as chunks of flesh flew off of their rotting hands and onto the booth tables on the other side. The hole caused by the bullet had grown so big that they were able to fit their wriggling hands through it and snap off small pieces of glass.

"Is this gonna clear the counter?" Duane asked, eyeing the small entranceway between the edge of the counter and the opposite wall. "It doesn't look good from here."

"Pray that it will, Duane. When this thing was delivered, it came in through the back, so God only knows. But pray that it will," Earl said.

They were able to push the fridge at a decent speed, establishing a nice momentum, and as soon they reached the opening in the counter, they were jolted to a halt. The fridge had hurdled into the counter and jostled its contents inside before stopping dead. Duane looked to see if they would be able to fit it through the awkwardly-angled opening between the counter and the opposite wall. Thankfully, he saw they could and that they had only mis-judged the angle through. But Duane knew it was going to take a miracle for them to reposition it in time for them to cover the window before the ghouls crawled in and devoured them all.

"Come on! We're close! Push!" Earl urged.

As the men worked the fridge through the opening, Duane turned to Francine and shouted to her. "I'm gonna need you to pull that booth away from the window, Fran! We can't waste any time!"

Francine ran over to the booth and grimaced at Marla's bloody body lying on top of it.

"I can't move this myself! Help me, Harold!"

Harold stumbled on his cane over to Francine and saw her hesitation at touching Marla's body. He tucked the gun into his pants.

"Come on, girl! She's gone now! Move!"

They moved the booth away from the weakened window, a few inches at a time, the table's feet screeching across the floor. With each shove of the table, Marla's lifeless head rolled back and forth, squishing this way and that. Her blood, now pooled on the table, dripped on their shoes and onto the floor. They pushed it into the corner, and Francine took off her apron and covered Marla's face. Beverly knelt down and picked up Georgie's body, his head slumping back in her arms. She turned and carried him to the corner of the room. She gently laid him on the seat of a booth, crying, placing him down out of sight.

"We need to rock this son of a bitch if we're gonna get it out of this hole, all right? So on three, we push with all our might against the wall, got it?" Duane asked each of them.

"Do it, Duane!" Earl replied, his right shoulder butted up against the side of the fridge.

Charlie hopped up on the counter and put his feet against the affixed register with his back against the fridge.

"One!"

A section of glass the size of a watermelon crackled from the window and fell to the ground.

"Two!"

The ghouls, still flocking around this weakened spot, continued to rip chunks of glass from the window, some of their hands so mangled from the shards that their fingers were skeletal white bone stained with crimson.

"Three!"

The men heaved against the refrigerator and freed it from its caught position on the counter.

"Yes! Now *move*!" Duane ordered, almost alive with euphoria. The men pushed the refrigerator, which was now rolling as smoothly as a baby carriage, and they slammed it against the window frame just as a ghoul was worming its way in over the cracked glass. The sheer girth of the refrigerator smashed the ghoul's head back through the glass, slicing its skull entirely in half from its jawbone to the top of its head, splattering greasy brains all over the back of the stainless steel fridge.

"The brakes! Jam the breaks!" Earl shouted. They kicked the brakes down over the wheels and rocked against the fridge to see if it would hold. The fridge didn't move, not the least bit, and its massive height stretched gloriously high. More than enough to secure the weakened window.

"Thank God for that," Charlie said, wiping away the sweat from his forehead. "Jesus, we might just make it!"

Marla stepped up behind Charlie, threw her undead arms around his shoulders, and with a thrust of her body, rolled her broken head around until she was able to clamp her open mouth around his neck. Before Charlie knew what was happening, Marla had bit deeply into his throat and ripped out his Adam's apple with one sick *pop*. As everyone shouted in surprise, Marla fell with Charlie's body and began to feed ravenously on him. Beverly screamed from her place at the counter, causing Marla to eye her sharply, her destroyed neck useless to hold up her head.

"Harold, goddamn it!" Duane bellowed furiously. He turned to see Harold staring at Marla with a look of sheer terror on his face from his place near a far window. He grasped his cane in front of him, frozen in fear, the gun still shoved into his pants.

Marla climbed to her feet and began walking towards Beverly, the motion of her steps causing her head to do full revolutions around her useless neck. She stepped into Charlie's crushed throat, making the sound one would hear when stepping on a sponge in the bath.

"Beverly, don't move!" Duane yelled, running to Harold and ripping the gun angrily from the man's pants.

"Make it count, Duane!" Earl shouted.

Duane responded to Earl's order by firing off a single shot into the back of Marla's head, the force of which spun her head entirely around and came to rest on her shoulder so she was facing *him*.

Bits of Marla's head cascaded down the wall behind her as she fell heavily onto a booth table, spilling leftover dishes and utensils loudly to the floor. Duane lowered the gun, his head slumping heavily to the floor, and wondered when this waking nightmare would end.

A soft gasp from behind him caused him to shut his eyes slowly as if cringing in pain. He didn't need to turn around to know what Francine was gasping at, and he especially didn't want to.

But he knew there was no choice.

He raised the gun out in front of him first, knowing it would be easier this way, and then slowly turned to face Georgie, who stood before him, his tiny hand grasping his toy gun. Georgie stepped closer, moaning, blood dripping from the bullet wound now clearly visible in his chest. He raised the toy gun even higher so that it was pointing at Duane's chest. Duane began crying then. It was the last straw, for all of it; this entire ludicrous day had led up to this one godless moment that he would give anything to not have to face. Duane wiped away his tears with the back of his hand, kept his other hand pointing the gun securely into Georgie's face. They stood there for several seconds, guns pointed at each other. Georgie moaned a soft, infant-like moan that his mother had probably heard dozens of times when doting on him when he was feverish, or tired, or having a nightmare.

Still clutching the tiny gun, Georgie doddered slowly towards Duane on uneven legs, blood dripping in layers down the front of his cowboy shirt. Duane squeezed his eyes shut, as did everyone else in the diner, and he very slowly squeezed the trigger until the Colt fired. And then there was a sound Duane knew would haunt him until the day he died. It wasn't the sound of the expulsion of the bullet, or of the squishing of flesh and crunching of bone as it tore through Georgie, but the sound following the bullet's exit from the small child's head and before his fall. It was the indescribably-heartbreaking sound of silence. The boy finally collapsed after what seemed like an eternity, and for a long time, no one spoke or moved. The only sound heard was of dull thudding on thick window glass and the moans of the dead coming from outside.

Duane finally opened his wet eyes, looked around from one window pane to the next, seeing all of the ghouls outside that wanted to maim, to murder, and to devour. He dropped the Colt onto the bloody floor behind him, the remains of mother and son mingling together on the dirty tiles of an old diner in Evanstown.

"I can't do this anymore," Duane whispered. "I can't stay here. I have to get in my car and go get help."

"You'll never make it, Duane. You said so yourself. There's too many of those things out there," Earl reasoned, stooping to retrieve the Colt.

"Then I'll take that truck out back. I'll, uh...I'll see if I can sneak over to one of the gas pumps and fill it without attracting their attention."

"And what if you do?" Francine asked.

"At this point, Francine, I'm willing to risk it. I won't stay here another second."

"What about us? You're just going to leave us here?" Beverly asked, stepping forward.

"This place is secure for now. If those things smash through the windows, you can all run into Earl's office and topple some of those cabinets against the door. It'll be cramped, but you'd be safe."

No one responded, but he could see the distinct look of betrayal on their faces.

"Trust me," Duane continued, "you'd be better off holing up here and waiting for me to bring back help. Out there on the road...who knows what could happen?"

"We don't want to stay here, Duane! We should leave together!" Harold argued.

Charlie stirred suddenly, his blood-stained eyes flipping open. He moaned, though it escaped through the hole in his throat with a wet wheeze. Beverly shrieked, and Harold held her instinctually. Earl raised the gun, but Duane waved him away.

"Don't waste the bullet."

Duane calmly walked over to the counter, grabbed the axe, and then moved over to Charlie, who was sitting up and staring at them with dull eyes.

"I'm so sorry, Charlie," Harold said, biting back tears as he held his wife.

Duane brought the axe down quickly over Charlie's head with such anguished fury that the blade came to a dead stop at the teeth of his bottom jaw. Duane kicked Charlie's head out from the axe's blade and let it fall back into the meaty mess it was, letting even more blood pool across the black and white tiled floor.

"I'm finished," Duane said.

He placed the axe on the counter and went into the back of the kitchen to wash the blood off his hands.

* * *

Duane, freshly dressed in a clean white shirt Earl had taken from one of the employee lockers, slid into the ratty, brown pickup truck. The key Earl had given him was clenched so tight in his hand that when he relaxed his fingers, the shape of the key was indented into his flesh. He started the truck, watched the needle, hoping it would climb just a little bit, just enough to give him some hope. The needle didn't move; it stayed firmly planted on **E**.

"Goddamn you," Duane said, staring at the stupid red little stick that was going to dictate to him if he lived or died. "Well," he muttered as he shifted the truck into drive, "it's still better than hanging around here."

He looked over to the back door and saw Earl and Francine, not daring to set foot out on the sandy lot despite it being clear of ghouls. The Colt Duane had refused to take with him was stuck into Earl's front pocket, slightly obscured by the apron he still wore. Duane had opted to take only what he came in with: his tire iron.

"Where will you go?" Francine asked from the doorway. Earl stood behind her, his hands on her shoulders.

"That way," Duane answered, pointing south on Route 10. "If I can't make it to the sheriff's, I'll stop at the first place that has lights on and I'll try to get some help."

"If things get hairy, get to our house. You remember how to get there?" she asked.

Duane nodded. "Two rights off of Route 10, right?"

Francine smiled. "Only right turn for miles. You'll see it. And tell Dora we're okay, would you? And that we'll see her soon?"

"You bet. Thanks, Frannie," Duane said, truly meaning it. In the thick of this madness, this poor woman was offering him her own home as a refuge while she had no choice but to stay behind, surrounded by death.

Harold showed up behind them suddenly and handed something to Earl. He took it, a smile crossing his face, and took a careful look outside before leaving the safety of the diner to bring the object to Duane. As Earl came closer, Duane could see it was his cardigan sweater, the one he'd thrown on the counter when he first arrived at the diner. Duane tried to wave the man away, nervous about his willingness to step into certain death just to return a sweater. He handed it to Duane through the driver's side window and smiled.

"Thanks, Earl," he said, slipping it on his shoulders despite the warm night, wanting to show his appreciation.

"Don't forget about us, huh?" Earl asked.

Francine waved, and Duane waved back. He shook Earl's hand and watched as he walked back to the door where Francine stood. They shut the door and Duane heard the deadbolt slide into place.

Duane drove off slowly from the sandy lot and around the corner of the diner to where the pumps were situated, careful not to turn the headlights on so as to attract their attention. He stopped, trying to decide if it was worth the risk of fighting off those things to fill up the gas tank, or to just test his luck and see if he could make it to the sheriff's station further down Route 10 with whatever gas was still in the tank. He decided it was worth the risk for the piece of mind and so he pulled up slowly to the closest gas pump. A few pumps ahead of him sat Ray's truck, its driver's side door still hanging open, and for the most part, it blocked the monstrous hordes' view of Duane's pickup. As he waited to make his move, he heard a voice, faint but clear.

Realizing it was the radio, he carefully turned up the volume.

"...began hours ago, an epidemic of mass murder, taking place all across the East coast and caused quite possibly by a contagion or a virus. People are warned to keep away from heavily-populated areas and to stay indoors. Do not venture outside for any reason."

Duane smiled at the irony of the radio's urgent orders as he watched small patches of the dead moving about, each finding an opening at the diner window on which to pound mindlessly against. He began to tense up, seeing his window to gas up his truck getting smaller. He debated on just lunging out of the truck and filling up before he lost the chance for good.

"Eyewitnesses say the attackers appear ordinary at first, and may even appear to be in need of first aid due to their clumsy motor functions..."

The ghouls, now close to a hundred in number, began to shift closer to his pickup truck, so he muttered a curse and shifted into reverse. He backed up slowly, trying to keep the engine undisturbed long enough for him to exit the parking lot. He made his left turn onto the road and cast one more glance into his side view mirror at Beekman's Diner. As he was wondering to himself if he would ever see the place again, if he would honor his promise to bring back help, he heard an ominous noise way off in the distance. It sounded how one might expect a Tyrannosaurus Rex to sound; a low steady roar that seemed to be coming at him from all sides. He could see in the mirror that this noise attracted the attention of the ghouls, and they turned from their various places around the diner to see what it was. Duane could just make out something moving in the distance, and whatever this object was, it was getting bigger. And as it drew closer, the noise grew even more prevalent. Finally, the mystery object revealed itself to be a gasoline tanker truck, barreling around a sharp corner and seemingly out of control. And it was coming straight at him. His eyes bugged out, not knowing where this tanker was going to end up. He jammed on the gas with the tanker truck now just a mere fifty feet away, and cut the wheel hard to the right. The tanker passed just behind him, screaming by so close that the motion of the passing tanker rocked Duane's pickup. He crashed through a guardrail and plummeted down several feet into a ditch. He lunged out of the driver's seat and crawled up the steep, wet incline of grass to try and gauge the path of the out-of-control tanker, worried that it could crash into the diner.

The tanker truck had close to fifteen of those things hanging on it, each trying to get at the driver inside. The truck dangerously veered back and forth on the road as the driver attempted to shake the ghouls loose. Now totally out of control, and as Duane feared it would, the truck barreled through a billboard before crashing directly into the diner's parking lot, smashing most of the cars in the lot like a sick act from God, tearing Charlie's big rig truck in half like wet toilet paper, to then jackknife directly into the gas pumps, taking them out with a simple swipe.

The explosion of the gas pumps was glorious, and even from a quarter mile down the road, Duane could hear the driver screaming; screaming for dear life, screaming as his face evaporated from the sheer heat of the inferno. The fire quickly spread to the tanker truck itself, and it then went up, exploding with such force that a large portion of the diner's roof lifted clean off like a tin can lid, allowing a wave of fire to spill directly into the tiny restaurant. The fire within the diner blew out every window with such force that, though Duane couldn't tell who it was, it sent one poor, unfortunate soul shooting out through the window to land on the windshield of one of the destroyed cars.

Duane could see that the ghouls backed away from the fire, disturbed by its presence. Whether it was the heat, or the brightness of the flames, he didn't know.

But it was something to remember.

The girth of the fire quickly subsided, having quickly consumed the fuel in which it had used to grow to immense proportions. Though the flames didn't stop burning altogether, they were small enough that the ghouls felt safe to move closer to the body stuck fast in the windshield of the car as smoke rose from the corpse. Whatever ghouls that were left untouched by the massive explosion fell quickly on their fresh meal simmering on the car hood. Duane's stomach turned as he watched them scoop handfuls of burning flesh and innards into their mouths, and as he stared in horror, he wondered who it was that was being fed to the dead. Was it Earl, perhaps? Or maybe Francine? Whoever it was, it had been a living, breathing person who was scared and confused and wanted nothing more than to just be at home away from the madness surrounding them.

Duane experienced a surge of emotions simultaneously; fear, regret, mourning, anger, and shame. From the moment he stepped through the front entrance to Beekman's Diner, everyone inside the restaurant became destined for death. And though it wasn't his presence that marked them all for the grave—that tanker truck would have barreled down the road regardless of where Duane was that day—it didn't make him feel any less responsible. And it didn't push away the pain.

He crouched over, suddenly feeling weak in his knees, and vomited up Francine's steak and eggs and his glass of Jack. It burned coming out of him as the fire at the diner burned every-thing else. He wiped his mouth with the sleeve of his sweater and looked at the diner again, at the car where the burned body of a former friend had landed. As the crowd of ghouls formed mind-lessly around the car, eager to get at the smoking mess, Duane, almost unaware of his actions, jumped in the pickup and shifted it into reverse. The powerful vehicle easily crawled backwards out of the ravine and pulled back onto the road, but not into the direction where he was headed, but instead pointed directly at the diner. He jammed his foot on the gas pedal and roared the pickup forward directly towards the undead horde. He flipped on his lights and then the high beams, flashing at them, getting their attention. He wanted their attention; he wanted them to see him coming.

They all turned, one layer at a time, and saw Duane barreling down on them. And even as he was pounding through them layer after layer, they didn't move, they didn't run. They just stood immobile, staring at him. Duane wanted to crush them, and he did. Upon the impact of the front grille against their chests, the ghouls flew through the air like bugs. He'd killed a few of them, maybe more than a few, but he hadn't killed them all, and he never would. Even if he stayed all night, running them over one at a time, more of them would materialize on the road, or from the surrounding woods, just to take their place.

Duane swept through them just the one time and it was enough. He turned onto the road now, making a screeching left, and he drove away. He looked down at the gas gauge again, knowing after gunning the engine to avoid the tanker, and to try and level the playing field, whatever gas still remained in the tank inside was probably gone and he was left with nothing but fumes. On his way down Route 10, he remembered what Francine and Earl had told him about their large farmhouse some miles down the road. It was in the middle of nowhere and wouldn't attract any attention. As he drove, the radio continued to repeat the same information over and over. Sometimes it rattled Duane from his thoughts just enough to sink in, other times it refused to permeate the hundred miles-an-hour thought process whirling inside his head.

Duane decided that the pickup would never make it the ten miles to the sheriff's station, and as if on cue, the truck's engine made a sputtering noise, giving Duane a verbal warning to not even attempt the drive. He cursed again, growing angry that no matter what he did and what he tried, he wasn't given a break. His best bet at that point was the farmhouse, so he set his sights on the right turn Francine told him about. And as he drove, thoughts of those he considered his friends drifted into his mind; Earl and Francine, Marla and Georgie the Cowboy, Harold and Beverly, Charlie the Trucker.

In the short time they knew each other, they had fought together and saved each other's lives, if only momentarily. And then they had died together. And from the minute he was looked upon as their leader, he knew the guilt he would feel would be immeasurable if something happened to them. And it was this guilt that was clawing at his insides now, the guilt that was flashing his friends' terrified faces on the inside of his eyelids when he squeezed them shut, trying to ward away his shame.

He spied ahead of him the dirt road leading to Earl and Francine's house. He banged a quick right and traveled down the bumpy dirt road, his high beams spilling out into the woods, lighting up the old gnarled tree trunks and reinventing them as gothic monsters set deep in the forest, as if awaiting weary travelers. Down the road a ways, as Francine promised, there was another dirt road on his right, which he turned down quickly. The road was a straight shot, and even in the darkness he could scarcely make out the beautiful, hulking figure of Francine and Earl's farmhouse, his home away from home, his salvation.

He finally pulled up in front of the large, faded white house and grimaced when he saw the ghouls stumbling around the property.

And then he saw the young woman.

She was dazed and terrified, dressed in a torn and dirty trench coat, standing on the porch, shielding her eyes from the bright headlights of Duane's truck. He could see by the fear on her face that she was normal. He didn't know if she was aware of the danger she was in, of those *things* surrounding her, but it didn't matter. Everything was going to be okay for her because he was there now. He wasn't going to lose another human life to those things. He grabbed the tire iron and jumped out of the truck, rushing to the porch where she stood, disoriented and terrified.

Come hell or high water, even if he had to do it with just the tire iron, he was going to save her. He wasn't going to fail her. Not like he'd failed the others. He wouldn't let that happen.

And he pitied anyone, whether living or dead, that would stand in his way.

THE AWAKENING

ANTHONY GIANGREGORIO

"Karl, we're going to be late," Marilyn snapped as her husband slowed the black, Ford, four-door sedan down just a little more. He was making sure to give himself two full car lengths behind the car he was following.

"Well, it's not my fault, Marilyn. I can't make the traffic go any faster, now, can I?"

In the back seat, their ten year old daughter, Kyra, shifted uncomfortably.

"I'm bored," she said as she stared out the window. It was a little after five p.m. and the sun was just beginning its descent, tinting the sky crimson.

"Oh, now, dear, I know you don't like car rides, but trust me, you'll love this play," Marilyn said to her daughter. She was wearing a simple black dress cut a little below the knees and had her hair done up in a bun. She was an attractive woman in her early forties with dark hair and a pleasant smile. Her figure was one most men would find attractive, though that didn't matter to her now. She was married and off the market, even though she wished her husband would treat her better.

As if he knew she was thinking about him, Karl glanced to her, taking his eyes off the road for just a moment. He was wearing a suit, the crisp white shirt seemingly sparkling in the high beams of the following cars' headlights. His bald pate made him look distinguished, but even she couldn't ignore the frown lines around his eyes. Those lines had been showing themselves more and more with each passing year, and she wondered what the next year would bring. Though she still loved him, their marriage was now strained. Karl always had a curt word for her or no patience whatsoever. Sometimes he would treat her like a child, more like his daughter; though in marriage they were supposed to be equals.

Looking over her shoulder, she could see the lights of Evanstown winking as the sun began to set. The play they were going to see was of Shakespeare's Hamlet. It hadn't been easy to convince Karl to go, but he finally relented, if just so she would leave him alone rather than out of any kind of respect. As for Kyra, she was coming because there were no sitters available. That was fine; they needed to do more things as a family, anyway.

Kyra was wearing a pink dress with a bow around her waist. Her dark hair, the same color as her mother's, was tied into two ponytails, one on each side of her head. Her pink shoes reflected the waning light and bounced it back to whoever was looking at them.

Karl placed a cigarette into his mouth and used the lighter in the dashboard to get it going. He sucked in two good puffs and handed it to Marilyn, who did the same and gave it back.

At least we have this in common, she thought as she handed the cigarette back to him. She glanced at him when she knew he wasn't looking at her, his eyes on the road. She studied his strong chin, his eyes that had once looked at her with love, the small dimple below his lower lip. He was a handsome man, and she felt her heart tug at her chest when she remembered how they had once been so close.

Karl broke her fugue dream by reaching out for the radio dial. Turning it on, he moved the bar across the stations until he found one he liked.

"*...authorities still don't know what to make of an unexplained attack which happened less than three hours ago. Reports are still coming in, but it appears a man and woman, while out for an afternoon walk, were attacked by unknown assailants. Both victims suffered mortal wounds and were pronounced dead at the scene. At this time the use of narcotics has not been ruled out. The attackers managed to get away and are even now being sought.*

The identities of the two assailants are still unknown, but one eyewitness account stated 'they were disheveled and devoid of emotion.' Stay tuned to this station for further updates on this terrible tragedy."

Karl turned off the radio, disgust on his face. "Damn nuts, all of them. The world's going to Hell, Marilyn, I swear to God. I don't know what to make of anything anymore. It's at the point you can't go for a walk without some yo-yo trying to jump you."

"Maybe it was about drugs?" Marilyn suggested. "You heard what the man said. It might be about something we have no idea about."

Karl shook his head. "No way, Marilyn, this is about chaos, pure and simple. The younger generation doesn't respect us. And this damn war, they want to protest instead of going over there and fighting. We should support Nixon, not ridicule him."

Marilyn frowned. She hated politics. "Do we really have to talk about the war, dear? You know I dislike it."

He waved his hand in the air, the one holding the cigarette. The smoke did rings in the car as he waved it about. "Oh, sure, Marilyn, just stick your head in the sand and ignore it. But it won't go away, you know. We all have to do our part. Why, if I was twenty years younger I would have gone over there myself."

Marilyn smirked, thinking of her husband crawling around in the jungles of Vietnam. She knew he would never have done it.

"Oh, sure, dear, you would have been a wonderful soldier," she said flatly.

"What does that mean?" he snapped at her.

"Oh, nothing, nothing," she said.

Karl grumbled some but let it go. Marilyn smirked wider. Though she did love him, she knew Karl was basically a coward. He would never fight if running or hiding was an option. A year ago he had a feud with their neighbor, John. It was about a fence and where the property line should be. At first Karl had yelled and screamed at John, being the pompous blowhard he was known for, but then John had lost his temper and had *actually* punched Karl.

Karl had gone down easily and had stared up at his neighbor in shock. After that, his gesturing had died down and they worked it out amicably.

Karl was one of those men who needed a slap in the face to put him in line. Otherwise he would rant and complain till the cows came home. She hated to know this about him, but it was there for all to see. She had come to accept it many years ago.

"Are we there yet?" Kyra asked from the back seat. She was twirling her hair in her right hand, the fingers spinning the tip.

"Do we look like we're there yet?" Karl snapped and Marilyn gave him a reproachful look. He saw it and his face took a down-turn. "Sorry."

"Don't tell me, Karl, tell you're daughter," Marilyn said.

He opened his mouth to say something, what Marilyn hoped was an apology, when the traffic took all of his attention. He stepped on the brake and the car began to slow.

Marilyn looked concerned. She knew this stretch of highway and there was nothing around; no exits for at least two miles. Maybe there had been an accident.

"What's wrong?" she asked.

"How the hell should I know, Marilyn? I'm in the same car as you, aren't I?"

"Well, you don't have to be so snip with me, dear."

"Don't I? Why the hell not?"

She closed her mouth, not wanting to instigate him. She knew how he was when he got this way. When he wasn't in control, he would lash out, and she and Kyra were easy targets. She did thank God he never raised a hand to either of them, but verbal abuse could be just as damaging. Still, she remained silent.

The car slowed until it was only a few feet from the bumper of the station wagon in front of it. Honking horns filled the interior as other upset drivers let out their frustration for being delayed.

"Maybe it's an accident," Marilyn said.

Karl only grunted, not having an answer. He checked his wrist-watch and frowned deeper than before. "If this doesn't clear up, we're going to be late for the play."

"You think so?"

"You know, Marilyn, I didn't want to go to this stupid thing in the first place. I wanted to stay home. But oh no, you kept nagging and so I gave in. And look where it got us, stuck on a highway miles away from anywhere."

"You act like this is all my fault, Karl. You know what? Maybe it is. That's right. I just wanted to get you alone with me so I cooked up this plan to block the highway so we could be together. Just the three of us, all trapped in our car. Is that what you really think?"

He inched the car forward a bit, as if that would make the station wagon in front of him nervous and the driver would move up a bit as well.

"No, of course I don't think that...that's ridiculous."

"Mom, I'm hungry," Kyra said from the back seat.

Marilyn ignored Karl to see to her daughter.

"Sure, honey, hold on a sec', I brought some snacks for the play, you can have them now," she said. In a small paper bag at her feet, she took out a smaller paper bag of crackers and cheese. Then she withdrew a thermos with ice tea. She poured some tea into the red cup that unscrewed off the top of the thermos and handed it to Kyra. Then she gave her some cheese and crackers.

"There you go, that should tide you over until we get moving again."

"Thanks, Mom," Kyra said and began eating quietly.

"You better make that last. If we don't get moving anytime soon that's all we're going to have to eat for who knows how long," Karl said. "If this is because of an overturned tanker truck or something, it could go on all night. They'll have to come at the wreck from the other side and it could take hours." He punched the steering wheel, causing Marilyn to jump in her seat. "Dammit, Marilyn, I don't believe this!"

"Well, yelling about it isn't going to solve anything. Please, calm down, you don't want to scare Kyra."

Karl glanced in the rearview mirror to see his daughter looking back at him.

"Sorry, Kyra, I didn't scare you did I?'

"No, Daddy, I'm okay, I know you get mad at stuff like this. Just don't yell at Mommy, though."

He frowned again and Marilyn smiled slightly in victory.

See? her smile said, *even your daughter knows what a pompous ass you can be.*

Karl nodded, trying to regain his composure. "I'll try not to, honey, you know Daddy has a short temper."

"Hmmph," Marilyn said askance of him.

He turned to her. "And what is that supposed to mean?" he snapped.

"A short temper? You have no temper. You fly off the handle at moment's notice. You need to see someone about it, too."

Karl threw his hands up and looked at the ceiling of the car, like he was talking to it. "You hear that, Lord? She wants me to see someone." He turned to stare at her. "Maybe if you got off my back I wouldn't have such a bad temper all the time. Maybe I will see someone and tell them how you drive me crazy. How 'bout that?"

"Fine, Karl, but make sure you tell the whole truth and not just what you think it is," she snapped back. She knew it was wrong to fight back; after all, he would only yell louder, force her to give in, but sometimes she couldn't help herself.

"Oh, I will, Marilyn, believe you me on that one. I'll tell him everything, and when I'm through, that guy will be on my side. He'll tell me how I'm a saint for dealing with you day after day and how ungrateful you are that I go to work every day and put a roof over your head and food on the table, and this is the thanks I get!" He was yelling now. He was so distracted he let his foot slide off the brake. He continued to yell at Marilyn and the car began to roll. It was just as he was at his peak, ready to really let her have it, that the car hit the bumper of the station wagon in front of them, the speed just enough to do some minor damage.

Immediately both Karl and Marilyn stopped yelling and he faced forward, seeing the brake lights of the station wagon glaring at him accusingly.

"Oh, great, now look what you made me do!" he yelled at her. "Now we have to deal with this!"

Marilyn crossed her arms over her chest, frowning. "Well, it's your own fault, Karl. If you hadn't been yelling at me and making a scene, this never would have happened." She pointed to the station wagon where a man was getting out of the driver's seat. "You better go talk to him. And please, for once, don't antagonize him. Remember, *you* hit him, not the other way around."

He held his right index finger up and pointed at her, his teeth grinding together he was so mad. But he held it in and turned to Kyra. "You okay, sweetheart?"

"Yes, Daddy, I'm fine. You hit that man's car, huh?" She was used to her parents yelling and took it in stride.

"Yeah, I did, your mom made me do it, but that's another story. You stay in the car with your mother and I'll be right back." He glared at Marilyn one more time, but she only glared right back at him, her lips pressed into a tight line.

Without another word to Marilyn, he turned off the engine and got out of the car to go see the driver of the station wagon, already thinking about what he was going to say and how he planned on blaming the accident on his nagging wife.

Darkness had fallen like a giant cloak over the area, and as Karl got out of his car, he had a better view of the highway. For as far as he could see there was nothing but brake lights. He could see for about a quarter of a mile; after that, the highway dipped and bent like a snake, but still, there were a lot of people other than him trapped on this road. To the right of him, on the shoulder, was a green highway sign with the words, **Bookman's Mortuary: For all your worldly needs. Next Exit**.

As he gazed out over the traffic jam, the driver of the station wagon was doing the same. For more than a minute, neither man looked at each other, both only staring at the sea of cars. Whatever was going on, no one was leaving anytime soon.

The station wagon's driver finally turned and walked back to the rear of his vehicle, scratching his head when he saw the dent in the metal bumper. He was a little taller than Karl, with dark hair and a sharp face, his nose angled so he took on the appearance of a hawk. He was well dressed with expensive shoes, telling Karl the man was no pauper.

"What the hell, buddy? How do you manage to hit someone in standstill traffic?"

Karl held his arms out to his sides. "Look, I'm sorry, all right? My wife was nagging me and I let my foot slip off the brake." He inspected the dent on the bumper. "It's not that bad. Tell you what. How 'bout I give you my address and you send me the bill, okay?"

The man nodded. "You damn well better believe that, pal. You're gonna pay, and how."

Karl lowered his arms, becoming defensive. "Now, just wait a second, there's no reason to be like that. It's just a little dent."

"Yeah, but you hit me, so it's your fault. Big or little, it doesn't matter. You're gonna buy me a new bumper.

"What? That's crazy. It's just a little dent. You're insane." Karl's voice was going up in pitch now. He had never had patience when people didn't agree with him. He had always believed he was a smart man and people would do well to listen to him. Only fools didn't.

"Well, if you're going to be like that, maybe I won't give you my address, how 'bout that?" Karl snarled.

The man folded his arms and glared at Karl. "Then I'll call a cop."

Karl laughed and gestured to the cars in front and behind them. "Go 'head, I don't see a cop, do you? In case you forgot, we're all stuck out here."

A few passengers from nearby vehicles were watching the argument. After all, there wasn't much else to do. Many had turned off their engines, realizing they weren't going anywhere, but most still had them idling. After all, gas was cheap and there was more than enough gas to go around, and idling for an hour or so was nothing. The man took a step closer to Karl, waving his right fist at him. "I could punch you out, at least that would shut you up," he growled.

Karl laughed some more. "Go 'head and try it, I can handle myself just fine."

Marilyn rolled her window down and stuck her head out of it. "Karl, for the love of God, just give him our address. You hit him, remember?"

Karl spun around; now glad to have someone he *knew* he could yell at. "Not now, Marilyn, let me handle this. Just be quiet, I'll be there in a second."

"Oh, what a big man, yelling at your wife," the driver said.

Karl spun on him, his right index finger pointed at him like a spear. "You just watch your mouth, mister. That's my wife and I'll speak to her any way I want to."

The driver was about to reply and tell Karl exactly what he thought about him, but a honking horn shattered the air. While there had been horns honking intermittently, this was one that had the distinct feel of panic. A second later, another horn sounded, followed by a third.

In less than ten seconds, there were more than twenty horns blaring, and now screaming could be heard. The entire cacophony was coming from further down the highway, and at first Karl couldn't see what was going on.

"Karl, what's happening?" Marilyn called out from the car. She, too, could hear the horns and it was making her uncomfortable.

"How the hell should I know, Marilyn? Just stay in the car...please."

"Hey, there are people walking down the highway between the cars," the driver of the station wagon said. Karl looked where the man was pointing and saw that he was correct. There were ten to twelve people stumbling down the pavement, between the cars and trucks, which were all lined up as if sitting in a parking lot.

Then Karl saw something he wouldn't have believed if he didn't see it with his own eyes.

One of the figures, a woman, if he was correct, stopped at a Ford hatchback with a family inside. The driver's window was open and the father was calling out to the walking woman, wanting to know what was going on, when the woman attacked him, sinking her teeth into the side of his cheek like she was starving and he was dinner.

The father screamed as half his face was ripped off, his cheek trapped between her bloody teeth, the flesh sagging over her lips and chin. The father opened his door, slamming the woman away from his car. Blood was pouring from his wound as he began to punch and kick at the woman. He was so angry about what happened to him, he wasn't thinking of staunching the flow of blood. Karl could see the father looked like a blue collar man, and when he moved closer, he saw he was right. The father's callused hands alluded to his sixty hour-a-week job working in a factory and his arms bulged with muscle.

Karl knew right then if he was going to pick a fight with someone, the father would be the last person on his list.

But the woman who had torn his face off wasn't in that same opinion, and as she was knocked to the road, she rolled onto her side. When the father tried to kick her again, she wrapped her arms around the leg like she was hugging it. No sooner did the father cry out, seeing he was trapped, when the woman sank her already bloody teeth into his leg. Her teeth tore into the material of his pants and plunged into the skin beneath, causing the man to cry out and fall over. As he fell, another shape came out from between two cars and fell on him. Meanwhile, other figures were reaching into the car where the man's family now screamed and yelled. Karl couldn't see what was happening, but he did see a dark liquid shoot out and spray the rear windshield. In the wash of the headlights from the vehicle behind the car, the coating on the windshield looked like paint—a paint that was dark in color.

Marilyn was out of the car now and she ran up to Karl, grabbing him by the arm. "Karl, what's going on? Why are those people screaming?"

"I...I don't know, Marilyn, but I think we should get back in the car."

The driver of the station wagon turned away from the chaos to face Karl. "Hey, wait a minute, pal, what about my bumper?"

Karl looked at the man as if he was insane. Something very unusual was going on and this man was still worried about a dent on his bumper?

And then the figures doubled in number and a shadow came out from behind the next car lined up beside the station wagon, tackling the driver. Karl watched the man go down and stared in horror as the figure on top of him tore his throat out.

Marilyn was screaming beside him and he thought he might have been screaming right along with her. Both of them stood stock still, not knowing what to do, when more shadows came out from between the idling cars.

"Marilyn, we need to get in the car, right now."

"But that man..." she began, but he cut her off.

"No, Marilyn, think about Kyra. Now *move!*" he yelled the last word, his tone shaking her from her stupor. Turning, they both ran back to the car and jumped in, just as shadows came for them. As Karl slammed his door closed, a figure bounced off his window.

What was startling was the man's shirt was open and he looked to have an autopsy scar, the V covering his chest resembling some form of bizarre ritual scarring, as if the man was from some lost tribe in New Guinea.

"Lock the doors, Marilyn, now!" Karl ordered, just as Kyra began to scream from the backseat. There were shadows all around them now, as they were also around the other cars and trucks.

Then Karl saw the driver of the station wagon standing in front of his car, his headlights bathing him in white light as the sun finished its descent. The man's throat was a mangled ruin and his shirt and pants were soaked with blood...his own blood.

Karl blinked, not believing what he was witnessing. The man should be dead...DEAD! There was no plausible reason for him to still be walking around. His throat was torn out to the point Karl could see his spine peeking through the blood and gore. And as the man turned slightly, the headlights to Karl's car reflected off the man's eyes and that was when he knew the man wasn't alive...at least not in the sense of the word used in the scripture he had read every Sunday for his entire life. The eyes were void of energy, gaping pools of what...nothing? Yes, nothing. There was nothing inside the man's eyes. It was as if his soul had flown away and left the shell behind, a shell that now wanted to kill him and his family.

Fists were pounding on the windows now as more arrived. He spotted a woman in a nice dress, her hair clipped in a bow. But as the woman pressed her face to the glass, Karl saw that her lips were glued shut and her eyes were open, though her eyelids were hanging from above, torn free of their flesh moorings.

He remembered seeing a documentary one time about how morticians prepared a body for a funeral; how the technicians would glue the eyes and mouth of the deceased shut. Well, that would explain why her eyelids were like that. She had been dead and ready for planting in the ground and somehow had gotten up.

She had gotten up and had begun to walk around; a dead person, walking around like they were alive. Impossible, yes—of course it was impossible—but if that was so, if that was the truth, then how in God's name could he answer the question of why dead people were on the highway attacking the passengers in the traffic jam?

Simple: he couldn't.

He remembered the sign on the shoulder of the road. The sign was for a mortuary. And if a mortuary was nearby, then all the people who had attacked them could have come from there and whatever cemetery was nearby.

Mortuaries and cemeteries were always located close together; it just made sense.

It was all ridiculous, yes, but when all rational explanations won't fit, then only the irrational remains.

The car was rocking back and forth now and Marilyn was crying out, as was Kyra.

"What do they want, Karl? Why are they doing this?" Marilyn screamed. She shrieked louder when a pale face slapped her window, and then dragged itself across the glass like a snail, leaving behind a residue of blood and gore.

Karl looked to the right where the woods lined the highway to see even more figures emerging. Through the trees, he could see the outskirts of a cemetery and a low fence, one that could be easily scaled by anything walking on two legs.

Then something hard whacked against the front windshield and Karl saw one of the attackers had a large tree branch the size of a human arm in its hand.

No wait, it wasn't a tree branch the size of a human arm...it was a human arm!

Each time the figure hit the window, blood and viscera remained behind, slowly dripping down the glass to pool near the top of the hood.

A steady staccato of hands beat on the hood and sides of the car, and Karl felt more than heard something heavy strike his driver's side window. Turning, he saw a man with a fist-sized rock in his hand.

Thump.

The rock bounced off the window inches from his head and he knew another one or two impacts would shatter the glass.

"Karl, what do we do?" Marilyn cried out as she stared at the blank faces of the people surrounding them.

"I don't know, let me think!" he yelled back. He started the engine and tried to drive away, but he made it no more than a foot before hitting the rear of the station wagon again, managing to trap one of the people between the bumpers. As he backed up, the car unpinned the trapped figure, letting it drop to the road. Karl backed up until he hit the car behind him, the impact cushioned by more bodies. But as he stared out into the night, using only the headlights of the other vehicles around him for illumination, he saw more and more figures on the highway. Some appeared to be the people who had been in the vehicles stuck in the traffic jam, only now they were covered in blood and riddled with mortal wounds.

Panicking, he drove the car forward again, everyone jolting back and forth when he rear-ended the station wagon yet again.

He was trapped! There was nowhere to go!

Shattering glass filled Karl's world and Kyra screamed behind him. A woman with a rock and ratty hair had managed to break the back window. Kyra was grabbed immediately by her hair and she shrieked in pain and terror as she was slowly pulled from the car.

"Kyra!" Marilyn yelled and dove over the back seat to save her little girl. Kyra was halfway out the window now, shards of safety glass spilling over the seat to fall to the floorboards. Marilyn grabbed her daughter by her right leg and yanked back for all she was worth. At first there was no give, but Marilyn was a woman possessed, fighting for the life of her daughter, and she screamed again and tugged harder. A voice in the back of her mind warned her to be careful, that she could dislocate or even break Kyra's leg. But she paid it no mind.

A tug of war ensued, with Kyra as the rope, as Marilyn fought to save her daughter.

Then Kyra was falling back into the car while hands clawed for her. Marilyn punched at them to knock them away from her child. She was terrified, but filled with strength to save her daughter.

Kyra fell to the seat and screamed again, her legs kicking out to stop from being grabbed again. There was blood on her arm, teeth marks apparent, but Marilyn couldn't see how deep the wound was. She could see the blood was barely enough to fill a couple of tablespoons. Kyra's rear side window exploded inward and hands reached for her and Marilyn.

"Get to the other side of the car!" Karl yelled out as he reached over to help Marilyn.

Both females scooted across the seat as hands reached in but could find nothing to grab. Karl realized, whoever these people were, whatever they were, they weren't very bright. None of the grasping hands thought to reach in and unlock the door; they merely continued to try and grab Kyra and Marilyn.

Then Karl heard a loud bang coming from behind him and outside the car. He glanced in the rearview mirror as the car bounced on its shocks to see a large fireball ten or so cars behind him. The orange and reds colored his mirror and a sense of dread filled him. He had never been a truly brave man and this was far beyond anything he had ever experienced.

"Karl!" Marilyn screamed as she was shaken back and forth. There had to be six or seven bodies now surrounding his car and Karl could see other vehicles on the highway in a similar state of attack. Not knowing what to do, he stepped on the gas again, the car surging forward to rear-end the station wagon again, and just as he moved forward, a rock came down on the frame of the window by his head. He suddenly realized that if he hadn't moved when he did, his window would have been shattered, and they would have gotten him. But no sooner did he try to back up when the car behind him rear-ended him, the driver also panicking and reaching for straws. Now he was wedged between two vehicles and his car was useless as a form of defense or attack.

Peering out the front windshield, the world had descended into utter madness. He could see shadowy figures silhouetted in the headlights of vehicles as they pulled open doors and yanked people out shattered windows. As unbelievable as it was to witness, the figures were eating their prey.

And by the looks of things, that would be the fate for himself and his family.

Suddenly, the car began to rock harder and he gripped the steering wheel with white knuckles. Panicking, he stepped on the gas but felt no traction. He floored the gas pedal and the engine whined, but there was no feeling of an engine wanting to break free of its prison.

Slowly at first, then faster, the passenger side of the car began to rise and he realized there was no traction because his back wheel wasn't touching the pavement.

"Oh God, they're tipping the car, Marilyn! They're trying to flip us over!" Karl yelled and Marilyn yelled back, terror filling her voice. She hugged Kyra tightly, brushing her hair as she tried to calm her down. Kyra wasn't hearing any of it. She was beyond terrified, screaming and kicking in fear, ranting that she wanted to go home.

"Hold on, they're really doing it!" Karl screamed as he felt the car lifting higher. His eyes were wide with panic and the back of his head was pressed to the driver's side window. The window finally shattered as a rock connected with it. He idly wondered if it was the same attacker who was holding the same fist-sized rock that had been trying to get at him moments ago.

Hands reached in and wrapped around his neck and he screamed, feeling cold hands pressed to his skin. He pulled himself away from the hands as he crawled across the seat.

Karl realized ironically that the tipping of the car had actually saved his life, for if the car had been on all four wheels, the attackers would have easily reached inside and pulled him out to join the dozens of other dead passengers.

The car was still going onto its side and as the two figures reached in to grab him, the car rolled over on its roof, crushing the two bodies and anyone else on that side of the car. Suddenly, up became down and all the remaining intact windows shattered as the roof bent inward, not able to support the weight of the automobile.

Marilyn and Kyra tumbled like laundry as they fell onto their heads and righted themselves. Karl was upside down now and he pulled his feet out from under the dashboard and dropped down to the car's overhead, which was now the floor.

"We have to go, Marilyn! We need to go right now!" he screamed as he reached over and pulled her to him.

"Where?" was all she could manage.

"I don't know, but anywhere's better than here." He spun around, careful not to cut himself on the safety glass.

Ha, what a laugh, he thought. *Pressed under your palms, it was just as bad as regular glass.*

He crawled out of the car, and the night seemed to wrap him in its embrace. He reached down and grabbed Marilyn, who handed Kyra to him first. He pulled her out while Marilyn crawled free. Karl held Kyra in his arms; she was catatonic with terror.

"Where do we go?" Marilyn asked. Her dark hair was a mess, bits of glass glittering in the firelight of the burning vehicle behind them.

Karl looked left, right, and then left again. Behind him stood the guardrail to the highway, as well as an open field. Beyond that was the trees and the edge of the cemetery, which at the moment, looked quiet and safe while the highway resembled a war zone.

To illustrate his point, another vehicle exploded, raining body parts and pieces of metal down on the road. People screamed, some begged for their lives, and above it all was a moaning that vibrated with a tone all its own.

Another high-pitched scream caused Karl to turn around, and he gasped in horror when he saw a figure running across the highway, waving in and out of cars. The figure was on fire, a flaming, moving funeral pyre, the face all but lost in crimson and yellows. The figure was neither man nor woman, the scream of neither gender. But it was filled with absolute agony as the immolated soul bounced off cars and trucks until finally tripping and falling to the road. The sickly sweet smell of burnt flesh filled Karl's sinuses and he felt the bile building in his throat. Marilyn was holding a hand over Kyra's eyes so she wouldn't see the horrible sight.

The figure fell only a few feet from Karl and he stared at its face as it seemed to blister and melt off the skull, the fat popping and sizzling.

He turned away, unable to stand it any longer.

Reaching out his right hand, he grasped Marilyn's arm. "Come on, Marilyn, we need to go."

"But where, Karl?"

He pointed into the field. "That way, it looks safe that way." He pulled her arm and she moved, Kyra beside her. Figures came at them from out of the shadows and Karl shoved and pushed them away. He found out quickly they were slow and alone; one on one, they were basically harmless. The trick was not to let them get a hold of you. But he also saw that when they cornered their prey and had numbers on their side, the hapless prey was doomed.

The only way was to run, to escape and hide, then wait for the authorities to handle things.

An old woman came at Karl on his right and he pushed her away, the frail body falling to the road, followed by a crack of bones breaking, probably her hip.

Marilyn cried out when a man in what appeared to be a black suit covered in gore and grime tried to grab her. Karl charged the man and used his shoulder to knock him off his feet.

Karl was terrified, his heart beating a mile a minute, and he wanted nothing more than to be free of this carnage.

"Go, Marilyn, go!" he screamed and pushed another figure away.

They climbed over the guardrail, Karl helping Kyra as she fought to get over the metal barricade with her dress on. With Marilyn's heeled shoes and dress, her attire was ill-suited for a hike in the woods, but there was no choice in the matter.

Shoving another attacker away from him, Karl backed away from the barricade, seeing they had followers. Four figures were now climbing over the guardrail, clumsily falling to the dirt lining the shoulder of the highway.

"Run, Marilyn, run!" Karl ordered as he began to leave the road. Marilyn was right behind him with Kyra by her side, but after fifty feet or so, she called out to Karl. "Wait, Kyra can't do it! There's something wrong with her!"

Karl turned and ran back to them, the waist-high grass parting for him. When he reached Kyra and Marilyn, he looked past them to see the four attackers in pursuit. They walked at a steady pace, but didn't run or jog.

"What's wrong, Marilyn? We need to go, they're right behind us," he snapped.

"Don't you think I know that? Kyra can't run!"

Karl grabbed Kyra by the arms and held her up. "What's wrong, honey? We need to run, the bad people are chasing us."

"I don't feel good, Daddy, and my arm hurts," she said, her face looking pale in the wan light from the moon and the glowing patches of fire coming off the highway.

Knowing there wasn't time for debate, he picked her up, feeling how light she was. She was frail on the best of days and now she was downright helpless.

"I got her, now come on. If we get enough distance, maybe they'll give up."

Marilyn nodded, touching her child's face lovingly, and they set off.

Their legs ate up the distance and soon they reached the trees lining the field.

Karl slowed and they ducked down in the grass, not wanting to dash into the trees and be spotted.

"What are we waiting for?" Marilyn asked.

"Shhh, I don't think they can see us. Let's give it a second and see what happens," he hissed.

She didn't argue, but ducked down and checked on Kyra, who was sweating heavily. "I think she has a fever," Marilyn whispered.

"Not now, Marilyn, quiet," he ordered.

He couldn't see over the tall grass and he risked raising his head to check on their pursuers. What he saw were the four figures wading through the brush, but they weren't going in the right direction, and when another vehicle exploded on the highway, the sound caused all four to spin around and head back to the highway.

Karl let out the breath he was holding and felt his heart slow just a little.

"It looks like they're going back to the road," he said. "We did it, Marilyn, we're safe."

She barely heard him, her attention on Kyra only.

"What now?" she finally asked.

"We go find a house or something and call for help. What else is there to do?"

"And we need to get Kyra to a hospital," Marilyn added.

"Of course, as soon as we call someone I'll ask for an ambulance. Come on, we better get moving while we still can."

Marilyn wiped Kyra's forehead with a tissue from her purse. She was dying for a cigarette but knew it wasn't the time. With Karl in the lead once more, they headed into the woods. While he carried her, his only daughter began to wheeze slightly, as if she was coming down with a bad cold.

*　*　*

Ten minutes later brought them to the outskirts of the cemetery. With full darkness, the ancient tombstones resembled shadowy sentries guarding the dead.

The moon was high and cast a pallid glow over every surface, while gnarled tree branches reached out like the fingers of long-rotted corpses. The trees themselves were losing their leaves, signifying the end of another year of life.

Karl leaned against the first tombstone he came to, breathing hard. He set Kyra down, his back aching from the dash across the field. Next to him, Marilyn knelt down and inspected her daughter.

"She doesn't look good, Karl. We need to get her to a doctor."

Karl waited to reply, needing to catch his breath. "Oh, fine, Marilyn, maybe there's one around here somewhere. Let me just call out and get him to come over here," he snapped irritably. He was hot and his formal suit was uncomfortable. He loosened his tie and waved his face. Despite the cool temperature, he was still perspiring.

"That's not what I meant, Karl, and you know it."

Karl pushed off the stone and took a step towards the tree line a few feet away. Through the trees he could see the flickering lights of the fires from the highway. Another explosion filled the night, but from the cemetery it seemed muted, less frightening. Screams could still be heard on the wind, but they were softer now, and if the wind shifted, he could barely hear them at all.

Turning, he went back to Kyra and picked her up. "Come on, Marilyn, we need to go. I don't want to be anywhere near that highway."

She merely nodded, deferring to his judgment.

They began walking again, weaving between the stone facades of the long dead, the faded carvings of lost mothers, beloved wives, and cherished sons, all lost in the shadows of the night.

A night bird called out from a nearby tree and Karl all but dropped Kyra in his terror. Realizing it was just a bird, he quickly regained what composure he had. Marilyn was crying now, though she tried to hold it in.

"Karl, what's happening? Why did those people attack us, attack everyone else? What do they want?"

Karl shook his head from side to side wearily. "I don't know, Marilyn. Does it really matter? Why do you always have to have an explanation for everything? Just accept it as fact and deal with it. *Why* doesn't matter."

"But if we can figure out why, maybe we can do something about it."

He turned to her, his face flush with anger. As he spun around, Kyra's small feet swung out as if she was on a swing.

"Marilyn, I don't care why it's happening. All I know is if we want to live, we need to get someplace safe. Now shut up and do what I tell you." His words were curt, short, and disrespectful. As usual. She glared at him, her chin rising in defiance, but then it lowered again. Since their marriage had begun to fall apart she had been more vocal in her opinions, but she knew now was not the time. Now she needed to be the good wife—for the well being of her daughter if for no other reason.

"Fine, Karl, I'm sorry."

He nodded, glad he won what he perceived as an argument. "Okay, follow me. It looks like there's a house on the other side of this cemetery. Can you see it?" He gestured to the north where Marilyn then looked. She strained her eyes through the sparse trees and finally she noticed a small light. A porch light, if she was correct.

He turned and began walking through the cemetery again, Marilyn right behind him. The night grew quiet the deeper they traveled and soon even the fires from the highway were completely lost from sight, as were the pleas for help and the screams of suffering.

Twenty minutes later, they slowed at the edge of a gravel driveway at the edge of the trees. The shrubs had been cut back, man keeping nature at bay. In front of them was the house Karl had seen. To the right of the driveway was a sign, and on this sign in faded script was the name **Bookman's Funeral Home**. And below that in smaller script were the words, *Let us usher you into the afterlife.*

"Thank God, we finally found help," he said as he began crossing the gravel. The rocks crunched under his now very scuffed black dress shoes. Marilyn followed, hugging herself as she went. Her eyes roved over the facade of the house, taking in the architecture. It looked to be about twenty-years-old, she thought, which would mean it was built in the late 40's. Wooden shutters sat beside each window, and the stone porch seemed to beckon to her, the nearby branches from the trees growing along the walkway like reaching arms.

Karl took the stone steps with a little hesitation, either from exhaustion or fear. Marilyn watched him and wondered which it was. She knew better than to ask him. Karl had never been one to talk about his emotions. Looking back to when they had been courting, he had always been like that. But she had believed she could change him, get him to open up to her. And there was good in him, too. But with his job weighing down on him as well as the war in Vietnam, where his younger brother was even now crawling through the jungles, he had become withdrawn. And every attempt she made to have him open up was only met with attacks and insults. It was possible she would have left long ago, just packed her bags and went home to Mother, but Kyra kept her with him. Kyra needed a father and she'd be damned if she was the reason her daughter would lose one.

Karl pressed the doorbell, and Marilyn could hear a faint buzzing coming from the other side of the door. Karl waited for almost twenty seconds before pressing it again.

"Give them a chance, Karl," she said, not wanting to anger the very people she hoped could help them.

But he ignored her, as if she had never spoken, something else he was wont to do. There had been times when they had been discussing something and he had decided the matter was over.

When she would then ask another question, he would ignore her, pretending she had said nothing as he concentrated on the CBS nightly news. There were times she believed Walter Cronkite was more important to him than she was.

He pressed the doorbell again and the faint buzzing could be heard once more. He waited another ten seconds and grunted, "I don't think anyone's home."

Marilyn opened her mouth for a rebuttal when Karl shifted Kyra in his arms and reached for the door handle. Pressing the lever with his thumb, the distinct sound of the latch popping came to her. Without looking to her for an opinion, he pushed the door open and stepped inside. She stood on the porch as his back disappeared into the shadows of the home, and with one brief glance over her shoulder at the darkness beyond, she followed behind him, closing the door behind her out of courtesy.

The first thing Karl saw upon entering the funeral home was a small foyer which branched off into two long hallways. One looked like it went deeper into the house, while the other led to viewing rooms. Each room had a sign over it, naming the room with some serene title, such as the **Eternal Life** room, or the **Forever With Us** room. There were three other rooms with equally over-the-top names. He wondered if anyone ever noticed how ridiculous they sounded, but figured anyone visiting would be there to say goodbye to a loved one, and thus probably didn't care about what the room was called.

Halfway down the hallway, he spotted a small table, and on this table was a standard rotary dial phone. Setting Kyra down on to the floor, making sure she was leaning against the wall, he told Marilyn to watch her and he dashed to the phone. Picking up the receiver, all he got for his trouble was dead air. Pressing the button in the casing, he still couldn't get a dial tone.

"It's dead," he said to Marilyn as he set the phone back on its cradle.

"What do you mean 'it's dead'? It can't be," Marilyn said as she brushed hair off Kyra's face, which felt clammy and cold. She was terribly worried about her daughter.

"Just like I said, Marilyn. It's dead. There's no dial tone."

But Marilyn wouldn't take no for an answer and she walked down the hallway, her heels silent as they crossed the carpeting. Picking up the phone, she saw Karl was correct.

"See? What? Did you think I was lying?" he demanded.

"No, I...I just..."

"Just what? It's always like you, Marilyn, to second guess me. I said there was no dial tone and I meant it."

Marilyn was about to reply when the electricity flickered, the lights buzzing back on a moment later.

"What's that?" she asked.

"Don't know. Must be a problem with the power lines," he replied. He turned and walked down the rest of the hallway and found a small kitchenette. A pile of dish towels lay on the counter next to a small sink and he quickly dampened three of them, filled two glasses with water from the tap; the glasses taken from a small cupboard. He drank one glass down and refilled it, then carried his finds back to Marilyn.

"Here, for her cut," he said to Marilyn, handing her a towel. "It might help if you clean it some. And I brought this too, for you or her." He handed her one of the glasses as he drank from the other one."

She said nothing, just took the glass and the towels. Kneeling down, she began cleaning the cut on Kyra's arm as well as wiping her face. She drank half the water for herself and then tried to give Kyra some. Her daughter only moaned and turned her head; spitting out the little bit of water Marilyn managed to give her.

"She won't drink it," Marilyn told him.

"Well, what do you want me to do about it?" He loved his daughter deeply, but she had never been *Daddy's Little Girl*. She had always been her mother's daughter.

"I don't know what you should do," she said as tears welled up in her eyes. She fought them back down. She was a strong woman and could control her emotions, even in a stressful time such as this.

"Look, Marilyn, whoever lives here will be back soon. They have to be. When they get here they'll have transportation. So we'll get them to take us to a hospital. Don't worry, everything will be fine."

She didn't reply, but continued to attend to her daughter.

"Look, I'm going to check the rest of this place out. Maybe someone's here and they're deaf or something. Will you be okay? The both of you?"

"We'll be fine, go and do your search," she said, barely glancing at him.

"Fine, just stay here so I know where you are, just in case there's any trouble."

She only nodded.

He gazed down at his daughter for a few seconds and then turned and headed off. Even if there was no one here, maybe he could find a gun or something to use as a weapon. He tried not to think that the attackers on the highway may have come from the very place he had brought his family. But he was out of options. Besides, he had yet to see anyone.

Moving deeper into the house, he left Marilyn and Kyra behind.

The hallway Karl now walked wasn't decorated like the other one. The first ten feet were, but then a curtain separated what was obviously the showroom part of the funeral home and the work area... the part customers weren't supposed to see. Here the paint was faded and the wood molding was scratched, the hardwood floor looking like it could use a refinish.

He followed the hallway to the other end of the home, and when he reached a final door, he opened it. Metal stairs led down into what had to be the basement, and with no other option, he began descending.

When he was halfway down, he began to hear a light pounding, like a fist on a door or a table. It wasn't loud and it could very well be the water pipes, but he knew he had to investigate. If it was the owner of the home then he needed to find them and hope they had a vehicle.

At the end of the stairs there was another hallway, the cement floor covered with a layer of old paint that was missing in more places than it remained. There was a fifteen foot open area and then a wooden door set into the wall. Karl walked to the door, trepidation filling him like a living entity.

When he reached the door, he could hear the pounding grow louder.

Whatever was making the noise, while still faint, was somewhere on the other side of the door.

Knowing he really had no choice in the matter, as his daughter needed help, he turned the doorknob and gritted his teeth as the door opened on creaking hinges.

As it swung open, he could see nothing. The room was entirely encased in darkness.

Reaching along the wall, he felt for a light switch. It took him a second, the switch lower on the wall than he would have expected, but when he flicked it on, stark-white ceiling lights illuminated what had to be the prep room for the funeral home. The metal gurneys, surgical equipment, and some sort of machine he believed was used for embalming filled the space.

To his right came the pounding again, and as his eyes shifted in that direction, his mouth fell open at the sight greeting him.

A middle-aged man was standing there, his right leg caught up in a sheet, the sheet then wrapped around the bottom of the steel table, like a dog on a leash. Every time the man tried to walk away, the gurney would thump and rattle. That was the noise he'd heard. Beyond the man he saw another door and the cool night of outside exposed. Whatever had been in this room had escaped through that door and into the surrounding countryside.

A low moaning came from his left and his head shot in the direction so fast he could have gotten whiplash. He was greeted by two more people, one a woman and one an old man, both also naked. The old man had a V stitched into his chest, and as he tried to walk, the stitches gave out, the wound opening to spill out his internal organs. They slapped the floor with a meaty sound reminiscent of a wet mop hitting the floor.

Karl felt his stomach flip-flop and he fought not to vomit right there. From the rear of the prep room, more bodies were shambling toward him, one dressed in a suit, another in a dress. Both had their faces done up with heavy makeup and they had that false look of life seen on cadavers when they were laid out at wakes for loved ones to say their last goodbyes.

Karl was frozen in horror as the bodies slowly walked and stumbled toward him, hands grasping empty air, arms upheld so as to wrap around him.

Finally, his stupor snapped and he screamed, long and loud, the entire night—which had just begun—already taking a toll on him.

Just as the first animated dead thing reached him, he stepped back and slammed the door shut, locking it with the key still in the lock. No sooner did the door close when the first fist pounded on it, causing it to rattle in its frame.

Karl took a step back, but as if his feet were made of clay, couldn't seem to turn and leave.

The door shook again and this time a small crack appeared on its chipped and worn facade. The door was cheap, hollow. It wasn't made for security and wouldn't standup to the ministrations of the walking dead for long.

Still Karl stared, as if mesmerized by the vibrating door. Another blow and the door shook, another crack appearing. Karl blinked but still didn't run.

Another fist connected with wood and this time a spot of light blazed through, a finger poking through the hole like a worm sniffing the air after a long sleep in the ground.

Another blow and the finger became a fist, the splinters of wood raining down onto the floor to cover the missing paint. When a head appeared, the teeth oddly white, the garish makeup and dead eyes seeming to peer right through him, Karl finally broke from his shock and bolted up the stairs.

As he took the stairs two at a time, he could hear the door fall in, then the sound of rustling bodies as they fought to be the first through the gap.

It was when Karl's foot hit the upper landing that he heard the sound of a bare foot slapping the first metal stair below and behind him.

They were coming.

Panic filled his insides like acid and he charged back to the foyer to get Marilyn and Kyra.

They needed to leave this place now, or they would find themselves trapped under a sea of attackers. As he ran, he wondered if the passengers who had been attacked and killed on the highway would end up being the lucky ones in the end.

Marilyn looked up as Karl came running down the hallway.

"Did you find help?" she asked.

"No," he said as he came up next to her, his hands slapping the wall to slow him down. He was breathing heavily now, his white shirt untucked from his mad dash. "We need to leave this place, Marilyn. There's more of those *things* downstairs."

"What?" she gasped.

He nodded. "A whole room of them and they're coming up here. Come on, we need to leave."

"But where will we go?" she asked, her eyes darting back and forth into the shadows, her mind conjuring images of demons.

"I don't know, but there has to be somewhere where we can be safe till whatever's happening is over."

He bent over and picked Kyra up. Her small face was pale, her eyes closed. She looked like she was sleeping. "This way," he said as he began to head for the door.

A crash from behind caused Marilyn and Karl to turn, seeing the first walking corpse stagger down the hallway. Pictures were knocked from the walls as flailing hands brushed them carelessly aside.

Marilyn screamed, though she barely heard herself doing it. Karl reached out and grabbed her, almost pushing her to the front door.

She opened it and he went through first, careful not to hit Kyra's head on the doorframe. Marilyn was right behind him and he spun around at her and said, "Close the damn door, Marilyn, we don't need them following us out here."

She did as told, slamming the door closed. As it clicked shut, she heard a thump of a body on the other side. Soon fists were pounding on the wood, but this door was made for security. Their followers wouldn't be exiting the funeral home by the front door anytime soon, unless they used the doorknob and figured out how to unlock it.

With Karl in the lead, the couple made their way through the woods. It was pitch black in many places thanks to the thick canopy of tree branches.

Karl still carried Kyra, cradling his small daughter in his arms. She was sleeping at the moment, her face very still. He didn't know what was wrong with her, but if he had to guess, it appeared she was in a coma.

Dread filled him as he weaved through the trees, branches reaching out to pluck at his suit. In the night, he was all but invisible. Marilyn followed close behind, making her way over the forest floor, her heels a hindrance. But she wouldn't take them off, not wanting to go barefoot.

They walked for what seemed like forever, their breath coming in gasps and finally they came to a small country road.

Karl had no idea where he was. If he had to guess, he figured the highway where his overturned car lay was maybe a couple of miles behind them. But for all he knew it was only a mile. It was hard to gauge distance in the woods, he quickly discovered. He was exhausted and wanted nothing more than to rest. But Kyra needed medical attention and that drove him onward.

The trees thinned finally and he stepped out onto a dirt road, packed down from years of use. At first he didn't know where he was. One second he was in the woods, and then he was on a dirt road, the sky overhead, the stars twinkling like a shimmering carpet.

Marilyn came out behind him and she gasped in thankfulness, seeing they had made it out of the endless forest.

"Which way do we go?" she asked.

Karl gestured with his head. "This way." He began walking down the middle of the road, the pale moonlight casting his figure in shadow. Without saying a word, she followed, the road making it easier for her to walk. Her eyes darted into the trees, imagining figures waiting for her, but other than a few cicadas and crickets, the road was quiet and devoid of life.

For fifteen minutes they walked, neither of them speaking. The horrors of the night flashed through their heads, though both did their best to force the images down into the dark pit of their minds.

Rounding a bend in the road, Karl let out a soft cry of relief when he spotted an old farmhouse. "Finally, I was beginning to think this road would never end," he said. Without waiting for Marilyn, he crossed the faded lawn, now dying due to the cold fall temperature, and stepped onto the small porch.

He glanced behind him to see Marilyn making her way across the grass.

He knocked on the screen door, Kyra still in his arms. He didn't want to put her down, not yet. When there was no answer, he opened the screen door and knocked on the faded wood of the main door. As soon as his knuckles struck the old wooden door, it swung inward. It was unlocked.

Way out here, no one probably locks their doors, he thought.

He heard Marilyn's shoes on the wooden planks of the stairs as he entered the house.

"Hello? Anyone home? We need help. We were attacked on the highway. Hello? Hey, there's people going crazy out there, you shouldn't leave your door unlocked." Karl waited but there was no answer.

The décor was plain; a threadbare rug, worn furniture and old wallpaper about to begin peeling. Immediately, his nose scrunched up at the smell of death. It was faint, but there nonetheless.

Marilyn did the same. "Oh my Lord, what is that?"

"It's not good, I can tell you that, Marilyn." He walked over to a worn couch and set Kyra down, laying her out. "Here, watch her while I check for a phone."

Marilyn did as she was told, going to her knees and pulling a handkerchief from her purse. She wiped Kyra's forehead with it. The little girl was still sleeping and she wouldn't wake when Marilyn shook her gently. Marilyn's stomach turned into knots with worry for her child. She inspected her surroundings and saw a quaint, if rundown, farmhouse, with ramshackle furniture and curtains on the windows. Whoever's home this was lived simply.

Karl began to explore the house, going to the refrigerator first and grabbing a cold beer from the top shelf. He downed it in a few gulps, wiping his mouth on the back of his sleeve. He looked at the wet spot then, realizing this was his best suit jacket, but at the moment he didn't care.

As he continued to search, he found there was nothing of use, as the phone was out here, too. Disgusted he set the receiver down. He went upstairs but didn't get past the top landing. In front of him lay the dead body of a woman. He could see her face and he tasted bile once more. The face was a mangled mess of torn flesh and gore, the eyes bulging like swollen ping pong balls. The white of skull could be seen peeking through the grizzly mess and he had to turn away or risk vomiting on his shoes.

He quickly ran back downstairs after calling out one more time. If there had been someone in one of the bedrooms, they would have come out, as there was no way they couldn't hear him.

"Did you find anything?" Marilyn asked as he came down the stairs. Karl shook his head. He decided not to tell Marilyn about the body. What would be the point?

Suddenly, the front door burst inward and a teenage boy and girl rushed in. When they saw Karl and Marilyn, the boy stopped cold, the girl moving instinctually into his arms. Karl gauged them at around seventeen or eighteen. The boy was clean cut, the girl pretty with long blonde hair.

Karl had panicked when they first barged in, having forgotten to lock the door, and fearing some of those *things* had gotten into the house, but he calmed down quickly enough when he realized they weren't like the crazy people, the dead people, as hard as it was to think, let alone say.

His right fist was raised in defense and the boy held his arms out to stop Karl from hitting him.

"No wait, we're okay, don't hurt us!" the boy yelled.

"Who are you?" Karl demanded.

"We're no one, just people from town. We were having a picnic when these people came out of the woods. They attacked us. I fought them off and we ran for it. We've been wandering in the woods for over an hour at least, and then we saw this house. Is this your house? Do you live here?"

"No," Karl said. "We just got here. Looks like what happened to you happened to us. We were on the highway a few miles from here. There was a traffic jam. Then these *things* came out of the woods and began attacking people. We ran for it and then we found this place."

A thump from outside caused everyone to look to the front door. Karl pushed aside the boy and looked out past the porch to the lawn. One of them was there, a man.

"They followed you, dammit. How could you be so stupid?" Karl demanded.

The boy looked chastised and scared. "I...I didn't know, it was dark in the woods. I thought we lost them."

"Well, you didn't," he said as he slammed the door closed.

He took a better look at the house, seeing all the windows, the bottom of the sills not far off the floor. The front porch would be easy access for *them*. He thought about hiding upstairs until help came but the body was up there. He knew he didn't want to go up there if he didn't have to.

His eyes spotted a door across the room. Walking to it, he opened it and was assaulted by the pungent odor of mold and moistness, like the smell of wet laundry left in the washing machine overnight.

It was the cellar.

He went to one of the front windows and looked outside again. Sure enough, there were now two of those *things* wandering around.

"There's another out there," Karl said to the boy. "What's you name, son?"

"Keith, sir, and this is my girlfriend, Judy."

Karl grunted at her.

"I'm Marilyn," Karl's wife said from across the room. "That's my husband, Karl, and this is our daughter, Kyra. She's sick."

Judy went to her and gazed down at the unconscious girl. "I'm so sorry," she said.

"I don't know what's wrong with her," Marilyn said as she felt a tear touch her left cheek.

Karl was checking the cellar door again, testing its strength. When he was satisfied, he went down the narrow stairs. It was dark and he had to feel around for a light switch. One anemic bulb came on, bathing the dingy basement in washed out-yellow light. He took one quick look around, nodded to himself, then headed back upstairs. When he stepped into the main room, Keith and Judy were looking out the front window, holding each other tightly.

"Are they still there?" Karl asked.

Keith turned and nodded. "They sure are. What do we do? I had to hit a few to get away and I tell you what, they don't seem to feel pain."

"I saw them tearing people apart," Karl said. "They're strong when enough of them are around. I say we go into the cellar and wait until help arrives. That door is strong and it opens in. We can board up the inside so those *things* will never get in."

Keith scratched his head. "Gee, sir, I don't know. Wouldn't we be trapped in there?"

"No, we'd be trapping those things out. We'd be safe," Karl said. He took a few steps across the room so he was standing next to Keith. "Listen, son, I saw those things killing and eating people. They might look human, but they're not. I know what I'm talking about. When we're out of sight, they'll probably just go away. Now get downstairs with your girlfriend and we'll board that door up good." He stared at Keith, using all his will to make the boy listen to him. "I know what I'm talking about."

Keith wanted to protest, but Karl glared at him. Keith was a good boy, raised to listen to his elders and the forty-year-old balding man staring at him was just one of those elders. He sighed slightly and nodded, then touched Judy's arm.

"Come on, Judy, let's go downstairs. The cellar should be safer than up here."

Judy didn't protest, listening to Keith. She brushed her blonde hair from her face and headed over to Marilyn.

"Can I help you with her?" she asked, gesturing to Kyra.

Marilyn smiled. "Thank you, dear. That would be a big help."

Karl went to the refrigerator and grabbed some supplies. A few beers, some cooked ham, and a jar of olives. He wasn't really thinking about what they might need, all he wanted to do was finally get somewhere safe where he could relax and not worry every second about what was coming up behind him.

Marilyn and Judy moved Kyra into the cellar, then Keith went down. Karl was last. He looked around the room one last time, glanced to the front door and the windows that seemed so inadequate against what was walking around in the darkness, then he closed the door and locked it. He stared at the door, content, but not entirely satisfied by its security. They would have to attach wooden supports to the doorframe so they could put two-by-fours across the door, thus strengthening it.

Reaching the floor, Karl walked over to the others. Keith had grabbed an old door from a wood pile against the wall and set it atop two sawhorses, making a crude table for Kyra to lie on. The girl was still unconscious, Marilyn hovering over her with worried eyes.

"What now?" Keith asked Karl as he pulled Judy closer to him, wanting to hold her, protect her.

"Now we wait for help to come," Karl said as he lit up two cigarettes, handing one to Marilyn and taking a hit from his. He finally felt calm enough to have one, feeling safe for the first time in hours.

Outside the lonely farmhouse, human shadows moved through the trees, unafraid of the darkness. It was as if they owned the night, and in a way, they did.

For they *were* dead...and though it was still hard to believe, despite everything Karl had witnessed this night, there was no question in his mind that this was truly the night of the living dead.

THE PICNIC

ANTHONY GIANGREGORIO

Keith stretched out on the red and white checkered blanket and reached for a sandwich. No sooner did he touch one, then Judy slapped his hand away.

"Not yet, you don't. Let me finish setting everything up," she said with a playful grin.

"But I'm hungry now," Keith said as he rubbed the back of his hand. One of her nails nicked him, and though she hadn't broken the skin, it was stinging slightly.

"Five more minutes and I'll be done. Go for a walk if you can't wait."

He sighed, staring at the food laid out on the blanket. Off to his right, leaning against a large oak tree, were their bicycles.

They were on a small hill, almost an incline really, and were surrounded on all sides by woodland. The sun was just beginning to set and they had about an hour before night would fall, casting their small glade in darkness.

But by then he planned on being well fed, maybe a little light kissing--no more than that as they were only dating--and some quality time spent with his best gal.

He studied her as she fiddled with the food, taking each item out of the wicker basket with almost infinite care. Her blonde hair caught the sunlight, making it resemble a golden halo. He admired the curve of her neck, and loved the way her hair would fall over her shoulders when she leaned forward to set something down. He watched her move slightly, her body filling out her shirt in all the right places.

Her skin was like porcelain, not a blemish to be seen. No freckle or pimple had ever touched her face for as long as he'd known her. And he had known her for his entire life. They had gone to school together since kindergarten and it had only been last year when he'd had the courage to finally ask her on a date.

He believed it was because they had been friends for so long that they were such a wonderful couple. They never argued and he respected what she had to say. She was very intelligent and the kindest person he had ever known.

In other words, he loved her deeply.

The plan was he would ask her to be his wife some day, not too far off in the future. He would graduate high school at the end of this year and when he did he was going to get a job at the steel mill in Evanstown. Once he had a steady job, he was going to marry Judy and spend the rest of his life with her.

She looked up from setting paper plates down to see him staring at her.

"What? Is there something on my face?" she asked, self-conscious when she saw him studying her.

"You look fine," he smiled as he felt his heart flutter in his chest. God, she was so beautiful.

"Then quit looking at me like there's a bug on my face or something."

He reached out to her hand and gently pulled her closer, a mischievous grin on his lips.

"Keith, what are you doing? Its going to be dark soon, we need to eat so we can get back to my parents' house."

"Food can wait for a few minutes," he said as he pressed her close to him. He felt himself lost in her blue eyes and his blood began to pump faster. He leaned in and so did she, and a second later they were one, kissing passionately.

He thought things couldn't be more perfect as he pressed his lips to hers, relishing their warmth, their softness, but then he felt her go stiff in his arms and he pulled away, wondering if he had done something wrong.

She was looking over his shoulder, into the tree line, and when he turned to see what was so interesting, he found a man was standing there watching them.

Breaking his embrace from Judy, he frowned deeply. "You stay here. I'm going to see what this guy wants."

"Okay, but be careful, Keith," she said with concern on her face. There was something about the man watching them that disturbed her, though she couldn't put her finger on it. Perhaps it was the way the man simply stood there, his arms at his sides, his head immobile.

Keith got up from the blanket and crossed the glade, his eyes studying the man before him. He looked disheveled; his suit wrinkled and spots of dirt on the knees and sleeves, as if the man had repeatedly fallen to the ground, only to pick himself back up again. His hair was unkempt, a dark rug of thin strands with a hunk hanging over his forehead. Keith knew what it was. It was a comb over, only this one was off by about four inches. The man looked to be in his late fifties or early sixties, his complexion pasty and pale, as if the man never went outside to get some sun.

Keith noticed the setting sun was at his back, and with the sun's rays in the man's eyes, he never so much as blinked once. That was certainly odd.

"Uh, hello there, sir, can I help you with anything?" Keith asked as the man stood perfectly still, like a soldier on guard duty. Keith took a step closer, feeling slightly uncomfortable. "Listen, mister, if you don't want to tell me what you want, how 'bout moving on, huh? See, me and my best gal Judy are trying to have a picnic."

The man still gave no sign of understanding. Keith was beginning to wonder if the man was one of those retards he'd read about. They had one in town, a boy named Richard Fennel.

Richard was slow in the head and could only carry out the simplest tasks. They let him work in the grocery store once a week to earn some spare money.

As Keith stared at the man, his eyes went wide when the man leaned forward, seeming like he was coughing or hacking or something along those lines. The cough was hoarse and raspy, like a chain-smoker who still didn't get that they were dying and continued to smoke three packs a day. Keith, always the Good Samaritan, stepped towards the man and placed his right hand on his shoulder, wondering if the man was having a heart attack or something similar. That was when the man popped back up and bared his teeth like a wild animal.

Keith took one step away, not understanding what just happened. Weren't they just talking? Well, he was anyway; the man hadn't said a word.

Before Keith could figure out what to do next, the man lunged for him, hands open, arms snapping out to wrap around him. Keith, totally caught off guard, felt himself wrapped in the man's embrace as they tumbled to the grass.

He could hear Judy calling out, scared when she saw him fall, but he didn't have time to quell her fears. He had to worry about himself for the moment. When he hit the ground, only the matted leaves covering the glade preventing him from losing all the air in his lungs. Still, the weight of the man on his chest was sufficient to cause him to gasp with pain and surprise. No sooner did they fall, then the man began trying to bite him. Keith was unsure how to handle the situation, but he knew if he didn't defend himself, he would end up with a bad bite or worse. Teeth clacked an inch from his nose as cold spittle slid from the man's mouth to fall on his chin.

Gagging with the feeling as it slid down his face and onto his neck, he kicked off with his right sneaker, bucking his hips as hard as he could. Young and strong, Keith threw the man off him, the body flying into the air to land two feet to his left. As Keith lay still for a moment, gasping for air, he wondered what that odd squelching sound he'd just heard was. It had happened as he tossed the man away from him.

Looking at the man, he saw the stranger wasn't getting up. His arm's and legs were moving but he seemed stuck for some reason. And when Keith rolled to his knees and stood up, he saw the reason why the man wasn't getting up.

A tree root, about an inch thick, had grown out of the ground. Over time the root had cracked and split, leaving what was basically a spear-like pole jutting from the earth. The man had fallen on it, the root impaling him and shooting up through his abdomen and out his back.

Keith could only stare in horror as the man tried to crawl towards him. As he did, he stretched his wound, tearing the flesh and muscle until ropy intestines began to slip out of the jagged opening. The stench of decay filled Keith's sinuses and he felt his stomach preparing to heave.

"Keith! What's going on?" Judy cried out, scared.

Keith shook himself from his stupor and took a step towards her, wanting to go to her, tell her it was all right. Meanwhile, the man continued to crawl, inch by bloody inch, as the wound opened more.

Finally, there was a tearing sound and the root was free, and a massive tear in the side of the man's side now glistened in the waning sunlight. Keith stared at the man, not understanding how this could be happening. And at the man's face, so impassive, so void of emotion despite the fact he was ripping himself in two. Why wasn't he screaming his head off in pain?

A low moan seeped from the man's lips and Judy cried out, terror filling her eyes. The man was attracted to her cries and he began to crawl towards her.

Keith knew that was it. He wouldn't let this *thing* hurt her. There were a few rocks lumped together at the tree line and he went and picked one up. The rock was a little bigger than a human head and he had to grunt a little as he picked it up. Bits of dirt rained down on his legs and sneakers as he carried the rock over to the crawling man.

"Judy, look away, you don't wanna see this," Keith bade her as he lifted the rock over his head. Judy turned away with tears in her eyes.

Keith had the rock over his head now and his arms trembled slightly from the exertion. Then he brought it down onto the man's head. A wet sound, such as when a watermelon is dropped from a high building, filled the glade and the head of the man went *splat*, brains and bits of skull seeping out of the sides of the bludgeon. Keith stood, heaving, unable to comprehend what he'd just done.

He turned away and was about to go to Judy when footfalls came to his ears, the rustling of dead leaves across the forest floor. He spun around to look at the same spot the man had appeared, and to his surprise, there were five more people slowly coming out of the woods.

He stared at them for all of ten seconds before deciding that whoever they were, he didn't want to meet them. They weren't acting normal, they were acting like the man who now had no head.

Turning, he went to Judy, grabbing her by the shoulders. She was still turned away from him and she let out a soft screech, jumping slightly.

"It's me, honey, it's me. We need to go, we need to get outta here."

She only nodded. He was about to get his bicycle ready, and hers too, when the people moved towards them, now blocking his path. If he wanted the bikes, he would have to go through the crowd.

He knew he didn't want that, so grabbing Judy's hand, he pulled her to the opposite side of the glade.

"Come on, we can't get our bikes, we'll have to hoof it back to town."

"But what about the man?" She hadn't looked back to him, Keith keeping her attention. Then she glanced over her shoulder and saw the five new arrivals. She whimpered, not knowing if she should be scared or not. Maybe they could help.

"Forget the bikes, we can get them later, for now follow me." He pulled her along, her blonde hair flying behind her as the last rays of sunlight caught the golden strands.

Together they headed off into the woods, while behind them, the five new arrivals followed. Their prey wouldn't get far and they were hungry.

*　*　*

"You need to move faster, Judy," Keith said as he stopped for the tenth time to wait for her to catch up.

"I'm trying," she said as she limped slightly. She had fallen a few minutes ago and had twisted her ankle by catching it under a hidden root. She was confident it would be better in time, but time was the one thing she didn't have at the moment. She stopped and leaned against a tree, wanting to take her weight off her foot for a few seconds. The air was cool and filled with a fresh, woodsy smell she had known all her life. Sections of the forest were so dense a person would be hard-pressed to traverse it, while other parts were more open.

"They're still behind us," he said. "We need to move faster."

Judy glanced over her shoulder to see how far back their pursuers were. The sun was setting now and the shadows were beginning to creep through the woods, the gloom becoming oppressive. She had to squint through the trees to see them, but yes, there they were. There were more than five of them now, too, she could see that for sure.

"There's more than five of them, Keith," she said in a hushed voice, speaking her thoughts.

"Yeah, I know. Some more joined them a few minutes ago from the north. I don't think it was planned, though. I think they were already in the woods and they heard us. But now we really need to keep moving."

She couldn't argue with his logic and she began to walk again, wincing a little each time her bad foot set down on the spongy softness of the forest floor. All she needed to do was rest. Just rest and rub the ankle for a few minutes and she was sure she'd be fine. But she couldn't and that frustrated her to no end.

Keith went back to her and put his arm around her shoulder. "Here, let me help you," he said as he began holding her up.

She nodded in thanks, feeling how strong he was as he flexed his muscles to move her along.

They began moving a little faster and she was feeling confident they would be able to outdistance their followers when Keith suddenly stopped. She looked at his face, now wreathed in shadows from the setting sun, to see he was staring forward, not backward at their pursuers, where she would have assumed he would be looking. She slowly followed his line of sight and let out a soft gasp when she realized what he was staring at.

There were more shadows weaving through the trees in front of them; slow, plodding figures that bumped into large trees, stumbled through the underbrush, and fell over fallen trunks.

"Who are they?" Judy asked as she watched one of the figures trip and fall face first into a pile of leaves. The figure looked naked, but that was hard to believe, given the chilly temperature. There was rustling as the figure regained its footing, then it continued forward. There were now bits of twigs and leaves in its matted hair and Judy realized it was a woman.

"I don't know, but if they're anything like that man back there, I don't want to know," Keith said flatly. He looked to the left and right, seeing the left was no good. There was a large tree fall from a past storm and the terrain looked treacherous. Maybe not so bad in the day, but with night falling, it would be too easy to turn a foot. Judy had gotten off lucky so far, she could have easily broken her ankle in a gopher hole or some such burrow, instead of only twisting it.

Judy was taking a step forward, her hand already leaving the support of the tree she was leaning against, when a hand fell onto her shoulder, the fingers squeezing into her flesh. She cried out in surprise and pain as she turned her head to see a shadowed face snarling at her like a slavering dog. Before she could try to escape, the attacker fell on her, shoving her to the forest floor where she felt a fallen tree branch dig into her side. Luckily, her shirt prevented it from piercing her skin.

Keith stared in horror as the figure forced Judy to the ground. With all the trees so close together, the attacker had snuck up on them, its stealth either on purpose or by accident. She was screaming now and Keith dashed to her side, grabbing the frail form, an old woman by the looks of it. The old woman had ash-gray hair and sunken eyes, her heavy brow now her predominant feature. Her face was pale, like the others he'd seen, and when she opened her mouth, a dull hiss escaped, like something foul and dead was finally escaping the pits of Hell.

With a yell and a heave, Keith yanked the woman off Judy, just as yellow teeth were seeking Judy's throat. The clacking sound was audible even over Judy's screams. Keith tossed the old woman as hard as he could and she hit a nearby tree with a loud *thump*, her form falling to the forest floor where she began crawling back to him, only now with a broken back.

Keith helped Judy to her feet and pulled her away from the crawling zombie, wanting to get as far away from it as possible. The zombie's hands dug into the soft loom as it pulled itself along, its legs dragging behind it like dried cordwood.

The young couple ran through the forest, seeking an avenue of escape, only to be stopped at every turn by shadowy shapes slowly plodding, one foot in front of the other. Keith found it odd how they never ran, never attempted to move a little faster and cut Judy and him off. No, they always moved at the same slow gait. It was only their numbers as they filled the woods that kept Keith and Judy from breaking free.

Pausing, Judy leaned against a thick maple tree, her breath coming in great gasps. It was complete darkness in the forest now, only an anemic moon waxing down on them through the thick canopy, sparse lines of light spearing the black every few feet where the tree tops were thinner.

"What do we do, Keith? They're everywhere?" she asked, her eyes darting back and forth in her head. For the moment, they were clear of the figures but their followers were still very close.

Keith ground his teeth as he posed himself that exact question. He decided there would be no escaping by simply fleeing. No, he would need to take the fight to his pursuers. Looking around on the ground, he spotted a half-buried tree branch. Its bark was flaking, resembling rotting flesh peeling from the bones of a corpse, and its tip was riddled from termite damage as was the middle. But it seemed survivable enough for what he had in mind.

"I have an idea, Judy. Just stay behind me, and when I say run, you run. Can you do that?"

She nodded. "Yes, my ankle doesn't hurt as bad, I think it's a little better."

"Good, you probably didn't sprain it then, it just bent the wrong way a little."

"That sounds right," she added.

"Okay, follow me and get ready to run when I tell you to. I'll grab you so you don't fall."

She nodded, the gesture barely discernable in the darkness.

Keith began walking in the direction he believed would take him out of the woods. He made it fifteen feet before the first shadowy figure appeared before him, seeming to pop up like a wraith. Behind it, three more waited for their chance at the frightened couple. Keith hefted the tree branch, and when he was as close to the figure as he thought he need to be for his plan, he raised the tree branch over his head and brought it down like he was chopping wood.

Upon striking the head, the branch exploded into a thousand pieces, the wood frail from termite damage. Dust and wood chips sprayed in every direction, some of it getting into the stumbling zombies' eyes. As for the one Keith had crushed with the branch, it dropped to the ground like a mail bag fallen from a truck bed.

"Now! Run now, Judy!" Keith cried out as he reached for her hand. She felt for him and for a moment couldn't find him. But then his firm grip had her hand and she was being pulled along the forest floor like she was on wings.

Keith shoved two of the temporarily blind zombies away from him and made a path they could squeeze through. This time their escape was free of obstacles and they ran as if their lives depended on it.

They kept running for the next half hour, barely slowing to rest. When Judy began to tire, Keith reached around her so his right arm was across her back and under her right shoulder, and half-carried, half-pushed her forward.

Their breathing came in harsh gasps, the night a solid blanket all around them, but still they ran. And when Keith dared risk a glimpse behind him, he always saw fleeting shapes darting between the trees. Though they weren't moving quickly, a fast walk the most Judy could handle, still the figures followed, relentless in their pursuit.

Time seemed to stand still as they made their way through the dense foliage, climbing over fallen trees and slogging through the clotted underbrush. But no matter how fast they moved, their pursuers were always there, just on the edge of their vision.

Keith was the first to realize they had reached an end to the woods when he looked up and saw a pale moon peering down on him. Judy, too, halted in her rush to escape to look up into the clear night sky.

Keith looked around to see they were on a dirt road, the tree line pushed back as if cleared by man. The road went off and over a slight incline, and Keith never hesitated, grabbing Judy's hand and pulling her along.

"We're safe, finally. This road has to lead somewhere," he said as he began to jog down the middle of the road. Judy said nothing, too exhausted to reply.

Just as they crested the hill, Keith glanced back at the tree line and frowned deeply when he saw dark figures emerging, stumbling out onto the road like drunks leaving a tavern at last call. They were still there, still following them like some kind of demons from Hell, inexhaustible in their pursuit.

The weary couple continued moving, only their drive to find safety and their love for one another ever moving them forward.

As they rounded a bend in the road, Keith was the first to see the old farmhouse, the ramshackle, weathered wood clapboards looking as if it had withstood a hundred winters.

"Judy, look, a house, we're safe!" he gasped as he began moving faster. He actually began to leave her behind until he realized what he was doing and slowed to help her.

Her ankle was better, time alone healing it, and she was almost back to her old self. Another few hours and it would be like it had never happened.

If only everything that had happened this night could be washed away so easily, she thought to herself as she followed Keith.

The light for the front room of the farmhouse was on, the light seeping through the old curtains, and Keith was filled with hope as he crested the dead lawn and began to climb the worn wooden planks that consisted of the front porch. An old door with a worn screen greeted him and he opened it, turning the knob easily. It wasn't locked, which to him was nothing new. Folks around these parts rarely locked their doors. No thief would dare to raid a farmhouse for fear of getting his backside blown in by a healthy dose of buckshot. Every farmer owned at least one gun, as the law wasn't just around the corner if help was needed. Out here, a man had to fend for himself most of the time.

"Do you think they can help us?" Judy asked as she prepared to enter the house with Keith.

Keith stopped, the front the door now open just an inch, and he turned to face her, then hugged her. Then he placed his hands on her shoulders and pushed her a little ways from him so he could look into her eyes.

"Sure they can, Judy, it's all over, this terrible night is finished. We'll go inside and even if no one's there we can still call for help. I'm sure they have a phone." He grinned at her, looking confident, despite his own trepidations. "All right?"

She nodded. "All right, Keith, I trust you. I love you, you know."

He smiled even wider, once more seeing her for her inner beauty as well as her outer beauty. Even in the darkness, she was his everything.

"I love you, too, honey." He turned away and placed his hand on the doorknob, then pushed the door open as the young couple stepped inside the house, both of them hoping salvation waited within, while behind them on the road, the slow, shambling figures followed, one faltering step at a time.

RIGHT BETWEEN THE EYES

JOE TONZELLI

As the beer-bellied, stone-headed, and dry-witted sheriff of Butler County leaned back in his chair, the phone on his desk rang.

Again.

Making no move to answer it, he stayed reclined in the chair in his cramped office, his hands creeping to his face in an overly-dramatic fashion. He groaned purposely loud and waved his hand over the phone in a dismissive gesture.

"What is it, a full moon or something?" he asked, covering his eyes with his flat palms, rubbing the sore spot at the bridge of his nose with his middle fingers.

"It's 10:30, Sheriff. In the morning."

"Thank you, Vince."

Deputy Vince Haig's young face warmed over red with embarrassment as he leaned over the sheriff's cluttered desk to answer the insistent phone.

"Sheriff's office," Haig said almost cheerily, and listened intently for a moment before rolling his eyes. "Yes, we're aware of the situation. Where did this happen?"

The sheriff slowly took his hands away from his face, his eyes on Haig, trying to determine if it was another one of *those* calls.

"Well, why didn't you call their station?" Haig asked, confused. He paused again. "I see. Well, thanks for your concern. We'll look into it."

Haig dropped the phone into the cradle and crossed his arms across his chest.

"Another report about someone going crazy and biting somebody else."

"You've gotta be kidding me," Sheriff George Kosana said, sounding defeated. "What on earth is going on? Did our boys lose the big game last night or what?" He began rifling through paperwork on his desk and muttered to himself. "People going crazy, giving me ulcers... How many reports does that make on this so far?"

"Six today, ten total since last night," Haig said.

The sheriff sighed again and stared at the pile of reports on his desk, all detailing the sudden outburst of random and unmotivated attacks on people. Nothing about them made sense. The assailants were ranging from the elderly to the very young, but they all seemed to have one thing in common: they all appeared crazed.

"Where were they calling from?"

"Willard," Haig answered, hands on his hips.

"*Willard?*" Kosana exclaimed. "So let Parkinson deal with it! What's his station doing over there? Picking out silverware?"

"They tried the Willard station, Sheriff. They said the phone just rings and rings. They said we were the closest station after them. They said..."

"Okay, okay, I get it." Kosana shook his head again. "Unbelievable. Put, uh...Pearson on it. And the new guy, Riley."

"Pearson's already on one. The one that Father Darien called about."

"And Riley?"

"He was following up on a call down on Route 10."

"Route 10? Where on Route 10?"

"Out near the reservoir, I think."

The sheriff grumbled, growing increasingly impatient. "That ain't our jurisdiction, Vince. That's Trooper territory. And who the hell sent him off by himself?"

"It was Shirley at dispatch, Sheriff. She had to. There was nobody to send with him. Hell, there's no one else even in the station. Just Shirley and us. Everyone else is out on calls."

"Oh, Lord," Kosana said. "Just wait till old Martha Riley hears about this one: sending her only boy—a rookie, no less—out to the ass end of Evanstown on the day the world's falling apart. She's going to give me an earful, I'll guaran-damn-tee you that."

Before Haig could respond, there was a sudden crashing noise at the double-door entrance to the inner office where Kosana and Haig stood. Another of the station's deputies, Murphy Preston, burst in. The front of his shirt was torn and covered in blood and he shambled towards them, weak, barely staying on his feet, small droplets of blood plopping onto the tiled floor.

"Oh, Jesus, God—Help me! Somebody!" he pleaded, helpless and frail, before collapsing on the floor in a heaping, bloody mess.

Shirley, the dispatcher who had been employed at the station for more years than she ever cared to discuss, came in just behind him, clearly rattled by what must have been an even more dramatic entrance from Preston at the main entrance to the station.

"Murphy, what *happened*?" she shouted after him. She ran and knelt down next to him, putting her hand on the small of his sweat-soaked back. Kosana also rushed to the officer's side, placing his hands underneath the battered man's arms.

"Vince, help me get him into a chair," Kosana said.

The two men lifted up the wounded deputy into a nearby desk chair as Preston hugged his bloody shirt to his chest and winced in pain. Shirley clasped her hands together in a worrisome manner and looked on as they seated the officer.

"Get him some water," Kosana ordered Haig, as he crouched on one knee and steadied Preston's face, trying to look into his eyes. "Easy now, Murphy, you're okay. Here, let me see."

Kosana slowly opened the young man's shirt to look at his wounds, getting only a quick look before Preston closed his shirt again, pressing his hands against his bloody chest.

"Don't, please, Sheriff. It don't hurt so much if I keep my hands on it."

"All right, kid, fine."

Kosana looked over at Shirley, the gaunt, brown-haired dispatcher's eyes filled with fear. He stood up quickly and removed the black suit jacket he was wearing that complemented his thin, black dress pants—an unorthodox uniform for a county sheriff, but

Sheriff George Kosana was as unorthodox as they came. He tossed the jacket on a nearby desk.

"It's okay, Shirl, go on back to the phones. I imagine they're ringing off the hook. We'll take care of him."

"Okay, Sheriff," Shirley said, taking a moment to lightly squeeze Preston's shoulder before disappearing through the double doors.

Kosana tipped the officer's drooping head up by his chin. "Tell me what happened."

Haig came back with a cup of water which Preston brushed away, instead trying to catch his breath.

"There were...dozens of them," he managed in between choked breaths. "They were...oh, Jesus..."

"Calm down," Kosana said. "You're safe now. Just relax and tell us exactly what happened."

Preston struggled to regain control of his breathing, and when he did, he finally waved the cup of water towards him. He drank it quickly and let the empty paper cup fall to his feet.

"I was on that call that came from D'Angelo's Bakery, up on 7th. So, I go in, and I see Tony. He's got a towel bunched up on his shoulder and I can see he's bleeding. 'Relax,' he says, 'it's worse than it looks.' So he starts telling me that he was waiting for his morning milk delivery out in his back lot. Sitting there smoking or whatever. Then, he sees the milk truck coming down the road, and *fast*. He said he could tell something was wrong just by how fast it was coming. The truck cuts into the back lot, and Tony says the guy gets out of the truck and looks real bad, said he was real pale and sweaty. Said the driver had seen some people out on the road a ways back. One was on the ground and the other was leaning over him. Said he got out to see what had happened, to see if he could help. Said the guy leaning over the other turned and groaned at him! Bit him on the hand! The driver, he knocks the crazy guy over, gets back in his truck and hauls ass to D'Angelo's, which was the nearest place down the road."

"Jesus!" Kosana exclaimed. "What the hell's going on in this town?"

"Might be rabies!" Haig said. "Or polio!"

Kosana rolled his eyes and turned back to Preston. "Okay, kid, then what?"

Preston looked dazed, more so than when he first entered the station, his skin now an alarming shade of gray. Sweat began flowing profusely from his hairline and was raining down the front of his face. His already-thin frame added to his masticated appearance. His head fell back sharply as if he had passed out and it rolled limply across his shoulder until his chin came to rest on his chest.

"Vince, get an ambulance over here right now," Kosana said, his concerned eyes focused on Preston's face. Haig ran off to make the call as the sheriff shook Preston's shoulder. "C'mon, Murphy, stay with me. Then what happened?"

"Tony, he, uh..." Preston started, weaker now, raising his head slowly up. "Tony brought the driver inside...said the guy was really weak. Almost had to drag him to his desk to let him sit. Said...the guy passed out. Tony, he went to call us from the register. Said he hung up with Shirley, turned to go tell the driver that help was coming, and he saw the driver standing there in the doorway. Tony goes to make the guy sit down again and the guy attacks him. Grabs Tony's shoulder and bites him...he tore a chunk clean out of him..."

Preston's head dropped heavily again and Kosana shook him several times before the man's head whipped up.

"Damn it, hang on, kid, help's coming. What happened to *you*?"

The kid widened his eyes and shook his head spastically, trying to keep himself awake.

"Well, that's when I got there...saw Tony. Tony said...he had no choice. Had to hit the guy. Grabbed a rolling pin and whacked him in the head a bunch of times until the guy dropped to the floor. He was looking real bad now. Tony, I mean. I was going to radio for an ambulance for him, but then he just dropped dead. Just like that."

Preston paused for a minute, confusion clearly present in his misty head.

"I don't get it. He seemed strong when I got there. Focused. He seemed okay. But then he just...died. He dropped dead. But...then he got up."

Kosana narrowed his eyes, confused.

"So Tony's okay?"

"No...no, Sheriff. Tony's not okay." He started panicking now. "Tony's *not* okay! If you see him, Sheriff, Tony is *not* okay!"

"You're not making sense, kid. What do you mean?"

"Listen to me, Sheriff," Preston said as he grabbed suddenly at Kosana's shirt, pulling him close to his sweaty face. "Tony was dead. Tony was as dead as dirt. I swear it. I checked his vitals; saw the blood pumping from his shoulder all over my shoes. He was stone-cold dead. But he got up. He got up and he came after me."

"Murphy, you're delirious," Kosana said in a reasoning tone. "You've been through a lot and it's messing with that head of yours, but everything's going to be fine now."

Preston began sobbing, shaking his head in response to Kosana's assertion. "He attacked me, Sheriff! And he got me real good, too!"

Preston ripped his already-torn and blood-stained shirt open and showed Kosana the damage done by Tony. A slash of flesh the size of a t-bone steak was missing from the upper right side of his chest, and what looked like a gnarled bite mark was pooling with blood in the middle of the pink wound.

"What in the name of..." Kosana trailed off in surprise. He stared at the exposed muscle mass that still secreted a heavy amount of blood.

"Don't...don't let him get you," Preston pleaded, his eyes rolling back in his head. "He's...not Tony."

Preston slumped back in his chair, not breathing, not moving. Kosana leaned over and felt for a pulse on his neck.

Nothing.

"Hell." Kosana got up and looked at Preston a moment. He turned and walked across the room to where Haig was trying to raise the hospital. Haig saw him coming and lowered the phone.

"I keep trying to get through but the switchboard's jammed or something."

"It don't matter," Kosana said. He sat down on another desk chair and put his head in his hands. He was still for a moment, letting the fact sink in that one of his men had died right in front of him—the first time in his history of law enforcement that had ever happened. At that moment, Kosana felt useless. And he didn't like feeling useless. He normally felt proud, and he liked feeling that way; he liked knowing that people looked to him as a strong figure of the community. Some of the townspeople even felt the sheriff was a bit brash in his attitude and had an all-around ego-maniacal attitude. And he liked that, too. Kept them in line, or so he reasoned. But he didn't like how he felt right then. He was frustrated at knowing nothing about what was causing these strange, unwarranted attacks. The feeling of futility that filled his heart surged within him, and quickly—almost alarmingly—mutated into a furious, even animalistic anger, and he swiped the phone from the desk at which he sat, sending it crashing to the floor.

"Don't you worry, Preston. Help's coming!" Haig shouted, putting the phone back to his ear, one eyebrow raised in response to Kosana's outburst.

"I said it's too late, Vince! Hang up the damn phone!"

"But…" Haig started, confused.

"He's dead, Vince!"

"But, Sheriff…" Haig started, motioning with the hand that held the phone to something behind Kosana.

He turned and saw Preston standing up, his battered shirt hanging open, his deep gash visible and dripping more blood onto the floor.

"Jesus, what happened to him?" Haig asked, the phone falling away from his ear, seeing Preston's wounds for the first time.

"Aw hell, now what's this?" Kosana asked, still, his jaw dropping open. The sheriff had felt for a pulse and found nothing, and not even someone twice as strong as Preston could have survived the wounds he had suffered. Kosana slowly stood up, his arms hanging heavily at his sides, hands slightly upraised; a position someone might make if crossing paths with a rabid dog one evening during a walk through the woods, knowing there was no help for miles.

"Murphy, you shouldn't be up and walking. Take a seat," Haig reasoned.

Preston didn't seem to hear him. He began shuffling towards them, groaning, his bloodied-wet shirt falling back and forth and slapping against his butchered chest.

"Damn it, Murphy, you're just gonna hurt yourself more," Haig said, setting the phone down on the desk and stepping towards him.

"Wait," Kosana said, holding his arm out in front of Haig's chest. "Something ain't right here."

"But, Sheriff..." Haig started. Preston continued to lurch towards them, his arms now outstretched.

"Preston, I said you need to sit down, boy," Haig said again, growing impatient.

Preston didn't sit, nor did he stop coming towards them, and as his bloody shirt continued to slap across his chest, he didn't seem to understand them.

Kosana drew his gun and pointed it at Preston. "Murphy, I need you to stop, boy. Right now," he ordered.

"Sheriff, what...?"

"Vince, draw your weapon, that's an order."

Haig drew his gun quickly but held it pointed to the ground at Preston's feet.

"Sheriff, that's Murphy!" Haig shouted, trying to reason with him.

"Not anymore, it ain't."

Preston took another dragging step towards them and Kosana cocked his gun, loading a round into the chamber.

"Preston, I will shoot if you take one more step. I ain't messing around," Kosana warned. Preston took another step towards them, now so close that he stood a mere three feet away.

"Goddamn it," Kosana muttered, pulling the trigger and shooting Preston once in the shoulder.

Preston fell back a few steps, but didn't otherwise react to the shot. He tilted his head ever so slightly, as if he was trying to understand what had just occurred. He paused for only a moment, however, before he began coming towards them again, his arms still outstretched, his mouth still hanging agape in a permanent expression of stupid confusion.

"Jesus, what is this?" Haig asked, finally pointing his gun directly at Preston's chest.

Shirley barged in through the door behind Preston, whipping her head around to follow the ruckus that had led her back into the inner offices.

"Sheriff? What's going on? I heard a shot!"

Preston turned sharply and looked at Shirley, spit falling in globs from his mouth onto his bloodied uniform.

"Murphy! Jesus, are you okay?" she asked, concerned, taking an alarmed step towards him.

"Stay away from him, Shirley! Get back!" Kosana yelled, his dark eyes never off Preston's face.

Preston began his shambling march towards Shirley, his arms reaching towards her. He groaned again, and wet drips of saliva again rolled out of his mouth.

"What is this?" Shirley asked fearfully, stepping back. "He looks hurt! Why aren't you helping him?"

Preston let out an inhuman moan and lurched faster after her, agitated by her frightened pleas.

"Murphy!" Kosana shouted one more time before putting a round between Preston's shoulder blades. The hulking figure stumbled slightly but continued to advance on Shirley.

"Shirley, get down!" Kosana shouted. She dropped immediately to the floor and covered her head.

Kosana fired several shots into Preston's back, none of which visibly affected him. Some of the bullets exited his chest and sparked off of various objects across the room. Framed pictures shattered on the wall and clattered to the floor. A desk lamp exploded, sending shards of glass misting into the air.

Kosana fired one more shot directly into the back of Preston's head, which sent him sprawling forward just a few feet away from where Shirley lay huddled on the floor. Blood, brains, and bone fragments showered across the office, lathering Shirley's brown hair.

"Jesus, Sheriff...what's going on?" Haig barely mustered, his eyes on Preston's dead body, his shaking hands still grasping the gun that he never fired.

Kosana also looked at Preston's motionless body.

"God only knows."

* * *

Sheriff Kosana sat behind his desk, the phone crooked to his ear as he pored over the reports having to do with the strange attacks flooding in. He examined each document more carefully this time, trying to understand what was taking place in his small town.

Preston's body had been covered in a sheet, which his blood was soaking through and slowly transforming from off-white into dark crimson. Attempts to get the hospital on the phone were unsuccessful. Every extension Haig tried resulted in a high-pitched tone. For the time being, they could do nothing with Preston's body except leave him on the floor.

Shirley had gone back to her desk, claiming to want to be near the phones, but more eager to get away from the bloody mess left after Preston's exit from the land of the living.

Kosana had punched in the last number of a neighboring police station several minutes ago and was letting the line ring and ring, hoping someone would pick up.

"Police," finally said an exhausted-sounding voice on the other end of the line. Kosana perked up, surprised to have gotten through.

"I'm trying to reach Sheriff Price. He around?"

"Might be. Hold the line. Things are crazy here."

"You ain't kidding," Kosana said, but the operator had already clicked off.

Kosana cast a glance to Preston's body, half-expecting to see it rolling and shuffling but it remained still.

"Price," a voice said after the line clicked.

"Price, it's Kosana over in Butler."

"Jesus, man. What in the blue hell is going on?"

"I was hoping you could tell me." He paused before continuing. "Listen, this is going to sound like a crock, but you've known me for going on fifteen years. The last time I made a joke, Eisenhower was president. But I need you to know that I ain't messing with you."

"Go on."

Kosana paused a moment, realizing how ridiculous it was going to sound.

"I just had to put one of my own men down. He came in from a call, real beat-up. He spun a wild tale about...being bitten, or something, and then he passed out. I thought he was dead, his vitals must have slowed to a crawl, and he woke up just a few moments later and tried to attack us. He looked...dumb. Brainless, almost. I put...well, I couldn't even tell you how many shots, but I emptied my damn gun into his back. And he kept going until I popped him one in his head. You tell me how the hell a man can do that?"

"Drugs, I reckon. I've run into that a couple times today. Men said they had to open fire on some assailants and it took like hell to get 'em down. There's a new drug out on the street—all the rage, called PCP. You take some of that stuff, hell, you could put your fist through a car window and not even feel it."

"This ain't like any drug I've ever seen, Price. And I can't swear to it, but it looked like he was trying to..."

"Bite *you*?"

"What are you, a mind reader?"

"Kosana, have you put on the radio today?"

"I haven't, Price. I've kinda had my hands full."

"Why don't you go ahead and give it a listen. You might learn yourself something."

Kosana lowered the phone to his shoulder and called behind him.

"Vince!" Kosana turned to see Haig still fruitlessly trying to raise the hospital on the phone. "Enough of that, Vince. Go put the radio on."

"What're you in the mood for, Sheriff? Big band?"

Kosana shut his eyes in embarrassment as he heard Price snicker on the line.

"Did your momma have any kids that lived? Just put the damn radio on."

Haig walked over to a small wooden table on the side of the room and flipped a switch on their small, rickety radio that was held together with pieces of duct tape, a typical Sheriff Kosana patch job. He fiddled with the knob and then raised the volume. An emergency news report was in progress.

"...*large packs of people taken over by some foreign object not yet known. Theories are in circulation claiming that this is the work of some kind of virus, while others are even more outlandish, suggesting that an organism from space is the culprit. While experts continue to unlock the mystery of what's causing this behavior among seemingly normal individuals, please remain cautious, as the threat itself is very real and very dangerous. There have also been reports of this contagion—whatever it is—being spread from the creatures to their victims through their saliva. While the closest explanation for this outbreak appears to be rabies, we are waiting for confirmation on this from the Centers for Disease Control.*"

"Well, that's fantastic," Kosana said dryly, sticking the phone back against his ear. "How widespread is this thing?"

"No way to tell. From what I hear, the first report came in about two days ago. Some seminary school in New York. Belport, I think. But who knows? If the bigwigs know, they're not telling us. I've been trying to get someone from the CDC on the line all day, but I knew that was going to be pointless before I ever picked up the phone. They have some snot-nosed kid on the line saying they'll be 'releasing all pertinent information through the media' or some crap," Price explained, emphasizing what appeared to be an exact quote, his voice dripping with disdain.

"How're you doing over there with your officers?" Kosana asked. "All my men are out on calls. I got Deputy Haig with me and a dispatcher, but other than that, I got nothing. They're all out in the field, and God knows what they're dealing with." Kosana tilted in his chair to verify Haig was still in the room, and he spotted him picking at his badge with his fingernails. Haig saw that he was being watched and quickly dropped his hands to his sides.

"We got a few extra officers running around here," Price said. "But I'm pretty much in the same boat. The calls started early this morning and they haven't stopped."

Just then, another of the station's officers, Bobby Blair, walked through the doors.

"What in God's name is going on in this town?" the officer demanded to know, sitting heavily in a chair for just a moment before getting up just as quickly, pacing up and down in between a row of desks. "I mean, holy Christ!"

"I gotta tend to something, Price," Kosana said. "Listen, you give me a call if you hear anything new and I'll do the same."

"You got it. Take care and watch your ass," Price said.

Kosana hung up the phone and walked to the pacing officer. "What happened?"

Blair, an older officer with a head of gray hair, which creeped down into a beard tinged with jet black, looked beside himself. He ran his hands through his hair as he seemed unable to settle with a direction in which to stand.

"It's bad out there, Sheriff. Real bad."

"Yeah...I know." Kosana motioned with his head over to Preston. Blair saw the blood-stained sheet and his eyes widened.

"Oh, no. Who is it?"

"Murphy."

Murphy Preston had been a fairly new officer; had transferred over from Philadelphia a few months ago in order to obtain a more peaceful existence. Blair hadn't known him very well, nor did many of the other officers, but that didn't matter if one of them fell in the line of duty. When one of them died, everyone felt it, and everyone took it personally.

"Oh, no, Murphy. Man had kids, didn't he?" Blair asked, shocked.

Kosana looked down at the floor, briefly ashamed that he didn't know the answer, and then angry at Blair for making him feel that way.

"So what's your deal, Bobby? What happened?" Kosana asked.

Haig came over with some water and handed it to the rattled officer. Blair nodded his thanks and took it gratefully.

"I was up at the library near the high school. Someone called and said they had to lock the janitor in the closet. Said he was acting real strange, sitting in one of the aisles and just staring at a row of books. No one knew what to do, and when someone asked if he needed help, he had attacked them or whatever."

"Like biting?"

Haig looked questioningly at the sheriff.

"Of course biting. That seems to be the newest thing. God forbid someone steals a car or runs a red light. Ya know, something *normal*." He paused. "Luckily, no one got hurt."

"Are you sure no one was bitten?"

"Yeah, positive. Why?"

"Radio says this thing making people go bonkers can spread in their spit or something."

For the first time since Blair had entered, Kosana could see blood flecks on the front of the officer's tan-colored shirt. Blair saw him looking.

"I had to put him down," Blair said. "The janitor. In front of everyone, too. It was just terrible. There were kids there and everything."

"Did he come at you?"

"Hell, yeah, he came at me," Blair said, sounding almost offended. "He had a damn broom in his hands, though he was dragging it behind him. Didn't look like he had any intention of braining me with it, but still he didn't let it go."

"So what then?" Haig asked, trying to sound like he was a part of the conversation.

"What do you mean *what then*? I shot the bastard. Right in the middle of the face. There was something not right about him. I know I should've put one in the shoulder, but...there was just something *off* about him, Sheriff. I got a bad vibe."

"It's fine," Kosana said. "Believe me when I say that it wouldn't have done any good. As for Murphy, well, it took a lot to get him down."

A scream suddenly came from the front office where Shirley's dispatch desk was located. The three men immediately hustled to the front, their hands hovering over their holstered guns. They burst through the swinging double doors that led to the front office and stopped immediately. Shirley cowered in her glass-walled cubicle as two men lumbered towards her from the entrance to the building. The first was wearing a policeman's uniform, and the second wore all black with a white collar—a priest.

"Sheriff," Haig began, slowly drawing his gun. "It's Hank. He's back from his call. And he brought the Father with him."

Haig was right. Hank Pearson was back from his call, and his mangled left arm bounced haphazardly against his body, hanging on by an extremely thin piece of flesh. His mouth was rimmed with blood and crimson-colored spittle coated his beard and rained down his chest. Father Darien was in even worse shape. His entire bottom jaw was missing, and his tongue moved within his open face like a possessed serpent. One eye had glossed over and was now entirely white and he held a small wicker basket lined with red felt: the collection basket from his church. As he walked towards the men, he unknowingly extended the basket out towards them as any usher would have done during Sunday mass.

"Shirley!" Kosana called, his eyes never leaving the approaching men. "You all right?"

"Fine, Sheriff. Just about to wet my pants is all," she responded, shrinking slowly down to the floor, her eyes on the approaching men.

"We'll have you out of there in a minute." Pearson gnashed his teeth at him in response to his shouting, and Kosana trained his gun on him. "Take 'em down, boys. You know as well as I do that that ain't Hank no more. And that ain't the Father, neither."

Blair fired his gun directly into Father Darien's chest without a moment's hesitation, having already experienced the madness firsthand. The Father stumbled back, but then continued approaching, raising the collection basket again.

"In the head, Blair," Kosana told him.

Blair fired again, this time into the right side of the Father's forehead. The man fell back this time, landing first on his butt and then teetering back, slamming his head against the wall and coming to rest in an awkward sitting position. Pearson continued to advance on Haig, who had his gun out and aimed but seemed unwilling to shoot.

"Boy, if you're gonna survive this thing, you're gonna have to learn to put them down. Hank Pearson ain't gonna be the last person you recognize who is gonna want to take a bite out of your hide."

Hank then fell on Kosana, who forcefully pushed him back against the wall but otherwise made no attempt to try and kill him.

Hank's back cracked against the blinds covering the window and snapped several of them off.

"Just take this one, Sheriff, please! I'll be okay in the future, but I can't do this one! Christ's sake, it's Hank!"

Blair aimed his gun at Hank, but Kosana waved him off.

"Stand down, Bobby. This is Vince's kill. He's gotta learn."

"Sheriff, please! Don't make me!" Haig whined.

"Are you a cop or not?"

"You know I am, but this ain't what I signed on for!"

"You signed on to protect and serve, Vince, and now you need to do both! Fire that goddamn gun!"

Haig reeled, stepped back until he hit the wall behind him, and fired the gun, his eyes squeezed almost entirely shut. The shot went wild and shattered the window near Hank, causing Shirley to scream in response. "Vince, you better shoot that bastard before I come over there and shove that gun so far up inside you not even Dr. Ford's gonna find it!" she shouted, furious.

Haig fired the gun again, sheering off the top of Hank's head, carving an awkward trench through his scalp and short-trimmed hair line, but he still kept coming.

"Again, Vince!" Kosana ordered.

One final shot from Haig's gun caught Hank in the temple, the force of which spun him around before he crashed into the gray metal folding chairs set up against the wall underneath the broken window. No one spoke for a few moments, and the only sounds heard were of Haig's ragged breathing and the tinkling of shattered window glass as it settled on the floor.

Kosana clapped Haig on the shoulder. "You did good, Vince. That was just fine. Now, don't stop doing it. Got a feeling this is gonna be a long day."

Kosana's feet crunched over glass shards as he peered out the window to see if there was anyone outside that were immediate threats; that could follow the sound of the gunshots directly into their dilapidated, aging police station.

The coast, at least in appearance, was clear.

He turned and looked at Shirley, who looked like she was ready to jump out the nearest window and never stop running.

"Shirley, I need you to get on the horn and get everyone back here ASAP. We need all the manpower we can get to deal with whatever the hell is happening."

* * *

The crowded police station was filled with officers who nervously murmured in their seats as Kosana, case files and a clipboard in hand, took his place at the front. The men ceased talking almost immediately, and a quiet hush fell across the room as they looked upon their sheriff, who they hoped was about to give them good news; who was about to tell them that this thing would be over soon and that they could go home to their families.

Their hopeful optimism didn't last long.

"I recognize those looks on most of you. You're hoping to hear some good news," Kosana said, beginning to pace back and forth in front of them. "If you're wondering if the higher-ups who sign your paychecks know what this thing is, they don't. And if they do, they're not sharing it with me."

Kosana was a brave man; strong, stubborn, and hardened by his years of service as a peace officer. He was a tough person to work for sometimes, and more than a few of his officers considered him to be of the arrogant sort. It was this arrogance that was a contributing factor to the sheriff's love of making speeches. He liked having the attention, and he liked giving a hard-ass speech to people below him. It was a chance to command the room and exert his power, so he never passed up the chance when one presented itself. However, of all topics that would have eventually come up that required one, putting down their fellow townspeople taken over by voodoo/rabies/magic space dust certainly wasn't the one he thought he would ever have to tackle.

"If you want good news, I can tell you this; you're still alive, which is a lot more than I can say for the two good men we lost today." Kosana had to catch himself before he added, *so far.*

He glanced over the many empty chairs in front of him and felt a jab of paranoia deep in his gut. "I worry for those of our men out in the field who didn't respond to our call to return to the station. I just hope it's because they're out there doing some good."

Kosana looked out over the thirty-or-so men that looked back up at him, eager to hear information that could shed some light on the strange occurrences of the day, and that it would hopefully all be over soon.

"Before I proceed, let me ask you this. How many of you out there encountered one of these crazy people while out on a call?"

More than half raised their hand. One of the men, Dean Jensen, called out, "Took a hell of a lot to put him down, too!"

Some of the men responded in flat murmurs.

"With *your* aim, Jensen I bet it did," Kosana quipped.

The men chuckled and Jensen muttered to himself as he folded his arms over his chest.

"Of those, how many had to kill one of them?" Kosana asked.

The men, whose hands were still raised, remained. One officer sheepishly lowered his.

Kosana turned his sights to the one officer that didn't raise his hand.

"What happened, Jake?"

"I, uh..." the brown-haired, pudgy officer named Jake Butler began. "I followed up on a call at a hou—at a...private residence. I got out of the car to approach the front door and one of those crazies saw me through the window in the house and started pounding against it. The glass broke and fell out of the frame, and the guy just fell with it. He cut his whole stomach open on a shard of window glass that was stuck in the bottom of the jamb. He just...stayed there, quivering, trying to free himself, but all he did was get cut up and empty out most of his insides. His guts were all over the place. I just...well, I ran."

A few of the men murmured in response again, and Butler looked around, embarrassed.

"Well, how was I to know what was going on? I'm not ashamed to say it! I got the hell out of there!"

Kosana shushed the officer. "Don't fret it, Jake. The Boy Scouts and metal shop don't prepare us for this, and they know it," he said, his eyes washing over the room of officers, boring holes into the eyes of those that didn't look away from him in fear and embarrassment. "Don't pay any mind to them. Just relax. What was the status of the occupants in the house?"

Butler flushed with red, looked down at his hands that he was nervously wiping on his pant legs. "I never made it inside."

The men traded even softer whispers until Kosana cast his steely-eyed glance towards them again. The men shut up quickly.

"Well, I got the call to return, so I did!"

The officer sitting next to Butler tapped his leg a couple times. He was a much older officer and he had seen his fair share of carnage during his time on the force.

"Don't get stressed, kid," Matty Bannon said, his hair silver and thinning. "It ain't the end of the world."

No one spoke for a moment after that, and the silent tension filling the room was unbearable.

Kosana cleared his throat to get the floor again. "I wanted to keep this short because poor Shirley is up at the front desk wrestling with the phones, and people out there need our help. Now, with that in mind, I'm going to pair you all up in twos and assign you a section of town to monitor. Shirley will be radioing you any calls she receives so you can respond immediately. Deputy Haig is going to stay behind with me so we can follow this damn thing and see if any new info comes our way. I want *all* officers to check in here every ten minutes. I'm not kidding around about that. If you fail to check in—if I have to chase down a single officer to see about their location—it'll mean your badge. Are we clear?"

The men muttered their agreement, their words meshing together to create a sea of unintelligible rabble.

"Now, before we go, some quick things to remember. If these infected people come at you, shoot them in the head. That seems to be the only way to bring them down. This disease, this virus, whatever it is—it's making everyone infected much stronger. And it's contagious. Flesh on flesh doesn't seem to spread it, but if one of these people manages to bite you, well...it's only a matter of time. It's fast-acting, and it doesn't play favorites. Any questions?"

No one spoke for a moment, but Butler raised his hand.

"Yes, Jake?"

"I, uh...folks are saying that these people...the ones going crazy and attacking other folks...Well, that they're dead."

"What you mean *dead*? Like, mummies?"

The men chuckled again, and Butler's face exuded hurt.

It was a ridiculous claim Kosana was shocked to hear was circulating in town, the rumor coming from people he once thought to be level-headed and intelligent, if maybe a bit old-fashioned.

Dead people walking? No way could that be the cause.

Not in a million years.

"That's what people are saying, Sheriff," Butler said defensively. "It's just something I've heard, is all."

The men exchanged varying looks of bewilderment and fear. A few men even exchanged smiles, as if this whole fiasco would amount to nothing more than a story to tell over tonight's dinner of meatloaf and potatoes.

"You need to stop talking to people, son, and just do your job," Kosana said. Butler shifted down in his seat, and Bannon gave him another comforting pat. "All right then. Deputy Haig will assign you your areas to monitor. If you need anything while you're out there, radio Shirley." He handed his clipboard to Haig, who took it from him and began reading off names immediately.

"Kenton and Davies, you have between Breakneck Creek and Front Street..."

Kosana gathered the case files he brought to the front, intending on referring to them during his speech before opting to keep it short.

Haig continued to read off names, as Kosana walked slowly into his office, his head swimming with paranoid thoughts about how bad this situation could become, and how quickly.

* * *

Sheriff Kosana had dismissed his men at 11:30 that morning, and they were instructed to check in every ten minutes. By the time noon had come and gone, many had not.

Shirley tried fruitlessly to raise the missing officers on the radio, but to no avail. Dead silence greeted her as she requested, then demanded, and then finally pleaded for them, to answer their radios. Her phones, alarmingly, had also become suspiciously quiet. The torrent of panicked calls the station was receiving suddenly ceased with no warning. A simple test of the phone lines had concurred they were still working, though a whiney tone greeted Shirley for each port she jammed her cord into on the switchboard. The phone lines in town were on the fritz and that didn't bode well for any of them. With only radio communication left to rely on, she continued her request to raise the missing police officers.

"Just a temporary thing, girl," Kosana reassured her. "Phones won't stay down long. Just you wait and see." But he didn't necessarily believe that, no more than he believed this ordeal would be over soon, and no more than he believed that his missing men out in the field were fine and dandy and would all soon return with wild stories to tell.

In a half-hour's time, Kosana had lost many of his men. He hoped it was for any number of reasons that they weren't checking in: aiding townspeople in distress, perhaps on foot patrol and away from the radio—even if they had parked their car down a quiet road to avoid having to encounter one of the infected.

But he knew it in his heart.

The men were dead.

Or...worse.

Would they be coming back to the station with that blank look in their eyes, infected with whatever it was floating around outside?

He stood with his arms planted on his hips trying to understand this ungodly situation. He felt useless, angry, and he looked like death warmed over. The stress was clearly present in his face, and his eyes darted back and forth around the station—his domain—as if seeing some inane, pointless object would trigger an "a-ha!" epiphany. Of course, one didn't come.

He walked over to the radio to see if newer information had been released. Haig was there, clipboard in hand, ready to take down anything deemed worthy. The blank white paper stared up at Kosana almost mockingly.

"Nothing, I guess, huh?" Kosana asked. Haig shook his head.

"Important men are in important meetings discussing important things. That's about the gist of what I've heard so far," Haig said. "It's like they're going out of their way not to have to tell us what's going on."

"Well, keep at it, Vince. Give me a shout if they say something that makes any sense."

"You got it, Sheriff."

Kosana looked at the radio a moment longer before pacing back to his office. He sat down, walked his fingers over the rolodex, and plucked out the card for the Centers for Disease Control and Prevention. He dialed the number and sat back in his chair, ready to wait for as long as it took for someone to answer. They did far quicker than he anticipated.

"Disease," a voice said; male, quick, flat, almost bored. The chaotic sounds of a sea of voices filtered in through the other end of the phone, and Kosana pictured a large room of people with high ceilings and row after row of tired men and women handling phone calls from terrified citizens.

"This is Sheriff Kosana from Butler County, in Pennsie. I was calling because..."

"We're aware of the threat, sir. The government is taking appropriate action," the man responded, cutting him off.

"I'm sure they are, but when are they going to tell us..."

"I'm told to instruct you that we'll be releasing all pertinent information through the media."

"Seems to be the thing to say with you people. C'mon, level with me, pal. What is this? You have to know something. I have people dying over here."

"I'm afraid I don't have any information available that hasn't been released through the media already."

"And why do I get the feeling that you're full of it?"

"Can I assist you with anything else, sir?" the man smarmily asked before clicking off the line without waiting for the sheriff's response. Kosana took the phone away from his ear and stared at it, as if checking to see if the explanation for man's inhumanity to man was written somewhere on its handle. He slammed the phone down and looked out into the empty inner offices, which were quiet and exuded an almost artificial look.

"The hell with it," he said. He opened his desk drawer, spotted the extra ammo in his desk, and filled his gun and the notches on his utility belt. He grabbed his trusty fedora, brown and worn, complete with a peacock's feather stuck in the black ribbon band—

a gift from his father—and placed it down carefully on his head, aware of the weak thread that was holding the hat together. He walked back out the front door and turned to see Shirley staring at him with an absolute look of fear in her eyes. He read her mind and tried to give her a reassuring smile.

"I'll be back before you know it, Shirl. And Deputy Haig is here if you need anything."

"Sheriff...is this going to be over soon?" she asked him hesitantly, unaware of how he would react. Her voice shook with heavy fear and her eyes darted around the street behind him as she spoke.

Kosana experienced a moment of sheer humiliation that he tried to shake off quickly, hating the feeling of questioning his instincts.

Was he abandoning her? Or was she just terrified of being alone?

He reasoned he had no choice but to leave. There was a thought drilling away at the back of his head and he wanted to see it through. But it still didn't quell his feeling of embarrassment and shame that he was leaving poor Shirley—a longtime friend of his mother's as well as a longtime employee of the police station—alone to man the phones and radio. She was put in charge of the insurmountable notion that those officers who hadn't yet checked in were going to any minute.

Because none of this was as bad as it seemed.

Because none of this was actually happening at all.

Kosana nodded at her and opened the front entrance doors. He cast a careful look up and down the street, and before turning to go, Shirley called out to him.

"Sheriff...please be careful."

He kept his eyes on the desolate street, and before letting the doors close behind him, he told her, "No worries, girl. I'm gonna sort this whole mess out. Just you wait and see."

* * *

Sheriff Kosana's police cruiser idled in front of the police station as he stared out the front windshield, keenly aware that at any time, one of those *people* could pop up out of nowhere. He raised his radio mic to his lips and clicked the transmission button, not knowing exactly what to say at first.

"This is Sheriff Kosana, boys. I'm leaving the station now. I got something I need to do, but there's something else I need first. Anyone out there see any of those...*people*?"

Kosana released the button which greeted him with an empty hiss. He counted to five in his head, then shut his eyes in intrusive, sudden prayer. He clicked the transmission button again.

"Goddamn it, there's gotta be someone out there."

Finally a voice responded. "Yeah, Sheriff! It's Bill Kenton here, out near Breakneck Creek! I, uh...I could use a hand!"

Kosana kicked his car into drive and sped off down the street, raising the radio mic to his lips again.

"I'm on my way. What's your status?" He released the button again and waited for Kenton's response.

"Uh...not good. I'm in my cruiser. Trapped. Davies...Davies is down. He's down and he's outside. He's got the damn keys. There's a lot of those crazies near me, Sheriff. *A lot.*" He clicked off.

"Hold tight, Bill. You just hold on. I'll be there in three."

"Better make it one, Sheriff. For the love of everything holy, make it one."

Kosana dropped the handheld radio in his lap and sped up to seventy-five mph; risky in such a small section of town. The streets were narrow and winding, but he'd been negotiating these turns for years. He could do it blindfolded if necessary.

He banged a left onto Dresden Street and the tires screeched in retaliation, his front bumper just a hair away from swiping a pick-up truck parked in front of the post office. His eyes darted up to his rearview mirror, exhaling with a startled laugh at how close he came to getting himself hurt—or worse. When his eyes settled back on the road, there was nothing he could do to prevent mowing down the bystander in front of him. A blur of gray hair was all he saw before the woman disappeared under the cruiser.

"Holy hell!" he shouted, jamming on the breaks and cutting the steering wheel hard to end up spinning in a half circle. The car hadn't stopped rocking from the extreme turn before he was out of the cruiser and running over to the jumbled mess of blue and red he'd left lying in the street.

"Hold on, ma'am! I'm coming!"

Thoughts of the end of his career zoomed quickly through his brain. He pictured his disgraced walk out of the station, sans his badge and gun. He pictured his ruined life in Butler County, and the whispers of the people who saw him on the street. He shook the thoughts out of his head, focusing on the innocent old lady that needed his help. He made it over to her and knelt down next to her twisted, battered body, grazing her neck with his two first fingers, feeling for a pulse. He held them there a moment before whipping them away when she moaned and raised her bloodied head to look up at him. Her mouth opened wide and black, bloody sludge sliding in chunks out of her mouth.

Despite the horrifying sight in front of him, he still sighed in relief. He hadn't killed a normal person.

It was one of *them.*

"Thank Christ," he said softly, pulled his gun from its holster, and blew the old woman's wire-framed glasses halfway through her forehead.

* * *

Sheriff Kosana's cruiser squealed to a halt, the sound muffled by the gravel which surrounded Breakneck Creek on either side. He saw Kenton's cruiser parked down a small ravine. It was at the entrance most people used to set up their fishing spots, where they would sit with their heads up, their hats down, and their fishing line dancing in the water as sonnies and other unimpressively-sized fish nibbled at their baits of hotdogs and bread.

Kosana saw that Kenton wasn't exaggerating. A crowd of people surrounded his car on all sides. Their hands slapped ineffectively at the windows of the cruiser, and one of them was sitting on the roof and pounding stiffly on it. Kosana jumped out of his cruiser, took out his gun, and fired it into the sky. The shot caught all of their attention, and they each began leaving the cruiser and stumbled towards him instead. It was only then that the sheriff's math skills caught up with him. He now had fewer shots in his gun than the number of opponents stumbling towards him. And there would be no way for him to reload in time. Knowing his only help was sitting terrified in the driver's seat of the beat-up cruiser parked crookedly at Breakneck Creek, Kosana raised his gun to the head of the nearest attacker coming towards him.

"Bill! Get your ass out here! I'm gonna need a hand!" Kosana screamed.

He fired off his first shot, splattering through the nearest creature's right eye, which exploded in a mess of clear, gelatin-like goo. The body pitched forward, head first, and a few of the others stepped blindly over the fallen body. He fired another shot into the head of an elderly man dressed in a topcoat and he collapsed to the wet grass.

Kenton still had made no move to get out of the car.

"Bill! If I have to ask you again, I'm gonna rip your door open and feed you to these people!" he yelled. Another attacker, a sickly-thin woman dressed in a hospital gown, crept closer towards him.

Kenton finally opened the cruiser's driver's side door slowly and stepped out with his gun drawn.

"Sheriff?" he asked, and seeing that the horde was now advancing on Kosana, followed up with, "Hey! Over here!"

Some of the people turned around and looked at Kenton before beginning their journey back to him, while some continued their march towards Kosana.

"Pick 'em off, Bill. And carefully, would ya?"

"You got it," Kenton replied.

Kosana and Kenton then began a back-and-forth shooting brigade, popping each slow-going attacker in the head like a bizarre carnival game. Each shot from Kosana's gun would catch their attention, and as they would slowly turn to attack him, Kenton would pick one of them off, and with the report of his gun, the sound would again attract them. Kosana recognized most of the people that came towards him, people he had known for years whose only intention now was to kill him. One of the Johnson brothers—Harry—sauntered towards him, his fishing hat adorned with bobbers stained with blood from the bite mark on his forehead. Kosana blew the hat and half of Harry's head off and the man crumpled at his feet. Meanwhile, Kenton took on Larry, the other, taller brother, and blew a hole through his bottom jaw and up through the back of his head.

With only two adversaries remaining—a fit-looking man dressed in exercise clothing and an overweight female in a baggy sundress, Kosana holstered his gun.

"What the hell are you doing, Sheriff?" Kenton demanded.

"Shoot the woman, Bill. Don't shoot the man. You understand me?"

"Yeah, but..."

"Don't ask questions, Bill. Just do it."

Kenton shook his head in confusion, but fired his last bullet into the woman's head. She collapsed forward, letting out a *whooooosh* as the hard ground forced all the stagnant air out of her lungs. The last remaining attacker reached his muscular arms towards Kenton, who backed up slowly and waited for whatever plan Kosana had come up with.

"Uh...Sheriff?" Kenton asked as he took unsteady steps backwards. Kosana began walking behind the man, slowly and quietly. He withdrew his set of handcuffs from his belt and readied them for a fresh set of wrists.

"Oh, Lord, are you kidding me?" Kenton asked, seeing what Kosana's plan had turned out to be.

"Shut up, Bill. Just let him keep coming at you. And when I say so, grab his arms and twist them behind his back."

"No, Sheriff, I don't think I can..."

"It ain't something you ain't done a hundred times before, now do it!"

"There's a difference between cuffin' old Dan Barnes when he's had a few too many and this."

"I ain't gonna ask again," Kosana said.

"Oh, Mother of Mercy," Kenton said. He took a giant step back, crouched, and waited. When the creature took one more step, Kenton lunged and grabbed his left arm, swinging it wildly and forcing it behind the man's back to apply one cuff. The confused man groaned and tried to reach his free arm behind his back to grab at the officer, and Kosana grabbed that same arm and forced it down close to the man's other freshly cuffed wrist. After Kosana snapped the cuff, he grabbed the man's shackled hands with one hand and the back of the man's neck with the other. Kosana began leading him to his cruiser, and when he got to the rear door, he saw Kenton standing dead still, a look of pure confusion on his face.

"Bill, open the damn door, would you?"

Kenton's eyes bugged out, but he shook himself out of his stupor and ran over to the sheriff's cruiser. He opened the door, holding his head far back from the man's gnashing teeth. Kosana kicked the man inside, who face-planted on the back seat, and slammed the door. He leaned against the side of the cruiser and exhaled in relief.

"What's your plan, Sheriff?"

"You said Davies is down?" Kosana asked, ignoring his question.

Kenton nodded sullenly.

"We were checking the creek to see if anyone was out here fishing, away from their TVs and radios. It was Martin's idea. He knew the Johnson brothers would be down here at least. And they were, all right. One of them—dunno which one—killed him."

"Where is he?"

"Down near the creek bed."

"You mean he didn't get up?"

Kenton put his hands up as if being accused. "If he did, I ain't seen him."

Kosana sighed, looking at his shoes. He slid out some bullets from his utility belt and loaded them into his gun. "Come on...let's go find him."

Kenton followed Kosana, straightened his blue policeman's cap, and loaded up his own gun.

"Has there been any more news about this whole thing?" Kenton asked, following Kosana as he strode towards the edge of the creek.

"Nothing yet. I called the CDC and spoke to a pretty unhelpful little prick. And the radio keeps saying the same thing over and over. If I have to sit here all day and wait for news, I'm going to lose my head. I got my own plans."

Kosana negotiated the steep decline to the edge of the creek bed and stopped when he saw Davies, with his back to them, sitting

Indian style by a toppled wicker chair previously belonging to the Johnson brothers.

"Oh, no," was all Kenton could manage.

"Come on," whispered Kosana over his shoulder. The two men took their place behind the officer and stopped a few feet away. The men could only see the back of Davies' head, which was hung low over his lap. He jerked it up every once in a while, only to lower it again.

"Martin!" Kosana shouted suddenly. Martin Davies stopped and slowly turned his head around until he was facing both men. He held a mutilated fish in his hand, with the hook that had caught it now snagged in Davies' bottom lip. The dying fish flapped tepidly in his blue hands, showing pathetically-little signs of life. Gray innards recently excised from the fish hung in drips and drools out of Davies' mouth. He muttered a barking groan and attempted to climb to his feet. As he did, the hook—which was still attached to the fishing line—yanked the fishing pole lying at the creek's edge across the overgrown banks. Kosana raised his gun to Davies' head and was about to pull the trigger when the fishing pole became snagged on some weeds. It jerked Davies' head back until he lost balance and fell flat on his back.

"Oh, Jesus," Kenton said, his gun upraised, waiting to see what Davies would do.

"I know, right? He's dumber than dirt now," Kosana replied, mistaking Kenton's sadness for disgust.

Davies slowly sat up, and because the fishing pole was still caught on the overgrowth of the creek, the fishhook ripped slowly through his bottom lip, tearing a three inch gash that ended in his left cheek. Blood filled the fresh wound and began flowing down the front of his uniform.

"Can I put him out of his misery? Or do you wanna arrest *him*, too?" Kenton asked, embarrassed and offended that both of them were letting this charade in the form of their ex-friend and fellow officer go on for so long.

"He was your partner, Bill. You take it."

Kenton forcibly pushed Kosana out of the way in a sporadic burst of anger and shot Davies once in the forehead. Davies fell back again, smashing his head on a protruding rock stuck deep in the orange clay of Breakneck Creek. Blood from the headshot diffused with the shallow running water of the creek in which he landed, and almost-perfectly round pink clouds began flowing down the current with each pump of blood from the bullet's exit wound.

Kenton kept his gun pointed in the position he had used to shoot his partner, and his eyes remained on the motionless body.

"Sheriff...what do you want with one of those people?"

Kosana's eyes remained on Davies' body for a moment before he knelt down at the dead officer's side and began patting the corpse's pockets.

"I need to know what's going on. I need to know what's wrong with these people, and if there's a cure, or if it's just a lost cause," Kosana answered.

"And how're you going to do that?"

"The one we caught? I'm taking him to Dr. Ford." He felt the small set of car keys in Davies' chest pocket and withdrew them, tossing them at Kenton. The keys bounced limply off his chest as Kenton stared at Kosana, shocked at his intentions.

"For what reason? What could you possibly want to know about them? They're here, Sheriff. And they're killing us. What does it matter?"

"There has to be a reason. A real one. And not that kinda talk Butler was going on about how these people are really dead or whatever. I don't know what that explanation could possibly be, but there has to be *something*. And I'm hoping the doc can tell us."

"I don't care why they're here, Sheriff. I just want them gone," was Kenton's response.

"So do I, Bill. C'mon."

Kosana grabbed the car keys off the ground and handed them to Kenton, then motioned with his head towards their cruisers. The two men left Breakneck Creek, newly exorcised, and as soon as the cruisers were lost from sight, the sounds of flowing water and chirping birds filtered back in to chase away the chaos from minutes before.

* * *

Having sent Kenton back to the station, Sheriff Kosana drove through the streets of his town with his reloaded handgun on the passenger seat next to him. It was suspiciously quiet. He saw not a single person—normal or not. The man in the backseat groaned softly, his hands still shackled behind his back. He chewed at the steel wiring that separated the backseat from the front. It was no stronger than those used to pen chickens, and it was the only boundary keeping the man from Kosana's certain, and undoubtedly messy, death.

As the streets grew narrower, he could see for the first time that wooden boards covered doors and windows of the houses and shops that made up Evanstown. The sight of the boards filled him with both dread and relief, somehow simultaneously. Relief because people were taking this thing seriously, and that even the most skeptical of the city's citizens would look upon the actions of their neighbor and think that it couldn't hurt to play it safe. The dread that filled him was due in part because Butler County's occupants—*his* friends and neighbors—were terrified, and alone, and some probably dead. Meanwhile, he cruised in front of their houses with one of the opposition shackled in his backseat as if he were nothing more than a small-time criminal. He shook away those thoughts as he made the turn onto Burgundy Street, where Dr. Ford lived.

He pulled up in front of the impressively-sized house—Camelot was what the townspeople had named it—and he got out of the cruiser. He holstered his handgun and withdrew his shotgun from the trunk. Pushing his hat down closer to his head, he gave a glance up and down the street, and then crossed the well-manicured front lawn to the peach-colored front door. He knocked, waited, and then followed up with, "It's Sheriff Kosana, Doc. You in there?" He waited a moment, but then heard some shuffling noises inside.

"Who is it?" the doctor asked in a small voice.

"I said it's the sheriff, Doc. Open up." He heard the sounds of several locks becoming undone before the doctor opened the door just a hair, the chain still in place.

"Are you nuts? What the hell are you doing out there?"

"My duty. I need your help."

"With what? Damn it, Sheriff, you're a sitting duck out there. Those people are all over the place!"

"An even better reason to let me in," he responded, though there wasn't a single one of those people in sight.

The doctor slammed the door, undid the chain, and swung it open quickly.

"Come on in, then!"

Kosana entered the house and the doctor slammed the door behind him, reapplied all of the locks, and then slid a heavy, pine chair under the doorknob.

"What the hell brings you out in the middle of this mess?"

"I need answers, Doc. I need to know what's wrong with these people."

Dr. Ford was flabbergasted, his mouth dropping open. "And because I took heartbeats and banged rubber hammers on knees for a bunch of farmers, you think I could figure out this thing while the government can't?"

"I don't know if they can't...or if they ain't telling us that they did."

The doctor began to rebut Kosana, but seeing the stubborn look in the man's eyes, he sighed instead.

"Come on, I just made some coffee," Dr. Ford said, turning and making his way back to the kitchen.

Kosana followed the doctor through his magnificently-decorated house, furnished in early-Victorian style, into the brilliantly-lit kitchen. Framed photographs of the doctor's family lined the wall, one of those being Margie, the doctor's wife. She had died years ago of heart-failure, and her death left the doctor all alone in his overly-spacious home. He retired soon after, citing his self-professed lack of worthiness to treat any other person when he couldn't save his own wife. The windows in the kitchen, even the very small set over the sink that was no larger than a breadbox, had a piece of plywood nailed over it.

"How bad is it out there?" the doctor asked.

"Pretty bad so far. Haven't you been following along? Radio or TV?"

The doctor shook his head. "Don't own either. Never had a need for them."

The doctor pulled out a stiffly-matted chair from the kitchen table and motioned to it before sitting down himself. When Kosana didn't sit, and instead laid down his shotgun on the kitchen counter, the doctor looked at him.

"Well...what can I do for you?"

"Well, Doc, is your examination room still in order? From when you used to see patients?"

"It is."

"Does it have a bed? Or a gurney or something with straps?"

The doctor turned his head slightly away from Kosana, yet kept his eyes sternly on his face.

"What do you have up your sleeve, Sheriff?"

"Not up my sleeve, Doc. In my car."

Dr. Ford, the tiny and frail man with swirling, snow-white hair, looked upon Kosana until his face dripped with a sudden explosion of realization.

"You're not telling me..."

"I'm telling you I have one of those crazy people in my car. I'm telling you that I want you to strap him down and give him a full examination, like you used to. I'm telling you that this county is depending on me and I need to understand why these people are the way they are...if it's a virus, drugs, or radioactive space dust."

The doctor stared at Kosana for what seemed like an eternity. His eyes remained wide as what the sheriff told him slowly worked its way around his brain.

"No. I'm sorry, no. Absolutely not. That's just insane, Sheriff."

"I lost a lot of good men today, Doc. *A lot.* Preston Murphy, Martin Davies, Hank Pearson. I saw the Johnson brothers earlier, down by Breakneck Creek. Father Darien. They're all dead. And a lot more will be dead, too, unless you help me. Now, I have one of them with me, Doc, like I said. I want you to examine him, like you would any other normal person that came in feeling sick."

"But what good is that going to do?"

"I don't know, but I feel like we've got to try."

Dr. Ford looked at him; saw that there was no reasoning with him. Kosana was adamant about seeing this through, and like it or not, he wasn't going to take no for an answer.

The doctor sighed heavily.

"Go get the...patient."

* * *

Sheriff Kosana secured the last strap across the thrashing man's ankle and pulled it taut. Dr. Ford, wearing his trusty white lab coat, turned with a stethoscope in his hand and approached the tied-down man. They huddled over the man who was secured to the doctor's examination table. A layer of white, crackling butcher paper separated the man from the vinyl-covered table and it was already torn in various places because of the man's fidgeting. The doctor's examination room was painted a sterilized white, and framed pictures of the town's local foliage lined the walls; pictures meant to relax those sitting on the table and undergoing an exam—routine or not.

Routine this definitely was not.

"Well, uh..." the doctor began nervously, "the first thing to do is to remove the patient's shirt."

As Dr. Ford reached over his tool tray to pick up a pair of surgical scissors, Kosana reached his hand to the top of the man's neck, grabbed the collar of the his red shirt, and ripped it down the middle. The man pushed his forehead against the leather strap tied down over it and tried to bite at Kosana's hand, but Kosana ignored it and spread the shirt flaps open, revealing more of the man's pasty white flesh. Dr. Ford sniffed at Kosana's primitive technique as he hooked the stethoscope around his head and cautiously reached the amplifier to the man's chest. The man flinched when it made contact with his skin and the doctor jumped back in fear.

"It's okay, Doc. He's not going anywhere," Kosana said.

Dr. Ford looked up at Kosana sharply before proceeding with the examination, angry that he was being put in this position. He again slid the amplifier up the man's stomach, resting it just over his heart. He pressed down and waited to read the heartbeat.

Kosana could see the doctor narrow his eyes, and after holding it there for several seconds, tried various spots surrounding the heart. He lifted the amplifier and tapped it with his fingernail.

"I don't get it," he said, looking confused.

"What?"

"I know I haven't been a doctor for a long time, but I'd like to think I'm still capable of at least finding a damn heartbeat."

"Are you saying there isn't one?"

"Of course not. Whatever it is that's changing these people...it could have slowed their nervous system down so low that the heartbeat is just too faint to read."

The doctor thought a moment before walking over to the table and placing his stethoscope down. He picked up a throat depressor and took a step towards the man before thinking better of it. He went to the cabinet, rummaged briefly, and removed a metal object shaped like a boxer's mouth guard. He rinsed it off in the sink thoroughly and then turned to the sheriff.

"Could you assist me with fitting this into his mouth?"

Kosana walked around the table and stood near the man's head. He carefully lowered his hands to lay them over either side of the man's face, and in response, the man gnashed his teeth and growled at him. Kosana whipped his hands away quickly.

"Yeah, right, Doc."

"This was your idea, Sheriff," Dr. Ford said impatiently.

Kosana cursed.

"What is that thing?"

"Keeps the mouth open. Used to use it on kids who would get scared and try to bite my finger off."

"Great." Kosana reached the device slowly over the man's mouth again, which resulted in another bite attempt. "The hell with this!" Kosana muttered and stormed over to the doctor's tray of tools and grabbed a large pair of metal sheers. He strode over to the man and drove the sheers into the man's mouth. He squeezed the handles together, forcing the man's jaws open.

"G'head, Doc, shove that thingamajig in."

Dr. Ford chuckled dryly and lowered the device into the man's mouth. Once in place, Kosana removed the sheers and dropped them on the counter behind him. The doctor stuck the wooden depressor into the now-secured mouth and held the tongue down, peering deep into the man's throat. He grabbed a small penlight from his pocket with his free hand and shined it into the mouth.

"This is getting weird, Sheriff," the doctor said, still studying the inside of the mouth.

"Why, what do you see?"

He removed the depressor and tossed it into a small waste basket behind him. He clicked off the penlight and let it fall into his pocket.

"I'd test his reflexes, but I have a feeling it's going to tell me the same thing."

"What's that?" Kosana asked.

"This is...extraordinary," Dr. Ford said, staring hard at the man wriggling on the table. The color had leaked out of the doctor's face, leaving him almost as white as a sheet. He began murmuring unintelligibly to himself.

"Talk to me, Doc."

Dr. Ford looked up at him, befuddlement in his eyes.

"Sheriff, this man, by all clinical definition, is dead."

This time, it was Kosana who was befuddled.

"Ohhh, no you don't," Kosana said, almost smiling. "I've heard that this kind of bullshit was circulating around the town. Some of my men came in saying the same thing. Don't you start now, either. Go ahead and do...something else, and you'll see that it ain't so."

"There's nothing else I can do, Sheriff. Believe me or don't, but I'm telling you, this man is dead."

"What do you mean *dead*?" Kosana asked. "That's ridiculous."

"I mean that this man has no heartbeat. And that the flesh inside him is the color of burnt wood, almost jet black. And if you take a step back and simply just look at him, you'll see he's not breathing."

Kosana did just that, staring at the man's chest intently. Though the man groaned, he didn't breathe. His chest didn't rise and fall, in spite of how agitated he was at being tied down.

Ford grabbed a fat syringe off his tool tray and stepped up next to the man. He rubbed two fingers across the underside of the man's arm and inserted the thick needle in between them. He began, slowly at first, to withdraw blood into the vial, but when no blood flowed, he withdrew with more force. A small, sucking noise emitted as brown chunks fired into the base of the syringe. The doctor filled half the tube with viscous goo before removing it from the man's arm. He looked at it for a moment.

"The blood's coagulated."

"*Coagulated...?*" Kosana said, emphasizing the word to show he didn't understand.

"It's a transformation the blood goes through after death. It turns into this chunky, congealed texture and turns from the usual crimson to a dark brown."

He dropped the syringe on the tray and grabbed the edge of the table it sat on.

"I don't know what else I can do for you, Sheriff," Dr. Ford said.

"Your little tests and theories ain't enough for me, Doc. You gotta open him up."

"Open him up? You mean like...an autopsy?"

"Exactly that."

"No, absolutely not. You came here for my help, and as far as I'm concerned, I helped. I'm not going to just cut this man in half because you say so. I'm not a monster, and even more, I'm not a mortician."

"But you *know* how to do it, Doc. I need more than what you've told me."

Dr. Ford looked over to the strapped man, hesitant.

"I don't think you have to worry about hurting him, Doc," Kosana reasoned. Now it was the sheriff's turn to look at the man. "I don't think they can feel any pain at all."

The doctor rubbed his chin for a moment, a nervous tic, and picked up a scalpel. The instrument hovered over the man as he gnashed his teeth at the doctor's white-gloved hand.

"What if I'm wrong, Sheriff? What if this thing is just a freak occurrence and these people can be cured? I don't know what this is, and neither do you. What if there's a cure? What if I'm about to kill a man that's just a pill or a flu shot away from being cured?"

The doc's reasoning gave Kosana pause, and he stood there a moment, unsure of what to say. But then he remembered the battles he'd already faced, and how he'd put down men he'd known for a long time. He saw in his mind putting a bullet in Preston's head, and the disgusting sound it made. But even more so, he remembered Preston's first day on the job, and how the men in his station had called in a phony report that one of the local farm-hands, Mackie Dawson, was drunk and wandering naked down Main Street. He remembered Preston had been sent out to look for Mackie, and obviously not finding him, returned to the station, nervous about not being able to conclude his first assignment as a Butler County police officer.

He returned to see the men smiling and laughing, standing around a table that had a tan-colored cake with two mounds in the shape of a human posterior (which Bannon's wife had made, as she had made the many other cakes that came before it) with the words "**Welcome to Butler County PD**" scrawled in cherry gel. It was a pathetic, immature joke they played on each new man, but Preston had laughed so hard that tears spilled from his eyes and he fell heavily backwards into a desk chair, having lost all control, and ended up sitting only halfway on the seat. He spilled to the ground, still laughing uproariously, and the station exploded in long, loud peals of laughter. The station had never experienced such camaraderie in its many years in operation—not since Kosana had been in charge, anyway.

"Doc, this thing strapped to your table isn't my concern. It's the people that *are* still breathing I'm worried about. Do it. I'll take full responsibility on whatever happens."

The doctor considered this for a full minute, then nodded solemnly, extended his hand, and inserted the scalpel into the man's flesh at the base of the groin, slitting upwards to the top of the neck. The man made no sign of experiencing pain, and he kept his glazed eyes locked on the doctor's hand hovering just over his face.

Dr. Ford sighed, shook his head ever so slightly in confusion, and then made another incision, this time in a zigzag pattern across the chest from the left to the right, the entire incision now a Y-shape. He breathed in a quick gasp, turned his head slightly away in disgust as the odor from the man's innards began to fill the room.

"Flip that switch behind you, would you, Sheriff?" Dr. Ford managed through a choked gag.

Kosana saw a small, white switch next to the door where they had entered. He flipped the switch and a small panel fan above their heads sputtered to life, eager to flush the disgusting odor from the room.

Ford waited a moment, as if gearing up for his next move, and then nonchalantly slid his gloved hands inside the incisions, rubbing them in and out as if massaging.

"Generates heat," Dr. Ford said, reading Kosana's mind. "Helps to separate the connective tissues."

He continued to rub his hands in and out of the incision before lifting the left half of the flap of flesh and laying it over the man's side. He did the same on the other side, and the man's midsection was now opened like a book. And yet he didn't struggle in pain, nor succumb to the surely-mortal dissection.

Kosana peered into the body's new opening and examined it. The underside of the flesh reminded him of a fish's scaly body, a pale green with tendrils of connective tissue that looked akin to the inside of a freshly-carved pumpkin. He took a hard swallow, trying to quell the nausea building inside him.

"Do you see that?" Dr. Ford asked, poking the same flesh that Kosana was looking at. "See that color?"

"Yeah."

"That's rotting flesh. And look at the lower intestines. They vary, from a light gray to a dark blue. See that?"

"Yes. What's it mean?"

"What it means, Sheriff, like I said before, is that this man's dead. He's been that way for, according to the coloring of his innards, maybe ten hours. Maybe more."

"Doc...no," was all Kosana managed at first, almost laughing at the shocking brevity and weakness of his argument, and at the audacity to question the man he had come to for answers. "It has to be this virus or whatever it is that people are getting. These people can't just be coming back from the dead. Something must be just taking them over. It's like...whatever this thing is...it just switches them from living to dead. That I can buy, that by some freak occurrence, the body continues to move. But for these people to just be dead...and come back. I can't buy that."

The doctor was growing visibly frustrated.

"Sheriff, I don't mean for this to sound...well, the way it's going to sound, but everything I've been telling you...you knew before you ever came here, didn't you? If I were to hazard a guess, you were coming here with this undead theory already in your head and you were hoping that I would *discredit* it, not validate it. Even right now I can see you trying to rationalize it in your head."

"Don't tell me what's in my head, Doc. You can't sit there and tell me to forget everything I know and leave my common sense at the door."

"Sheriff, science discovers new things almost daily. To suggest that everything we currently know about the world encompasses the absolute and final word is sheer ignorance. For instance, about fifteen years ago, two scientists were able to complete an experiment that proved living, organic matter was able to, due in part to various chemical reactions, materialize from nonliving, inanimate objects. Do you recall this?"

"Mmm, yes," Kosana said, cockily. "I believe it was the experiment by Dr. Frankenstein, and his assistant, Half-a-Man."

Dr. Ford glared at him, but continued onto his point.

"It was called abiogenesis, and it's heavily theorized *that's* what began the origin of life on this planet, Sheriff. What we're dealing with here isn't that dissimilar. Life spawning from a nonliving organism."

"Ridiculous," Kosana said, though the doctor's words were drilling their way into his brain and planting roots. It sure would explain everything he'd seen; the seeming immortality of the people that had accosted him, their strange, awkward movements, not to mention their appearance.

The doctor looked Kosana sternly in the face, could see that his words were beginning to work, and so he grabbed the large set of sheers from the counter that Kosana had used to force the man's mouth open and plunged them into the dissected man's ribs. He squeezed them open, forcing the ribs through which they were impaled to stretch to the point of cracking. He withdrew the shears and then shoved them in again, prying out a section of the right rib cage, which sounded like heavy tree branches as they fell apart and clattered to the floor in wet sections. He then inserted the tool around the man's heart, closed the shears around it, and with one mighty yank, removed it. He dropped the organ into a small, metal dish that lay on the tray and grabbed it, pushing it into Kosana's chest.

"You know what this is, don't you?"

"Don't get smart, Doc."

"It's time for you to get smart, Sheriff. Look at our patient."

They both did then; looked the strapped man in the face who regarded them as nothing more than easy prey. He showed no signs of slowing down, nor the flame of his life extinguishing.

"He's still going, Sheriff. And if I untied those straps, this man would pursue us to the ends of the earth, even as his organs fell out around his feet. He's still struggling, still wants to come at us, and meanwhile I'm holding his heart in my hands." He turned and dropped the metal dish directly into the man's open chest and looked at Kosana again. "Look, you came to me, remember? You came to me because you're the sheriff of this county, and as the sheriff, you know your business. This is my business. I've been a doctor before your folks ever moved to this county. And I'm telling you that according to the definition of clinical death...this man is dead. Why he continues to walk around, and attack, and why he thinks that biting chunks out of us is going to provide him any kind of nourishment is beyond me. I can't tell you that. I don't think anyone can. But what I can tell you is that this person in front of us is a human being in physicality only." He looked to the man, still struggling under his confines. "At this point...he's more of an animal than anything else."

Watching the heart slide across the bottom of the uneven metal dish, a frigid wave of sudden fear washed over Kosana. He'd tried to ignore the signs, and tried to make his common sense overrule what his instincts were otherwise trying to tell him: this was for real. He'd seen the transformations for himself, heard their un-dead, soulless groans as they shuffled towards him, and smelled the wicked odor of the grave. He'd touched their cold, grimy flesh, and now was feeling a familiar taste in the back of his throat.

Kosana spun and barely made it to the small waste basket in the corner of the office before letting loose a torrential explosion of his morning's breakfast. He leaned on the wall for support and tried to bite back each wave of nausea as his mind worked tirelessly to sort out this revelation in his reeling mind. Suddenly, he realized he was keenly aware of the fluorescent light buzzing over his head. He heard water drip from the faucet in the sink on the other side of the room. He could hear the man's—no, the *thing's*—flesh rub against the leather straps attached to the bed as he tried in vain to free himself. All these noises at once became almost unbearable, and Kosana shut his eyes against them all.

He tried his best to ignore them, to shut them out.

But he couldn't.

They were in the room with him, confronting him, assaulting him.

And they weren't going to stop.

"This is unbelievable, Doc," Kosana said, still leaning against the wall, his eyes shut tight. The odor of his vomit wafted up in his face and it made his stomach again lurch.

"Believe it," Dr. Ford said solemnly.

Kosana yanked a paper towel off the counter next to him, blotted his mouth, and balled it up tight in his fist. With one hand still pushing against the wall, he turned his head to look at the doctor.

"Why isn't this being reported, Doc? No offense to your skills, but if you were able to figure this out, why haven't scientists from Washington?"

"Who knows? Would it surprise you at all if our government was suppressing this information in hopes of avoiding a panic? Hell, I wouldn't be surprised if there was a big meeting going on right now with the left side of the room shouting to those on the right with absolutely nothing being agreed upon. Politicians are barely useful when things are fine. Plop them in the middle of a crisis and you've got a bunch of scared kids in grown-up clothes."

"Christ," Kosana breathed heavily, dropping the balled-up paper towel into the trash can. "This thing is for real..."

Dr. Ford motioned with his eyes to the phone that was affixed to the wall behind Kosana, before snapping off his rubber gloves.

"I imagine you have some calls to make."

* * *

By the time Kosana had discovered that the phones were useless in this part of town, huddled around the table in Dr. Ford's kitchen, it was just after three in the afternoon. His men—whoever were left—were probably wondering where he was. And Shirley was probably a nervous wreck.

Dr. Ford walked into the kitchen, sans white lab coat, wiping his hands. "You get through to your station?"

"Phones are dead. Clinically dead, you might say."

The doctor rolled his eyes and reached for the phone. "Let me."

Kosana grew annoyed at the presumption that he wasn't intelligent enough to know when a phone was working, but he said nothing and handed the phone to him. The doctor heard for himself the high-pitched tone that greeted him. He tapped the receiver a few times to see if he could vanquish the tone away, but to no avail. He disgustedly dropped the phone in the cradle and picked up his room-temperature mug of coffee.

"I'm gonna head back to the station," Kosana said, taking his shotgun from the counter where he left it.

"Wait a minute. You're not going to leave Patient X here, are you?" Dr. Ford asked, tipping his head behind him, referring to the dissected body strapped to the table in the other room.

"Heh," Kosana chuckled. "Almost forgot about him."

The strapped man groaned loudly, suggesting it was offended by Kosana's dismissal.

"Stitch it up and I'll get rid of it on the way."

Dr. Ford rolled his eyes and opened a nearby pantry door, and grabbing a roll of duct tape with his free hand, he handed it to Kosana.

"Done," he said, sipping his tepid coffee.

Kosana grabbed the duct tape from the doctor and let a smile sneak through his hardened face.

"Come on, Doc. Give me a hand."

The two men went into the examination room, and together, they used the entire roll of tape to keep the strapped man intact. They even taped across its mouth for good measure.

"Now there's an idea," Kosana said as he loaded the man into the backseat of his car. "We can just tape all of their mouths shut. Problem solved." He shut the door and the living dead man looked at them from the backseat, a pathetic sight covered almost head-to-toe in tape.

"What are you going to do with him?" the doctor asked, still sipping from the coffee.

"Find a quiet place, I guess. Let it have some dignity."

Kosana swung open the driver's side door and was about to lower himself in when he paused and looked at the doctor.

"Thanks for your help, Doc. Although I sure didn't like your prognosis."

"Who would?" he asked, raising the mug in salute.

"Are you going to be okay here?" he asked, concerned.

"Who knows, Sheriff? What are my options?"

Kosana looked past the doctor and saw someone in a football uniform stumbling up the road; the jersey was splashed in blood. The player held a helmet in his battered, raw hand. The football player spotted the two men, moaned at the sight of them, and began stumbling towards them again, only faster. Kosana withdrew his handgun and fired a single shot, startling the unaware doctor. The football player dropped to his knees and fell over backwards, the helmet rolling away from the body.

"You sure you won't come to the station?" Kosana asked, holstering his gun nonchalantly.

The doctor, shocked, only stammered. "How bad is this going to get?" he managed.

"Bad?" Kosana replied. "Phones are dead, and so are these things. Think we skipped bad and went right to worse."

Kosana got into his cruiser and started the engine as the duct-taped dead man in the backseat began bouncing its head off the wire frame.

"Come with me. I could use your help down at the station. You'd be with people at least," Kosana reasoned.

The doctor considered it for a moment.

"Guess it's better than sticking around here," he said finally. He walked to his front door and locked it, and before turning to make his way back to the cruiser, took a strange, long look at his house, as if he was getting ready to never see it again. He plopped into the passenger's seat and shut the heavy cruiser's door.

On the way back to the station, Kosana tried not to notice that the number of those *things* wandering around had increased since he set out only a few hours ago. They pounded against doors, windows, and cars. They stared stupidly at small forest critters jumping from tree branch to tree branch. They formed small packs that moved about together, though there seemed no reasoning behind it. One followed the other that followed the other. A few times he came across several of them standing in the street blocking his way, but instead of running them down or driving around them, he would merely slow the cruiser down to a crawl and lightly bump them until they moved out of the way.

Kosana leaned down and flipped on the radio. This slight activity caused the bound creature to groan loudly from its place in the backseat.

"Shut up," Kosana said impulsively. He fiddled with the knob until he found a station that was still broadcasting.

"...*outbreak has spread largely up and down the east coast, with these attacks reported as far south as Gainesville. The National Guard has begun dispatching units to each area in which an attack has been reported to attempt to quell the seemingly growing outbreak. Reports coming in now conclude that reports consisting of these attacks have resulted in the blood-chilling fact that murder victims have been partially devoured by their killers. The President has called an emergency meeting with representatives from the scientific community that is said to include the National Aeronautics and Space Administration.*"

"You think they're gonna tell people about it soon? About them being dead?" Dr. Ford asked.

"Who knows, Doc? I hope they do. You can say the weirdest stuff on the radio and people will believe it. But when it's coming from two men they've known their whole lives? You'd be surprised how easily your own friends and neighbors can distrust you."

"What about you? You know the truth. Are you going to tell them?"

Kosana shook his head, his eyes on the road in front of him.

"Not my place. Anyway, what would be the point? They know what they need to know: these things are dangerous, contagious, and can be killed by getting them in the head. Everything else is just a mundane detail, way I see it." He grabbed the radio mic from its perch.

"Shirley, it's Sheriff Kosana. On my way back to the station with Dr. Ford. What's the status? Have any of our missing boys checked in yet?"

Dead air greeted him.

"Shirley, come in."

More dead air. The empty hissing caused the knot in his stomach to tighten.

"Got a bad feeling, Doc. When your own dispatcher doesn't answer the radio, that ain't a good thing."

When they passed a wooded spot free of people living or dead, Kosana stopped the car and freed his prisoner/patient before shooting him in the face with his handgun. The man toppled to the side, the lifeless eyes staring into Kosana's hard orbs. There was nothing behind those eyes. No flicker of its former life or the understanding of what it had become.

Kosana got back behind the wheel and peeled away, hoping that was true.

* * *

Sheriff Kosana and Dr. Ford pulled up to Butler County Police Station and were greeted with a chaotic mob scene. All of the windows of the police station were shattered and several of the dead shuffled in and out of the front door, occasionally bumping shoulders, like they were in a bread line.

"Oh, Jesus, no," Kosana said, grabbing the door handle to let himself out of the cruiser.

"Wait," Dr. Ford said sharply, his eyes on the movement of the creatures inside the building. "We're outnumbered, Sheriff. Just...let's just get out of here."

"But those are my people in there, damn it!"

Kosana grabbed the shotgun from its holder and opened the car door.

"No, Sheriff!" the doctor yelled, making no move to get out of the car. He reached out and grabbed Kosana's sleeve to hold him back, which was quickly ripped out of his grip as the man got out of the cruiser. Kosana then withdrew his handgun from its holster and handed it through the open driver's side window to the doctor, handle first.

"Let's go, Doc. You're up."

The doctor grabbed the gun frantically and got out of the cruiser.

"I knew I should've stayed at my damn house," he muttered, examining the gun in his hands.

Two creatures that had stumbled out of the front entrance spotted the men. They began their undead hobble over to them and Kosana opened fire with his shotgun, obliterating the first creature's head, spraying fragments of brain and blood all over the other one's face, who barely noticed the splatter and instead advanced quickly on Kosana. Seeing the dead man coming, Kosana swung his shotgun like a bat, slamming it into the dead man's face. The doctor, meanwhile, grasped the handgun nervously and kept quickly spinning, trying to avoid being caught off guard. Except for the stragglers that wandered out of the station doors, the street in front was clear.

Kosana fired off another shell into an advancing attacker and blew the right side of its skull away, creating an almost perfect half-circle. The hard fall to the ground shattered the rest of the creature's head and the bits of brain left intact oozed from the skull onto the concrete sidewalk.

"I'm going in, Doc. I need you behind me."

"Don't depend on me, Sheriff. I'm a terrible shot," the doctor muttered.

"Well, lucky for us they're slow and dumb."

Kosana kicked open the formerly glass-filled double doors, now only metal frames covered in a set of blood-misted blinds. The first thing he saw was Shirley's glass cube, spiderweb cracks spreading throughout, but still intact. Shirley wasn't in sight, but the back wall of her desk was splashed with blood, which trickled in slow drops to the floor, and the small door—the only entrance to her desk—hung open.

"Oh, no," Kosana said, his eyes on the blood covering the wall, the desk, and the phone.

Shotgun aimed out in front of him, he kicked open the sturdy double doors to the inner offices to see that the dead were all over the place. They wandered around, aimlessly ripping chunks of flesh off of dismembered body parts. Kosana's stomach lurched when he saw that there didn't seem to be a single spot in the office not covered in blood and human remains. No matter where he looked, a piece of a human life was in his sights.

His nausea turned to rage.

He cocked the shotgun and set his sights on a small crowd of the walking dead leaning over a body and ripping chunks of flesh off with their mouths as others reached their hands into the mess and withdrew intestines from the body's stomach. They ripped through the tough organs with their teeth and chewed them slow, as if savoring the taste. Bodily fluids dripped from the torn ends and lathered the front of their faces as they shoved the meat sloppily into their fetid mouths. Kosana fired an unfocused shot into the crowd and managed to kill two of them. The dead, with warm food at their fingertips, didn't react to the shots and instead continued to feast.

"Damn it, Doc, fire that gun!" Kosana shouted, taking aim at another group of feeders.

Dr. Ford finally obliged and fired shot after shot at any attacker that came close to him as Kosana continued to fire shells into heads of the feeding dead. Kosana reached for his belt for more shells for his shotgun only to tap empty leather notches.

He was out.

"Keep firing that gun!" he called out to the doctor, shotgun-whipping the empty weapon into an approaching creature's face as he cleared a path to the police station's armory. He grabbed the doorknob but found it was locked. Muttering a curse, he patted his pockets in frenzy until he located his keys and unlocked the door. He slammed the door hard behind him and locked it so he could locate the shells needed for his shotgun. As he filled the weapon, he heard gunshots continue to sound off in the offices, but more so than Dr. Ford was capable of shooting at one time. He peered through the metal door's screened window and saw for the first time that there was a larger crowd of creatures surrounding a group of trapped police officers, who had toppled and stacked several desks which they used to surround themselves, creating a temporary barrier from the creatures. Of the three officers desperately fighting against the advances of the dead, two had guns drawn and were firing shots into the creatures' heads while the third was beating them away with a flagpole bearing the state flag. The three officers did their best to fight off their attackers while shouting angrily at them.

Kosana finished loading his shotgun, grabbed a box of ammo for Dr. Ford's handgun, and kicked the supply room door open. He sent a creature that was watching him curiously through the door's window sprawling over a desk and landing face-first on the floor.

"Don't shout, boys!" Kosana called to them from the doorway. The men looked up at once and spotted Kosana. "It only pisses 'em off!" He strode across the room, the shotgun still aimed out in front of him, and fired at the creatures surrounding the officers. He kept calm, concentrated, and when he pulled the trigger, held his breath. The glorious, sheer power of the shotgun exploded each of the creature's heads that had turned to face him when he bellowed to the men from the doorway. A few of the creatures were some of the local townsfolk that he recognized, while others wore the uniforms of Butler County police officers. His stomach warmed over with each face he recognized to be a former officer, and friend.

Working his way close to Dr. Ford, he tossed the box of bullets to him, which the man miraculously caught in one hand.

"You got that?" Kosana asked, his eyes on the opposition surrounding him.

"I got it," the doctor said, easily refilling the borrowed gun.

With Kosana's help, the trapped officers were able to pick off more of the creatures as the doctor ran up and fired single point-blank shots to the heads of those standing off by themselves in the large room. Finally, the last creature, dressed as a school teacher with her hair up in a bun, shambled over to Kosana. He saw her and recognized Linda Alexander, the local grade school English teacher.

"Sorry, Mrs. A," he said, and blew the top of her skull off in a puff of red mist, leaving her head only a bottom jaw and a furiously wagging tongue. As she crashed to the floor, he turned to look at his men.

"Boys, I believe you know Doc Ford," Kosana said, as if he was making introductions at a social event.

The doctor, dazed from his new position as a hunter of the un-dead, barely mustered a hello.

"Are we all that's left?" Kosana asked, again taking in the red-spattered, macabre scene that was formerly his police station.

The men looked down at the floor, ashamed, as if it were their fault.

"Yeah, Sheriff," Nick Harrison said; he was a young officer, barely a year on the force. "At least we think so. None of them answer their radios. We saw some cruisers abandoned out on the roads leading into town. We saw Bannon's cruiser. He's dead for sure. Miller. Evangelista. Kenton, too. And a lot of other officers are still missing."

"Bill Kenton? How? I just saw him a couple hours ago," Kosana said, almost despondent.

"On his way back to the station, he must've driven off the road," Cliff Barton said, an overweight officer who hadn't gotten up from his desk for the better part of the last five years. "We saw him on the way back. Had to put him down. He was in real bad shape."

Kosana said nothing in response and merely looked at the floor. He began to speak to the men when he looked up and realized for the first time that he hadn't recognized one of them. The man saw Kosana looking at him and spoke up.

"Name's Al Crothers. I'm an officer over at the Youngstown sta-tion. Things got real bad, Sheriff. I had to get out of there. We lost almost every man. I came up here looking for my brother; he lives in Evanstown. Figured I'd pop in to your station to see if you could help me out."

"Looks like you helped us out instead, Al. I appreciate it," Ko-sana replied. He shook the man's hand, giving just one single pump, as was his style. "Well, I figure we ought to regroup and we can..." he began, and then just as quickly stopped, seeing the look on Barton's face.

"Sheriff..." Barton began, extremely hesitant. "Shirley..."

Kosana's mind began reeling, having temporarily forgotten that she was the reason he stormed back to the police station in the first place after she had failed to answer the radio.

"What about her?" Kosana interrogated him, becoming more impatient with each depressing response Barton and the rest of the men gave him. "Where is she?"

It took a moment for one of them to answer.

"Shirley's gone, Sheriff," Barton said. "Poor old girl. She fought to the end, but there were too many of 'em."

Kosana's heart felt heavy, and it surged with mourning for his old friend, whom he'd known for years.

"Where is she now?" he asked again.

Barton looked almost afraid to answer at first, but then he did.

"When you first came in...you stopped and killed the ones that were eating?"

Kosana nodded yes. But then realization set in.

"Oh, sweet Jesus," Kosana muttered, as images of the horror he had seen when he first entered flash-flooded through his mind; the tearing of flesh and the ripping of bloody insides. He forced it out of his mind, trying to mentally regroup; to see what the men who were spared from grisly death could do to help him fight off this growing army.

"What about Deputy Haig?" he asked, checking Haig's desk as if he would find him sitting there.

"That freak is running around out back with his gun out like he's John Wayne or somebody," Harrison said, sounding almost annoyed.

"Well, good for him, I say. So long as he doesn't get his fool-self killed," Kosana added. As if on cue, Haig entered the back entrance of the door covered in blood, his gun holstered.

"Sheriff! Hey, Sheriff!" he called and ran over to the men. "I've been shooting them left and right!"

"Good, Vince. That's good. But you got men in here that could've used your help."

Haig looked at the men who had begun to push the toppled desks to the side of the room.

"Ah, they were all right, Sheriff. These things're dumb as hell!"

161

Kosana didn't respond to Deputy Haig's statement, but instead looked over his shoulder and spotted the police station's beat-up radio.

"Word on the radio says they're sending the National Guard out to infected areas," Kosana said. "Anyone see something like that? Maybe a squad of soldiers, or you might have heard some whirly birds whizzing by overhead?"

"Nothing yet, Sheriff. Hope they get here, soon," Haig said, wiping his sleeve across his face to remove a smattering of blood. "We're all that's left, I think, and we could use the damn help."

Dr. Ford, who had remained quiet, still in shock from his ordeal, suddenly cried out and backed away from the rest of the men in fear. "Look out!" was all he could manage.

A gunshot rang out and Kosana spun quickly, his hand lunging to his holster for his gun. He saw that a creature who had been lying on the floor had attempted to reach out and grab him. The creature, its arm still outstretched, fell heavily back to the hard floor.

"Close call, Sheriff," Sully James said. He was a local farmer and was holding a smoking rifle in his hands. A few more men poured through the front entrance just behind him, each with rifles and handguns. Kosana recognized them as farmers from the community. Dressed in their typical outfits of dirty jeans and dirty flannel shirts, the men all nodded to Kosana, who nodded back.

"Thanks, Sully," Kosana said, his heart pumping wildly. "I owe you for that one."

"No sweat, George. We figured you could use the help sortin' out this mess."

Kosana smirked, realizing Sully was the only man in town to ever call him by his first name

"You know I appreciate it, Sully, but I can't ask you to do something like this. Word is we got the National Guard coming in. I couldn't look any of your wives in the face if I let you in on this thing and you got hurt or worse."

"You ain't lettin' anyone, George. You got no choice in the matter. And if you wanna put the cuffs on us when this thing is all said and done, I leave that up to you. But we lost some good people today, and I'll be damned if we're gonna lose anymore."

Kosana was about to respond when spats of gunfire from outside suddenly cut him off. They all ran to the entrance with their guns out, ready to fight, but another group of men, five in a line across the road, were shooting down a small crowd of the approaching dead. These men, hunters on their own time, easily took all of the approaching attackers down. They hooted and hollered in enthusiasm as they high-fived each other.

"Friends of yours?" Kosana asked.

Sully nodded, his eyes on the men.

"They're friends of yours now, too," he replied.

Kosana stuck out his hand to Sully again.

"Welcome to the team, Sully."

* * *

Within a half hour, the National Guard had finally roared into Butler County, and with them they brought troops, jeeps, trucks, packs of German shepherds—and belligerent egomaniacal generals. They barked orders, chewed cigars, and smoothed out the front of their heavily-medaled, military-issued jackets. Despite the unspoken power struggle, Kosana was grateful to see them, and when he saw the first camouflaged jeep driving towards him down the street, he had let out a breath that he'd been holding in for the entire morning.

And with the National Guard came TV crews, eager to feed the terrified world their own coverage of the outbreak and to permanently cement their image with the events of the day. They all stood in front of Army vehicles as they read off the same information they'd been repeating for hours: random attacks perpetrated by infected civilians, the risk of contagion, and the unusual revelation that they were also eating their victims. Unsurprisingly, the extra tidbit that the attackers were also *dead* didn't come up. But it was only a matter of time before the truth was revealed, and then Kosana knew the shit would really hit the fan.

Soldiers were interviewed incessantly, giving off the strange and slightly frustrating notion that they had nothing better to do, that while people cowered behind locked doors and boarded windows, these men—their salvation—preened for the camera and answered the same questions over and over.

When the National Guard's presence became known around the county, members of the community stepped up to volunteer in any way they could. It was refreshing to see townspeople—some of the more selfless of the community as well as those Kosana had previously written off as deadbeats—opting to come out of their homes and assist in an uncertain and potentially dangerous situation. Some of them merely brewed coffee for the troops and other volunteers, but even for such a meaningless task, the idea that they were out in the middle of the madness was inspiring and it made him proud of his community.

Kosana leaned against an army vehicle, shotgun now affixed to a leather strap swung over his back, and smoked a cigarette. He had quit years ago after his father died of lung cancer, but with all that had gone down today, he figured the universe wouldn't begrudge him a smoke. He watched as his remaining officers—some of whom had finally filtered back to the station after hours of being missing in action, and with wild stories to tell—wandered around the open field with their weapons, trying to lend a hand where possible.

As he smoked, his thoughts drifted back to his time spent with Dr. Ford, and of the stunning revelation that had sent him reeling into the corner of the room, feeling momentarily helpless—a feeling he hated. He opted not to tell the other men what Dr. Ford told him—that these things they hunted were the living dead. As wildly strange as the prognosis had been, it didn't change things. These things were still a threat, and they were still murdering people in his county, and they had to be stopped. There was no need to complicate matters further by making his men think he'd finally lost it after all his years on the force.

Sully James walked by him while talking with another man, but when he noticed Kosana, he turned and walked over to him.

"Thought you quit," Sully said, taking out his own pack of cigarettes.

"I did. Few times."

Sully withdrew his smoke and lit it with a tattered book of matches he had slipped inside the pack.

"Real mess this thing, ain't it?" Sully asked, puffing and darting his beady eyes across the landscape filled with National Guard and TV crews.

"Sure is," Kosana agreed. "Hopefully it'll be over soon."

Sully chuckled dryly. "What makes you think it'll be over soon?"

"I don't think—I just *hope*. Why, you don't?" He crushed out his cigarette under one of his boots and tossed it away.

"You don't wanna hear what I think, Connie." Sully continued to look off into the distance, but it was obvious he wasn't looking at the men scurrying about in the open field. He was looking beyond that, to the uncertain fate that had a strange, blank face and didn't stop coming when you fired bullets into its flesh.

"Out with it, Sully. I know you. You're achin' to tell me, so tell me."

Sully looked at him finally, and though his voice slightly quivered, his eyes were calm.

"It's the rapture."

Kosana smiled faintly and looked down at his shoes, and at the tall, wheat-colored grass that cropped up from the ground.

"I take it you're not a Bible-readin' man?" Sully asked, clearly offended by Kosana's reaction.

"I got the gist of it, yeah."

"The gist," Sully sniffed, before dropping his smoke to the dirt and crushing it out under his boot, and as he did so, proved his devotion to the word of God. "*And I looked, and behold a pale horse: and his name that sat on him was Death, and Hell followed with him. And power was given unto them over the fourth part of the earth, to kill with sword, and with hunger, and with death, and with the beasts of the earth.* That's Revelation."

Kosana didn't speak for a moment, not because he didn't know what to say, but because he didn't know how to say it without sending Sully, a man who had saved his life not even two hours ago, off in an angry huff.

"I don't believe what you believe, Sully," Kosana finally managed. "We both look at this huge mess—you see God and I don't. Think we better leave it at that."

Sully considered this a moment and pushed off the truck to walk away, and as he did so, he patted Kosana on the shoulder. He left him without another word, and without looking him in the eye.

*   *   *

As the sun began its downward course so the darkness of the night could roll in and swallow the town whole, Kosana stared hard into one of the many bonfires that were lit. The fires were a way to quickly rid themselves of the infected bodies they encountered. Deputy Haig, Harrison, Barton, and even Crothers, who agreed to stay with them until the mess was sorted out and he could find his brother, had left with another band of men to help hunt in an area not too far from where the National Guard was camped.

Kosana, ever their leader, had ordered them back before the sun fell. The way he figured it, the National Guard had the money and the means to work in the dark. Butler County PD did not.

The men had agreed and walked off hours ago, leaving behind the circus of soldiers that had invaded their town. Kosana was almost amazed at how many soldiers were traipsing around, and he wondered how many had been deployed in the entire country.

Dr. Ford had also joined the fight, but as a man of medicine, not as a hunter. Insisting he would be better equipped to assist the Guard with injured men rather than out in the field with a gun, he bid goodbye to Kosana.

The sun's journey behind the tall trees of the wooded area where society was attempting to regain control soon left them all in darkness, and the only light came from spotlights located in the National Guard's central hub; the headlights of vehicles, and the bonfires, which were fed long into the night.

Kosana sipped from a cup of coffee and sat on the hood of a National Guard jeep. His men, back from their hunt as ordered, trudged past him, having just filled their bellies with hamburgers and hotdogs cooked up by some of the volunteers. They made their way to the tents filled with rows of uncomfortable cots in which exhausted men could grab a few hours of shut eye before getting back to the fight.

"G'night fellas. Take it easy. This thing'll be all over soon," he told the men, believing those words a little less each time that he said them.

"Sure thing, Sheriff," Barton said. "See you in a few." He ducked inside the large, brown canvas tent and let the flaps of the entrance fall behind him. Deputy Haig merely nodded at Kosana and followed Barton inside with Harrison behind him. Crothers made no attempt to go in, and instead folded his arms and stared at one of the roaring bonfires.

"Go on, Al, get some sleep," Kosana said, touching the cup to his lips.

"Worried about my kid brother, Sheriff. The lines are down and I haven't talked to him all day." He continued to watch the embers of the roaring fire as orange light from the dancing flames flickered over his face. "He's the only family I got left, you know?"

"He's all right, Al, I'm sure of it. These guys..." Kosana said, motioning to the National Guard presence. "They're gonna get this thing taken care of. No worries."

Crothers looked at him, still unsure.

"They don't even know what this thing is yet, Sheriff. I saw a bunch of Washington higher-ups on TV coming out of a meeting. Even they couldn't agree what was causing this craziness. You shoulda seen it, these reporters were asking these guys questions after the meeting as they were walking to their car and they all disagreed with each other! One guy said it was radiation coming from this Venus Probe Satellite or something and the other guy looked like it couldn't be further from the truth." Crothers let out a heavy sigh. "Frankly, I think we're all dead already. It's just taking us a bit to realize it. I don't think we have a chance."

A cold shudder washed across Kosana's shoulders and he shook the feeling off.

"Go on, get some sleep," was the only response Kosana could muster. "Back to it tomorrow morning."

Crothers waited a moment more, but then nodded goodnight and disappeared inside the tent.

Kosana considered the man's fears a moment and was shocked to see that it was a struggle to disregard them as irrational; merely the thoughts of a man scared and paranoid. He hopped off the hood of the jeep and slipped inside the opening of the canvas tent where the other men had earlier retired.

What little sleep the men did get was routinely interrupted by the sudden gunfire that thundered throughout the night, some of it off in the distance while some sounded like it was just outside their tent. And some of it was. More often than not, the sound of gunfire was usually preceded by shouts of alarm from the soldiers who didn't see the creatures approaching until they were enveloped by the harsh white shine of the army's spotlights. The dogs, exhausted from their day of tracking scents, were mercifully quiet as they slept in stacked cages in the back of one of the military trucks.

For the rest of the night, creatures were shot and thrown in groups into the bonfires. Thankfully, the sickening smell of the dead, burning flesh was carried off by the cool autumn winds, and as Kosana drifted off to sleep on one of the brown, simplistic cots within the large tent, the crackling sounds of the fire flooded his head with memories of summer nights spent sitting around the campfire and listening to his Uncle Darren's tales of ghosts and ghouls.

"They ain't real, Georgie," his Uncle Darren had always told him as they would roast wieners and marshmallows over the fire following the tales that always made him shiver in fear. "Ain't no such thing."

He smirked slightly before finally falling asleep.

*   *   *

The next morning, Sheriff Kosana slid out of his cot and re-dressed in his plain black suit that was lying on another empty bed from the night before. He liked wearing his suits to work, instead of the boring brown button-up shirts with the patches and the badge that screamed, "Sheriff!" People never quite understood his penchant for wearing such clothes while on duty, but then again, not many people understood him in general.

He slid the tie knot up under his collar and straightened it. There was no mirror in the tent, but he felt confident enough to straighten his clothes without one. He looked around the tent to see if any of his men were still sleeping. Several men slept in their cramped cots, but he didn't recognize any of them. He pushed open the tent flap and stepped outside, seeing that despite the early morning hours, the place was abuzz with activity.

But of course it would be.

You don't take the morning off when the undead come knocking.

One of the guardsmen who had spent most of his time in Butler County smoothing his shirt and combing his hair for the TV cameras, General Wick, saw him exit the tent and strolled over to him.

"Morning, Sheriff," he said, smiling as if the two were old friends.

"Sure is," Kosana replied, denying the general even this pleasant formality.

"You sleep well while my men did all the heavy lifting?" Wick asked through a gritted smile.

Kosana spit into the tall grass at his feet as a response.

"You're a real piece of work," Wick continued and then added, "A bit too much like me, I'm afraid."

"I'm just concerned about my town, General. I see a lot of your guys mugging for the camera and standing in circles around the barbecue pit. Meanwhile, the people in my county are behind locked doors waiting to be rescued."

"Well, if you wanna play hero so bad, then let's go. Our helicopter spotted a farmhouse back through the woods about a mile or two from here. Says the activity there is pretty high. I'm taking some men through in a few minutes. Think some of you civilians can handle coming along?"

General Wick, a rigid man who towered six inches over Kosana, walked away without a response. Kosana's angry eyes burned holes into the man's back before walking off. He spotted Deputy Haig sitting on the grass with his rifle leaned against his legs. Crothers sat next to him and the two men were making idle chatter. Kosana, already sweating under the hot summer sun, blotted his head with the handkerchief from his breast pocket as he approached them. He gathered them to him, and also spotting Harrison and Barton, recruited them as well.

And so Sheriff Kosana, along with Deputy Haig, and the rest of the men—his new posse—set off across the Plainfields Farm to the nearby tree line. Kosana had opted to give themselves a head start, leaving General Wick and his platoon behind. The men didn't complain because Kosana hadn't told them about what the general had described as "high activity" in the area. They were on a need to know basis, as far as he was concerned.

And they didn't need to know.

After having marched a half-mile through the woods, pushing branches out of their faces, the radio on Kosana's belt squawked to life.

"Sheriff, this is General Wick. Come in."

Kosana snapped the radio off his belt.

"This is Sheriff Kosana," he muttered into the radio, knowing there would be hell to be pay later if he didn't.

"What's your position?"

"Making my way through the woods towards the farmhouse," he responded curtly through gritted teeth.

"Just couldn't wait to get started, could you?" General Wick asked through the radio as the sounds of men shouting orders in the background petered through the small speaker. "Well, watch your ass. I have men following just behind you. I told you the threat level in that area is high."

Deputy Haig and Harrison exchanged worried looks as Barton marched on, pretending not to have heard the transmission. The men cast their eyes to the ground, almost seeming to purposely look like they hadn't overheard Wick's ominous warning over the radio.

"Fantastic," Barton muttered, already winded despite the short walk.

"Keep an eye out. We'll be all right so long as we watch each other's back," Kosana reasoned.

The sounds of helicopter rotors roared overhead as they continued their walk. The men looked up and saw the helicopter pass by over the trees. Wick wasn't exaggerating, as even over the sounds of the rotors the men could hear the groans of what sounded like an army of the dead. The men stopped in their tracks and each pointed their guns in different directions, as the sounds of the groans seemed to be coming at them from all angles.

"Christ, where are they?" Barton demanded, slowly spinning in circles with his gun drawn.

"Hang on, guys. We got the Guard coming right up on us, so just relax and don't shoot each other," Kosana spat.

The creatures finally made their appearance, coming at them from the direction in which the men were heading—from the farmhouse.

Kosana took aim at a bloodied woman dressed in a pink night-gown with a large flap of flesh hanging loosely from her thigh. He fired off a shot, taking her face off and spilling her backwards into the brush. The other men followed suit, and they all took their place next to each other in a line and picked off creature after creature.

"Holy hell, take a look at that one," Harrison gasped, his eyes on a stark-naked woman coming right at them. "Bet she was a fox before she ate her daddy."

No one laughed, and Harrison wasn't smiling when he said it.

"Sorry, honey," Harrison said before putting one in her forehead.

Despite their markedly good aim, the number of the creatures didn't seem to diminish. Wave after wave of attackers came at them, bumping into each other as they advanced on their prey, and though the men were putting them down fairly steadily, the creatures were still able to advance closer and closer. Their numbers were close to fifty now, and an aura of impending death wafted across each of the beleaguered men.

"Nick, reload in two," Kosana nervously barked, his eyes on the dead man coming at him, dressed in hospital scrubs that were ripped and tattered in such a way that it looked instead like a toga. Harrison fired off one more shot before slipping ammo out of his utility belt and reloading his gun.

The creatures, now a scant fifteen feet away, caused the men to begin taking weary steps backward as they continued to fire. The horde of ghouls that approached them snapped their jaws in the air threateningly, almost knowing how garish their appearances were, and what effect they had on their prey in front of them. They continued their undead shuffle towards them, dressed in bathrobes, work uniforms, or fine eveningwear. They were all mangled and torn, some more than others. Limbs hung dumbly from broken bones or ripped flesh, while some were missing them entirely. Though they ranged from the small to the tall, they all approached with that same blank look, and with that same mouth hanging agape.

As the men continued to fight, it occurred to Kosana that they might be one of the very few people to see these creatures up close...and hopefully live to tell about it.

"We gotta fall back, Sheriff!" Deputy Haig stammered.

Kosana fired off another shot through the wide-open mouth of an approaching creature, this one dressed in a fancy black-and-white tuxedo and wearing shiny, black shoes. The creatures were very close now, and though Kosana had wanted to push on, to prove that he and his few men were perfectly capable of accomplishing what the far more expansive National Guard had set out to do, he finally relented.

"Fall back!" Kosana barked.

But the order came too late.

A dead man, wearing a flannel shirt and canvas safari vest, grabbed Barton around his wide stomach as he turned to run and bit deeply into the back of his fatty neck. Barton screamed loud and long as yellow teeth ripped off his thick skin and continued to hold him from behind as the dead man sloppily chewed the warm flesh.

"Jesus, help me!" Barton shouted, falling on his face into the hard, rooted ground of the woods. The feeding dead man fell with him and took one more bite from Barton's neck before Harrison shot him in the face, splattering red bits onto the back of Barton's head. The mutilated police officer continued to scream bloody murder, blood flowing heavily from his wounds. More creatures, spotting the easy meal before them, advanced quickly. Kosana took one step towards Barton but then took a step back, seeing there would be no way to get there in time to help him. He fired a single shot into the back of Barton's head, sparing him the pain that was soon to follow.

"Run!" Harrison cried, high-tailing it across the wooded floor, jumping over fallen tree trunks and dodging around trees. Kosana saw him stop suddenly for a moment, his arms going up almost in surrender before diving to the ground, and as he did so, a line of soldiers marched through the trees and opened fire at the approaching creatures.

"Get down!" Kosana ordered and dove to the ground along with the other men. The Guard's machine guns worked quickly, and a torrential assault of whizzing bullets tore chunks from the bodies of the dead as they jostled and convulsed from the gunfire. The creatures had been close enough to Kosana and his men that as he lay on the ground covering his head, he could hear the vibrations of their dead bodies hitting the ground.

Finally, the shooting subsided, and Kosana slowly raised his head to see General Wick looking down at him, an unlit cigar clamped firmly in his mouth, a look of exuberant spite plastered across his face.

"You all right, fellas?" he asked, his tone more snide than concerned.

Kosana, from his position on the ground, looked behind him and saw the sea of dead bodies that began three feet from him and seemed to stretch on for miles into the woods.

"Call in the meat wagon, boys," the general said as he walked by Kosana to the direction of the farmhouse, not offering his hand to help the sheriff up. "Why don't you boys hang out for a moment and let us get in there first. We'll let you know if it's safe," Wick continued, his eyes twinkling with righteous indignation. Kosana climbed to his feet, ignoring the general's pompous remark, and his men did the same.

"Y'all okay?" Kosana asked them. The men nodded sullenly as Kosana watched General Wick and his men walk off into the woods.

"What about Barton? Is he gonna get up?" Crothers asked, his eyes on the dead police officer's decimated body.

Kosana shook his head. "Don't think so. Think I took care of it before he could. Hope so, anyway."

They all then looked over to Barton's body as if waiting to see if it would prove the sheriff wrong.

It didn't.

"Come on," Kosana said.

The men trudged on, Barton's death weighing heavily on their minds. Though they were in the middle of the madness, they hadn't yet experienced the death of one of their group firsthand; till now.

After another mile, they finally made their way to the end of the woods and stepped into the wide clearing that was the farmhouse's surrounding property. The large, white house with a weathered look sat in the middle, leaving wide open space all around it that encompassed the front and back yard.

General Wick squawked through Kosana's radio at him again.

"Found something on the side of the house. Looks like a truck caught fire here sometime late last night."

As Kosana began searching the side of the house, he immediately spotted the shell of an old truck that was hollowed out and burnt to a crisp.

"I'll check it out," he answered Wick as he lowered the radio and raised his gun.

He approached the truck, and soon detected the faint aroma of barbecued meat. His stomach growled in response, having lived only on greasy hotdogs and coffee for the time being. He peered back into the charred vehicle, which by the looks of it had roasted until it eventually burned itself out. He rather doubted people had been running around with buckets of water trying to put it out. There had been more pressing matters at hand, he was sure.

On his way to the farmhouse, Kosana could see two creatures walking side-by-side, their backs to Kosana and his men. He popped off a single shot with his revolver and one of the creatures toppled. A barrage of gunfire from his men brought down the other creature as well. It was a regular shooting brigade. Bullets whizzed back and forth across the field and these simple farmers and volunteers almost always hit their targets. Creatures dropped left and right, some with perturbed looks on their faces and some simply dropped with no discernible reaction at all.

Kosana shot another ghoul through the back of the head, this one grabbing at its face in confusion before tumbling to the ground. He ran over to it to make sure it was dead for good, and seeing that it was, he straightened up and took another look at the farmhouse.

"Drag that outta here and throw it in the fire," he ordered, scanning the property quickly to see what could be shot next.

The men with him complied and they dragged the corpse away.

Kosana turned back to the men with him. "Let's go check out the house."

The men nodded at him and they marched towards the house. As he got closer, he could see boards covering the windows, the sight of which filled him with hope.

Maybe whoever had been inside was okay.

Maybe they had survived the night.

However, upon closer examination, he could see that the front door was wide open, and that on several of the windows, the boards hung loosely, as if the house had been under siege. As they got closer, Kosana was able to see through the weakened sections of the boards directly into the house.

It became severely evident that whoever had been inside when the creatures broke in were dead. No question about it. They, like every other unfortunate soul to cross paths with one of these *things*, had been bitten, ravaged, and ripped apart. And they were probably still conscious as the things began to eat them, and slurp sloppily on pieces of them that were ripped greedily from their ravaged bodies.

But instead of rage, sadness, or even pity, it was a strange calm that washed like warm bathwater over Sheriff Kosana. He likened it to taking a walk during a foggy day, feeling around blindly with his hands until the clouds had suddenly dissipated, leaving everything clear and brighter than when the fog had come in the first place. He thought for a moment more about this strange epiphany before he realized what it was. It was the notion that he was ready to dedicate the rest of his life to hunting these creatures—the walking dead; that if he had to search the entire world, he was going to kill every single one of them and toss their soulless bodies to the flames. He owed that to his men, to his community, and to his friends—both living and dead. Kosana, cocky and arrogant, was a man who would not only contain the madness spreading throughout his county, but he was looking forward to the challenge.

Each burst of the soldiers' gunfire from different parts of the property sent shivers of delight through him as he visualized in his mind the exploding heads of the creatures as they tumbled to the ground in piles of dead meat. With each dead creature face-planting into the stony ground of Butler County, Sheriff Kosana came that much closer to redemption. He was going to fight this thing. And he was going to win.

Peering at the house again, he could see movement inside; movement of a figure that shuffled clumsily over its own feet, something that approached the window closest to where they were.

"Vince!" Kosana said, motioning for Deputy Haig to step up next to him. "See it in there moving around?" Kosana's eyes were on the shape he spotted through the broken boards.

"I see it," Haig answered, aiming his rifle.

Kosana wouldn't take this shot. He would watch. He would be, at this time, an audience; a spectator to the decimation of the walking dead. He wanted every skull-shattering, blood-misting moment ingrained in his memory.

"Hit him in the head. Right between the eyes," Kosana ordered.

Deputy Haig aimed, squinted, and pulled the trigger. The bullet tore through the opening in the window and slammed home into the hapless creature unfortunate enough to be standing in front of it. Kosana relished the sound of the body tumbling away from the window and it sent more shivers of delight through his body.

He was now one dead creature closer to the end of the madness.

Deputy Haig made his way into the house to retrieve the body, ready to shoot anything that came at him. As the other men followed him inside, Kosana remained outside on the lawn so he could watch as the National Guard prepared a new bonfire in which to dispose of the creatures killed in the area. During this time, other men dragged dead bodies across the wide fields with large, curved hooks. The sharp, rusty blades were plunged directly into the corpse chests as no one wanted to touch the infected directly. Some of the volunteers ran around with cameras, trying to document the momentous occasion. The living were winning the battle, and their victorious actions were going to be splashed across every front page in the country.

Despite everything Sheriff George Kosana had seen, and the people he had lost, he smiled, and planted his hands firmly on his hips as he watched the taking-back of civilization.

Gunshots punctuated his confidence that the whole mess would be over soon, that these *things* would soon be back in their graves for good.

It wasn't just going to be extermination.

It was going to be a massacre.

And it was going to last all night long.

ABOUT THE WRITERS

Anthony Giangregorio is the author and editor of more than 30 novels, almost all of them about zombies. His work has appeared in Dead Science by Coscomentertainment, Dead Worlds: Undead Stories Volumes 1, 2, 3, & 4, and an upcoming anthology (Zombology) by Library of the Living Dead Press and their werewolf anthology titled Wolves of War. He also has stories in End of Days: An Apocalyptic Anthology Volumes 1 & 2, and 2 anthologies with Pill Hill Press. Check out his website at www.undeadpress.com

Joe Tonzelli is a writer of short stories and screenplays and has a short story featured in Book of the Dead Volume 1 by Living Dead Press.

He currently resides just outside of Philadelphia and works as an editorial coordinator for a publishing company in Sewell, NJ.

BOOK OF THE DEAD 2: NOT DEAD YET
A ZOMBIE ANTHOLOGY
Edited by Anthony Giangregorio

Out of the ashes of death and decay, comes the second volume filled with the walking dead.

In this tomb, there are only slow, shambling monstrosities that were once human.

No one knows why the dead walk; only that they do, and that they are hungry for human flesh.

But these aren't your neighbors, your co-workers, or your family. Now they are the living dead, and they will tear your throat out at a moment's notice.

So be warned as you delve into the pages of this book; the dead will find you, no matter where you hide.

CHRISTMAS IS DEAD: A ZOMBIE ANTHOLOGY
Edited by Anthony Giangregorio

Twas the night before Christmas and all through the house, not a creature was stirring, not even a. . . zombie?

That's right; this anthology explores what would happen at Christmas time if there was a full blown zombie outbreak.

Reanimated turkeys, zombie Santas, and demon reindeers that turn people into flesh-eating ghouls are just some of the tales you will find in this merry undead book.

So curl up under the Christmas tree with a cup of hot chocolate, and as the fireplace crackles with warmth, get ready to have your heart filled with holiday cheer.

But of course, then it will be ripped from your heaving chest and fed upon by blood-thirsty elves with a craving for human flesh!

For you see, Christmas is Dead!

And you will never look at the holiday season the same way again.

DEAD HOUSE: A ZOMBIE GHOST STORY
by Keith Adam Luethke
Welcome to Dead House

The old mansion on the edge of town, aptly named Dead House, has a history of blood, pain, and death, but what Victor Leeds knows of this past only scratches the surface of the true horrors within.

But when his girlfriend is attacked by a shadowy figure one rainy night, he soon finds himself caught up in a world where the dead walk and ghostly wraiths abound.

And to make matters worse, a pair of serial killers are fulfilling carefully made plans, and when they are done, the small town of Stormville, New York will run red. The last ingredient to open the gates of Hell, and plunge this small upstate town into madness, is rain.

And in Stormville, it pours by the gallons.

The Zombie in the Basement
by Anthony Giangregorio
Illustrated by Andrew Dawe-Collins

The spooky house at the end of the street was the one all the kids avoided. With its overgrown shrubs and weeds, the place was a modern day haunted house. Especially at night. So when Ricky sneaks into the yard to retrieve his favorite ball, he comes across something he'd only seen in movies and bad dreams. He sees a zombie in the basement window of the old house, but when he tells his friends, no one believes him. Ricky knows what he saw, that something lurks in the old house, something that isn't supposed to exist.

With his best friend Eric by his side, Ricky will find out the truth and prove to everyone that zombies are real. And when the night is done, everyone will know about the zombie in the basement.

Note: This book is for young adults and for those who are young at heart.

DEADFREEZE
by Anthony Giangregorio
THIS IS WHAT HELL WOULD BE LIKE IF IT FROZE OVER!

When an experimental serum for hypothermia goes horribly wrong, a small research station in the middle of Antarctica becomes overrun with an army of the frozen dead.

Now a small group of survivors must battle the arctic weather and a horde of frozen zombies as they make their way across the frozen plains of Antarctica to a neighboring research station.

What they don't realize is that they are being hunted by an entity whose sole reason for existing is vengeance; and it will find them wherever they run.

VISIONS OF THE DEAD
A ZOMBIE STORY
by Anthony & Joseph Giangregorio

Jake Roberts felt like he was the luckiest man alive.

He had a great family, a beautiful girlfriend, who was soon to be his wife, and a job, that might not have been the best, but it paid the bills.

At least until the dead began to walk.

Now Jake is fighting to survive in a dead world while searching for his lost love, Melissa, knowing she's out there somewhere.

But the past isn't dead, and as he struggles for an uncertain future, the past threatens to consume him. With the present a constant battle between the living and the dead, Jake finds himself slipping in and out of the past, the visions of how it all happened haunting him. But Jake knows Melissa is out there somewhere and he'll find her or die trying.

In a world of the living dead, you can never escape your past.

DEAD MOURNING: A ZOMBIE HORROR STORY
by Anthony Giangregorio

Carl Jenkins was having a run of bad luck. Fresh out of jail, his probation tenuous, he'd lost every job he'd taken since being released. So now was his last chance, only one more job to prevent him from going back to prison. Assigned to work in a funeral home, he accidentally loses a shipment of embalming fluid. With nothing to lose, he substitutes it with a batch of chemicals from a nearby factory.

The results don't go as planned, though. While his screw-up goes unnoticed, his machinations revive the cadavers in the funeral home, unleashing an evil on the world that it has not seen before. Not wanting to become a snack for the rampaging dead, he flees the city, joining up with other survivors. An old, dilapidated zoo becomes their haven, while the dead wait outside the walls, hungry and patient.

But Carl is optimistic, after all, he's still alive, right? Perhaps his luck has changed and help will arrive to save them all?

Unfortunately, unknown to him and the other survivors, a serial killer has fallen into their group, trapped inside the zoo with them.

With the undead army clamoring outside the walls and a murderer within, it'll be a miracle if any of them live to see the next sunrise.

On second thought, maybe Carl would've been better off if he'd just gone back to jail.

ROAD KILL: A ZOMBIE TALE
by Anthony Giangregorio
ORDER UP!

In the summer of 2008, a rogue comet entered earth's orbit for 72 hours. During this time, a strange amber glow suffused the sky.

But something else happened; something in the comet's tail had an adverse affect on dead tissue and the result was the reanimation of every dead animal carcass on the planet.

A handful of survivors hole up in a diner in the backwoods of New Hampshire while the undead creatures of the night hunt for human prey.

There's a new blue plate special at DJ's Diner and Truck Stop, and it's you!

DEAD WORLDS: Undead Stories
A Zombie Anthology Volume 2
Edited by Anthony Giangregorio

Welcome to a world where the dead walk and want nothing more than to feast on the living. The stories contained in this, the second volume of the Dead Worlds series, are filled with action, gore, and buckets and buckets of blood; plus a heaping side of entrails for those with a little extra hunger.

The stories contained within this volume are scribed by both the desiccated cadavers of seasoned veterans to the genre as well as fresh-faced corpses, each printed here for the first time; and all of them ready to dig in and please the most discerning reader.

So slap on a bib and prepare to get bloody, because you're about to read the best zombie stories this side of Hell!

THE DARK

by Anthony Giangregorio

DARKNESS FALLS

The darkness came without warning.

First New York, then the rest of United States, and then the world became enveloped in a perpetual night without end.

With no sunlight, eventually the planet will wither and die, bringing on a new Ice Age. But that isn't problem for the human race, for humanity will be dead long before that happens.

There is something in the dark, creatures only seen in nightmares, and they are on the prowl. Evolution has changed and man is no longer the dominant species. When we are children, we're told not to fear the dark, that what we believe to exist in the shadows is false.

Unfortunately, that is no longer true.

SOULEATER

by Anthony Giangregorio

Twenty years ago, Jason Lawson witnessed the brutal death of his father by something only seen in nightmares, something so horrible he'd blocked it from his mind.

Now twenty years later the creature is back, this time for his son.

Jason won't let that happen.

He'll travel to the demon's world, struggling every second to rescue his son from its clutches.

But what he doesn't know is that the portal will only be open for a finite time and if he doesn't return with his son before it closes, then he'll be trapped in the demon's dimension forever.

SEE HOW IT ALL BEGAN IN THE NEW DOUBLE-SIZED 460 PAGE SPECIAL EDITION!

DEADWATER: EXPANDED EDITION

by Anthony Giangregorio

Through a series of tragic mishaps, a small town's water supply is contaminated with a deadly bacterium that transforms the town's population into flesh eating ghouls.

Without warning, Henry Watson finds himself thrown into a living hell where the living dead walk and want nothing more than to feed on the living.

Now Henry's trying to escape the undead town before he becomes the next victim.

With the military on one side, shooting civilians on sight, and a horde of bloodthirsty zombies on the other, Henry must try to battle his way to freedom.

With a small group of survivors, including a beautiful secretary and a wise-cracking janitor to aid him, the ragtag group will do their best to stay alive and escape the city codenamed: **Deadwater**.

DEAD END: A ZOMBIE NOVEL
by Anthony Giangregorio
THE DEAD WALK!

Newspapers everywhere proclaim the dead have returned to feast on the living!

A small group of survivors hole up in a cellar, afraid to brave the masses of animated corpses, but when food runs out, they have no choice but to venture out into a world gone mad.

What they will discover, however, is that the fall of civilization has brought out the worst in their fellow man.

Cannibals, psychotic preachers and rapists are just some of the atrocities they must face.

In a world turned upside down, it is life that has hit a Dead End.

DEAD RAGE
by Anthony Giangregorio

An unknown virus spreads across the globe, turning ordinary people into bloodthirsty, ravenous killers.

Only a small percentage of the population is immune and soon become prey to the infected.

Amongst the infected comes a man, stricken by the virus, yet still retaining his grasp on reality. His need to destroy the *normals* becomes an obsession and he raises an army of killers to seek out and kill all who aren't *changed* like himself.

A few survivors gather together on the outskirts of Chicago and find themselves running for their lives as the specter of death looms over all.

The Dead Rage virus will find you, no matter where you hide.

BLOOD RAGE
(The Prequel to DEAD RAGE)
by Anthony Giangregorio

The madness descended before anyone knew what was happening. Perfectly normal people suddenly became rage-fueled killers, tearing and slicing their way across the city. Within hours, Chicago was a battlefield, the dead strewn in the streets like trash.

Stacy, Chad and a few others are just a few of the immune, unaffected by the virus but not to the violence surrounding them. The *changed* are ravenous, sweeping across Chicago and perhaps the world, destroying any *normals* they come across. Fire, slaughter, and blood rule the land, and the few survivors are now an endangered species.

This is the story of the first days of the Dead Rage virus and the brave souls who struggle to live just one more day.

When the smoke clears, and the *changed* have maimed and killed all who stand in their way, only the strong will remain.

The rest will be left to rot in the sun.

The Lazarus Culture

by Pasquale J. Morrone

Secret Service Agent Christopher Kearns had no idea what he was up against. Assigned on a temporary basis to the Center for Disease Control, he only knew that somehow it was connected to the lives of those the agency protected...namely, the President of the United States. If there were possible terrorist activities in the making, he could only guess it was at a red alert basis.

When Kearns meets and befriends Doctor Marlene Peterson of the Breezy Point Medical Center in Maryland, he soon finds that science fiction can indeed become a reality. In a solitary room walked a man with no vital signs: dead. The explanation he received came from Doctor Lee Fret, a man assigned to the case from the CDC. Something was attached to the brain stem. Something alive that was quickly spreading rapidly through Maryland and other states.

Kearns and his ragtag army of agents and medical personnel soon find themselves in a world of meaningless slaughter and mayhem. The armies of the walking dead were far more than mere zombies. Some began to change into whatever it was they ate. The government had found a way to reanimate the dead by implanting a parasite found on the tongue of the Red Snapper to the human brain.

It looked good on paper, but it was a project straight from Hell.

The dead now walked, but it wasn't a mystery.

It was The Lazarus Culture.

END OF DAYS: AN APOCALYPTIC ANTHOLOGY
VOLUMES 1 & 2

Our world is a fragile place.

Meteors, famine, floods, nuclear war, solar flares, and hundreds of other calamities can plunge our small blue planet into turmoil in an instant.

What would you do if tomorrow the sun went super nova or the world was swallowed by water, submerging the world into the cold darkness of the ocean? This anthology explores some of those scenarios and plunges you into total annihilation.

But remember, it's only a book, and tomorrow will come as it always does. Or will it?

DEADFALL

by Anthony Giangregorio

It's Halloween in the small suburban town of Wakefield, Mass.

While parents take their children trick or treating and others throw costume parties, a swarm of meteorites enter the earth's atmosphere and crash to earth.

Inside are small parasitic worms, no larger than maggots.

The worms quickly infect the corpses at a local cemetery and so begins the rise of the undead.

The walking dead soon get the upper hand, with no one believing the truth. That the dead now walk.

Will a small group of survivors live through the zombie apocalypse?

Or will they, too, succumb to the Deadfall.

DARK PLACES

By Anthony Giangregorio

A cave-in inside the Boston subway unleashes something that should have stayed buried forever.

Three boys sneak out to a haunted junkyard after dark and find more than they gambled on.

In a world where everyone over twelve has died from a mysterious illness, one young boy tries to carry on.

A mysterious man in black tries his hand at a game of chance at a local carnival, to interesting results.

God, Allah, and Buddha play a friendly game of poker with the fate of the Earth resting in the balance.

Ever have one of those days where everything that can go wrong, does? Well, so did Byron, and no one should have a day like this!

Thad had an imaginary friend named Charlie when he was a child. Charlie would make him do bad things. Now Thad is all grown up and guess who's coming for a visit?

These and other short stories, all filled with frozen moments of dread and wonder, will keep you captivated long into the night.

Just be sure to watch out when you turn off the light!

BOOK OF THE DEAD
A ZOMBIE ANTHOLOGY
VOLUME 1
ISBN 978-1-935458-25-8
Edited by Anthony Giangregorio

This is the most faithful, truest zombie anthology ever written, and we invite you along for the ride. Every single story in this book is filled with slack-jawed, eyes glazed, slow moving, shambling zombies set in a world where the dead have risen and only want to eat the flesh of the living. In these pages, the rules are sacrosanct. There is no deviation from what a zombie should be or how they came about. The Dead Walk.

There is no reason, though rumors and suppositions fill the radio and television stations. But the only thing that is fact is that the walking dead are here and they will not go away. So prepare yourself for the ultimate homage to the master of zombie legend. And remember... Aim for the head!

DEAD TALES: SHORT STORIES TO DIE FOR

by Anthony Giangregorio

In a world much like our own, terrorists unleash a deadly dis-ease that turns people into flesh-eating ghouls.

A camping trip goes horribly wrong when forces of evil seek to dominate mankind.

After losing his life, a man returns reincarnated again and again; his soul inhabiting the bodies of animals.

In the Colorado Mountains, a woman runs for her life, stalked by a sadistic killer.

In a world where the Patriot Act has come to fruition, a man struggles to survive, despite eroding liberties.

Not able to accept his wife's death, a widower will cross into the dream realm to find her again, despite the dark forces that hold her in thrall. These and other short stories will captivate and thrill you. These are short stories to die for.

REVOLUTION OF THE DEAD
by Anthony Giangregorio
THE DEAD SHALL RISE AGAIN!

Five years ago, a deadly plague wiped out 97% of the world's population, America suffering tragically. Bodies were everywhere, far too many to bury or burn. But then, through a miracle of medical science, a way is found to reanimate the dead.

With the manpower of the United States depleted, and the remaining survivors not wanting to give up their internet and fast food restaurants, the undead are conscripted as slave labor.

Now they cut the grass, pick up the trash, and walk the dogs of the surviving humans.

But whether alive or dead, no race wants to be controlled, and sooner or later the dead will fight back, wanting the freedom they enjoyed in life.

The revolution has begun!

And when it's over, the dead will rule the land, and the remaining humans will become the slaves...or worse.

KINGDOM OF THE DEAD
by Anthony Giangregorio
THE DEAD HAVE RISEN!

In the dead city of Pittsburgh, two small enclaves struggle to survive, eking out an existence of hand to mouth.

But instead of working together, both groups battle for the last remaining fuel and supplies of a city filled with the living dead.

Six months after the initial outbreak, a lone helicopter arrives bearing two more survivors and a newborn baby. One enclave welcomes them, while the other schemes to steal their helicopter and escape the decaying city.

With no police, fire, or social services existing, the two will battle for dominance in the steel city of the walking dead. But when the dust settles, the question is: will the remaining humans be the winners, or the losers?

When the dead walk, the line between Heaven and Hell is so twisted and bent there is no line at all.

RISE OF THE DEAD
by Anthony Giangregorio
DEATH IS ONLY THE BEGINNING!

In less than forty-eight hours, more than half the globe was infected.

In another forty-eight, the rest would be enveloped.

The reason?

A science experiment gone horribly wrong which enabled the dead to walk, their flesh rotting on their bones even as they seek human prey.

Jeremy was an ordinary nineteen year old slacker. He partied too much and had done poorly in high school. After a night of drinking and drugs, he awoke to find the world a very different place from the one he'd left the night before.

The dead were walking and feeding on the living, and as Jeremy stepped out into a world gone mad, the dead spotting him alone and unarmed in the middle of the street, he had to wonder if he would live long enough to see his twentieth birthday.

DEAD UNION

BOOK 6
by Anthony Giangregorio
BRAVE NEW WORLD

More than a year has passed since the world died not with a bang, but with a moan.

Where sprawling cities once stood, now only the dead inhabit the hollow walls of a shattered civilization; a mockery of lives once led.

But there are still survivors in this barren world, all slowly struggling to take back what was stripped from their birthright; the promise of a world free of the undead.

Fortified towns have shunned the outside world, becoming massive fortresses in their own right. These refugees of a world torn asunder are once again trying to carve out a new piece of the earth, or hold onto what little they already possess.

HOSTAGES

Henry Watson and his warrior survivalists are conscripted by a mad colonel, one of the last military leaders still functioning in the decimated United States. The colonel has settled in Fort Knox, and from there plans to rule the world with his slave army of lost souls and the last remaining soldiers of a defunct army.

But first he must take back America and mold it in his own image; and he will crush all who oppose him, including the new recruits of Henry and crew.

The battle lines are drawn with the fate of America at stake, and this time, the outcome may be unsure.

In a world where the dead walk, even the grave isn't safe.

DEADTOWN

BOOK 8
by Anthony Giangregorio

The world is a very different place now. The dead walk the land and humans hide in small towns with walls of stone and debris for protection, constantly keeping the living dead at bay.

Social law is gone and right and wrong is defined by the size of your gun.

UNWELCOME VISITORS

Henry Watson and his band of warrior survivalists become guests in a fortified town in Michigan. But when the kidnapping of one of the companions goes bad and men die, the group finds themselves on the wrong side of the law, and a town out for blood.

Trapped in a hotel, surrounded on all sides, it will be up to Henry to save the day with a gamble that may not only take his life, but that of his friends as well.

In a dead world, when justice is not enough, there is always vengeance.

THE PLACE TO GO FOR ZOMBIE AND APOCALYPTIC FICTION

  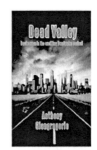

LIVING DEAD PRESS

WHERE THE DEAD WALK

www.livingdeadpress.com

Revolt of the Dead
Keith Gouveia

The Undead World of Oz
L. Frank Baum & Ryan C. Thomas

Anna Karnivora
W. Bill Czolgosz

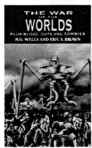

The War of the Worlds
Plus Blood, Guts and Zombies
H.G. Wells & Eric S. Brown

Adventures of Huckleberry Finn
and Zombie Jim
Mark Twain & W. Bill Czolgosz

Vicious Verses &
Reanimated Rhymes
edited by
A.P. Fuchs

Emma and
the Werewolves
Jane Austen & Adam Rann

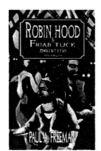

Robin Hood and Friar Tuck:
Zombie Killers
Paul A. Freeman

LaVergne, TN USA
10 June 2010
185704LV00004B/17/P